The Drowning

By the same author

In Search of Adam
Black Boxes
Like Bees to Honey
99 Reasons Why (ebook)

With Nik Perring and Darren Craske
Freaks!

CAROLINE SMAILES

The Drowning of Arthur Braxton

THE
FRIDAY
PROJECT

The Friday Project
An imprint of HarperCollins*Publishers*
77–85 Fulham Palace Road
Hammersmith, London W6 8JB
www.harpercollins.co.uk

First published in Great Britain by The Friday Project in 2013
Copyright © Caroline Smailes 2013

10

Caroline Smailes asserts the moral right to
be identified as the author of this work

A catalogue record for this book
is available from the British Library

978-0-00-747909-2

Typeset by Palimpsest Book Production Limited, Falkirk, Stirlingshire

Printed and bound in Great Britain by
Clays Ltd, St Ives plc

www.harpercollins...

First published ... by ... in 20...

I got a whole world where you'll never find me.
('Yours', Gaspard Royant, feat. Marie-Flore)

Laurel

AIR: (*Earth. Water. Fire.*)

A Tiny Bow and Arrow:

I'll say, 'Why don't you just kill me?'

And I'll mean it. I'll wish he would.

He'll say, 'No point, you're going to die within the year anyway.'

And I'll say, 'What?'

And he'll say, 'Dead, within a year.'

But right now I'm running, sweating like that fat bloke who drinks cans of Diamond White in the bus stop – down the road, around the corner, over the sand dunes and onto the beach.

'Cause it was Mum who first told me about the advert. She'd been queuing to buy a pound of mince from the butcher and spotted it on the corkboard. I'd just that second walked in from school when my mum handed me the advert, said it'd be a nice little job for me and something that I could squeeze in between school and looking after my little brothers.

'You never took it down from the corkboard?' I asked.

'I didn't want no other bugger getting it,' Mum said, then we laughed.

The advert's for a part-time job, for someone to take the money off folk wanting to see the water-healers at The Oracle, the public baths on the seafront. 'Apply in person', and Mum said that I'd best hurry. And 'cause I'm a good girl and 'cause I always do what

I'm told, I'm running like a mental over the sand and sweating like that fat bloke, to try and get this job.

The Oracle had been a community swimming baths, had been around for years, then it closed down and started being derelict. The local council had put it up for sale and that's when some out-of-town folk bought it. They said that the Males 1st Class pool was built over a spring that was full of magic water. It's the same water that does that holy well up the hill, the one all them religious poorly folk from all over the world travel to. They reckoned the water had healing powers, I mean there's people who'll swear the water made their diseases disappear. None of us local folk knew the spring went under the Males 1st Class pool, but those out-of-town folk did and they bagged themselves a right bargain. That's when the swimming baths changed its name and started charging loads of money for folk to go in.

Apparently, someone was once cured of being fat and that's why every local lass pays their weekly subs to have a float. I've never been in before, but Mum and her friends are regulars. There's three water-healers who work there. They're local celebrities; they never pay for nowt in the shops, mainly because everyone thinks they'll be cursed if they're ever anything but ridiculously nice when the water-healers are around. They're like those baddies in the second Superman movie, those three that were banished from Krypton in the big mirror prison that shattered, letting them come to Earth via the Moon and be proper terrifying. It's our Bill's favourite-ever film, so I must have watched it at least a million times. Well Ursa, the female baddie, looks exactly like one of the water-healers, the one who goes by the name of Madame Pythia, and then there's Martin Savage, the main male water-healer, who's a bit like General Zod, the one who liked to say 'Kneeeel before Zod' in the film. The other one, the one that would be Non, is an old man, known as Silver. He's said to be quite nice. He refuses to give bad news when he picks up some psychic energy mid-heal; instead he bursts out crying and tells the poor customer to run for their lives.

If I'm honest, I'm a bit scared of The Oracle and the water-healers, I mean I've heard stories from Mum about all these local people who've had their now torn apart 'cause the water-healers have told them that they have nowt good in their future, that their futures are set to be proper rubbish and they can't ever be healed. Me, I'd prefer not to know. All I want in my future is to work hard for the next two years and then to get into college, maybe even go to university and train to be a teacher. I'd like to be one of them teachers that makes a difference, 'cause they 'proper under-stand' kiddies. I don't want some nutter putting their hands on me and telling me I can't be healed and my dreams won't be coming true and I'm best off jumping off the pier. My English teacher says I've the brains and I'm used to being around kids, what with being the oldest of seven kids by four different waste-of-space dads, 'cause even though Mum's proper useless at picking nice blokes, she's proper perfect at getting pregnant.

So, I'm running through the sand and up the steps onto the seafront. I can see The Oracle. It's a massive mansion of a building that's all orange and yellow like a bumblebee that's transformed into a building, but really we all know it's still a bumblebee. There's fancy stained-glass windows and a clock tower that chimes out every hour, even though it's something like seventeen minutes slow. There's three wooden doors in, for the three different water-healers and the three different baths, but mainly people make their appointments through the posh door, the one that leads to Madame Pythia's pool. But even when it's sunny, the place still freaks me out.

I get to the metal gate and I can see the main man-healer, Martin Savage (General Zod), sitting on the stone steps leading up to the Males 1st Class entrance. He's got a cigarette in one hand, a bacon butty in the other and the zip of his shell-suit top's undone, showing off his hairy belly.

'Hi,' I say.

'Hi,' he says. He smiles and I'm thinking, *Kneeeel before Zod*.

'I've come about the job,' I say, handing him the advert that my mum's ripped off the corkboard in the butchers.

'You're not what I expected,' Martin Savage says. 'How old are you?' Martin Savage asks.

'Fourteen,' I say.

'You got a boyfriend?' Martin Savage asks.

'No,' I say.

'Got any experience?' Martin Savage asks.

'No,' I say. 'But I learn fast,' I say.

He smiles (*Kneeeel before Zod*), then he flicks his ciggie butt onto the pavement, stands and walks up the steps and through the open wooden door into The Oracle. I don't know what to do so I start kicking the tips of my DMs against one of the steps.

'What's your name?' a voice asks.

I look up and the woman one, Madame Pythia, is standing at the top of the steps, all elegant and mysterious. She walks down the steps, without making a sound, so I reckon that she must have no shoes on, but her violet dress is long and flowy.

'Laurel,' I say. 'I've come about the job,' I say.

'So Martin tells me,' she says, she stops. She looks me up, she looks me down. 'You're pretty,' she says.

'Thank you,' I say.

'Can you start now?' she asks and when I nod she begins telling me all that I need to know about my hours and expected duties at The Oracle.

The Daughter:

'I'm to work every night after school, from four until eight. Madame Pythia reckons that's the busiest times. They open at two, but they've got their cleaner, Maggie, covering until I get there,' I tell Mum.

'What about weekends?' Mum asks. Mum's sitting on the sofa, a can of Diamond White in one hand, a ciggie in the other.

'They're open from two until eight, but then I've got to do full days and nights three days every month when Madame Pythia is "absorbed of everyone's sins",' I say.

'You what?' Mum says.

'I've no idea, the woman's cuckoo, Mum,' I say. 'I'm to take money, check appointments, sit at a desk in the Males 1st Class reception and pretend like I'm hard as nails and scary.'

Mum laughs. She pushes her ciggie butt into the almost-empty can.

'Piece of piss, our Laurel, and you get paid for doing it. Don't know how I'll manage with the kids without you, though,' Mum says.

'We can give it a go for a bit, Mum, see how it all works out. Two pounds fifty pence an hour, cash in hand, that'll really help out,' I say and Mum nods. Mum's all about the money.

And I reckon that the pay's okay for the job I'm doing. I mean I don't tell Mum, but really I think that working at The Oracle is going to be better for me than being at home looking after my brothers. The youngest is two, Sammy he's called, and he's a proper handful, into everything, and I spend all my time running after him and stopping him from climbing out windows. Madame Pythia even said that she's okay with me doing my homework at my desk in reception. 'Course I don't tell Mum that, mainly 'cause I don't want her thinking that I'm having it too easy, and 'cause it's almost too good to be true. I'm going to be able to do all my homework while I'm at work. I'll be able to read books and hear myself think. I reckon it's possibly the best job in the world.

When I get to really thinking about it, I don't even know how I got the job. Mum reckons it's fate, that it was meant to be, but I don't even know if I believe in all that sort of stuff.

Silver and Elsie Hughes:

It doesn't take long before I realise that most of the people who come to The Oracle are desperate, I mean proper desperate. It's only my second day, I mean I've only been at my desk for fifteen minutes and I'm trying to figure out algebra, but Elsie Hughes has turned up sobbing. My mum and Elsie used to be best mates, before Mum shagged Elsie's brother and got pregnant with our Sammy.

'I don't have an appointment, Laurel,' she says.

'Who do you want to see?' I ask.

There are three pools, Males 1st Class, Males 2nd Class and Females, and each of the water-healers works from one pool. Men or women can go in the male pools, it's not strict, just has them labels 'cause they're carved in stone over the entrance doors. I think it used to be a lot stricter in the old days. Only Madame Pythia's pool has water direct from the spring in it, the other pools have a mix of local water and seawater and magic water. That's why proper poorly people tend to go to Madame Pythia for healing.

'I need to see Madame Pythia,' Elsie Hughes says, wiping snot on her red coat sleeve. Elsie's a bit plump and her hair's all scruffy, with some of it still in rollers. She's holding a plastic bag with a blue towel not quite fitting in it.

I look at Madame Pythia's appointments, I shake my head.

'Soz, Elsie,' I say. 'She's booked solid for the next two days.' I turn the pages and look at Silver's bookings. 'Silver's got a cancellation in fifteen minutes,' I say.

She stops her crying. I think she might have been holding her breath.

'Okay,' she says, sighing. Then she moves to stand outside. I see her taking a ciggie from a blue packet and cupping her hands round it. She's trying to light it but her whole body's proper shaking.

I watch her. I mean I'm supposed to be doing my homework, but something about the way she shakes, something about how desperate she is to light that ciggie, something about the way she stares down to the stone steps, makes me want to cry with her. I've never seen anyone that sad before. I mean Mum's been in floods of crying, especially after one of her loser boyfriends has dumped her, but there's nothing deep about her tears. I've always known that she'll be out down The Swan on the pull the following night. Mum's bed's never empty for long. But with Elsie Hughes, her pain's different. It's like it's all the way around her and covering her like a shower curtain. I think she might be trapped and I think she might be desperate for someone to make her better.

I hear Silver coming. He always whistles the same tune. I think it's from an old film but I don't know him well enough yet to ask.

'Elsie Hughes is your next appointment,' I say to Silver, pointing out the door to Elsie.

Silver looks at Elsie Hughes and frowns. He walks out the wooden door but I can still hear them talking.

'You going to run away again?' he asks Elsie Hughes.

'No, Silver, I'm hoping you can help me last a bit longer,' she says to him.

Silver starts whistling again. I hold my breath until they've gone down the steps and they've turned left towards the Females bath entrance.

No Swimsuits Allowed:

It's been nearly a week now and I'm proper shattered. I've got no energy and I feel proper sad inside. There's so much pain and upset in the air in The Oracle. Some days I've wished I was wearing my fluffy pink earmuffs. Apparently that's normal. And that's why Madame Pythia came in earlier to tell me that part of my job was to take a weekly swim in the Males 1st Class pool. She said the spring water would take away all the weight I'd absorbed during my first week here. That was a couple of hours ago.

Now I'm practically being carried by Silver and Martin. They've each got me under one of my arms and my DMs are off the ground. I'm worried that they can see my knickers 'cause my dress is silly short and with the dragging it's going up and up. I'm practically making tiny running steps in the air as they take me to Madame Pythia.

She's standing next to the wooden steps going down into the deep end of the pool. Martin and Silver let me go, my knees buckle, and I fall to the mosaic floor.

'You're being ridiculous, Laurel, this is for your own good, and hiding—' Madame Pythia says.

'I wasn't hiding,' I say, and then, 'I don't have a swimsuit.'

'No swimsuits allowed,' Madame Pythia says.

I feel sick. I don't like my body. I don't like the hairs, I don't like my tiny titties. I don't like how the three of them are staring at me, waiting for me to strip down to starkers.

'Strip, or Martin'll do it for you,' Madame Pythia says, and then, 'I know this is making you uncomfortable, but there's no other way. Let the water help you, Laurel.'

I look to Martin Savage and he licks his lips. I can't let him be touching my skin, I can't let him be getting that close to me. There's something about him that I don't like, there's something about him that makes my stomach do hula-hoops.

'Can I change in there?' I ask, pointing to the blue changing cubicles that line the side of the pool. I like their pink-and-white stripy curtains.

'Strip, now. It's for the best, it has to be now. Please, Laurel,' Madame Pythia says. Her voice is gentle, yet firm. Her voice, her eyes, they make me trust her. I trust that this needs to be done, but still Martin Savage is staring and I hate that he's staring.

So I do what Madame Pythia asks me to do. I do it because I want this job, I need this job and, if I'm honest, I want the pain and sadness to go away. I start undoing the buttons of my little flowery dress. I slip out of my DMs 'cause they're never done up tight, I let my dress fall to the floor. I fumble trying to undo my bra at the back. It used to be Mum's but it don't fit her no more. I'm still rubbish with the catch. I take my bra off, let it fall to the floor and I cross my arms over my titties so that Martin Savage and Silver can't see my nipples. I feel stupid.

'Now your panties,' Martin Savage says.

I do as I'm told. I feel their eyes on me and my little-girl nipples. I wish I had big brown nipples like Mum.

'Get in the water,' Madame Pythia says. I look at Silver and he nods his head.

I walk to the edge of the pool, not sure whether to put my

hands over my titties or my fanny, and grab the metal handrail. I take the wooden steps slowly, worrying that I'm going to slip and drown and Mum'll always be wondering why I've died swimming with my titties out.

One, two and my feet are in the water. It's icy. It nips at my breathing. Three, four and the water's to my waist. I hate cold water; I'm shaking already and can't stop myself from wondering why on earth I even thought about getting a job with these nutters.

'Swim,' Madame Pythia says.

'Swim?' I ask. She nods.

I let go of the metal handrail and I flop forward into the cold water. I hold my breath and I flap my arms about. It's ages since I've been swimming.

'Swim,' Madame Pythia says again. I don't look at her or Silver or Martin Savage. I look down through the water; the white tiles are too far away for my toes to touch. I look to the shallow end, I see the wooden stairs, and I reckon that I'll swim to there and then out.

I swim badly. Mum never could afford the lessons and the ones I had with the school were pretty basic and more about avoiding being drowned by Sheldon Frances.

'I'll do it,' Martin Savage says. I think that's what he says. I look up with water splashing on my face, dripping from my fringe, and I see that he's undoing his jeans. I feel sick. I'm going to throw up into the water and I know that'll get me in proper trouble off Madame Pythia. I don't want him near me, I don't want him with his willy near me. I start to panic. I flap my arms up and down through the water, trying to make me go faster, trying and trying. But the more I flap my arms, the more it feels like I'm being pulled underwater. It's like the water's trying to stop me escaping and it feels like there's fingers grabbing my ankles and pulling me down. The water's filling my mouth and my ears and covering my head and I want to scream. I think I'm dying, I'm definitely sinking.

And that's when I hear Madame Pythia.

'Stay calm, Laurel, let the water help you,' she says.

And that's when I feel his arms around my waist. I try to kick him but my legs aren't working like I need them to work and them fingers are still squeezing my ankles. He pulls me to the side, the fingers let go of my ankles, and then he puts his hands on my naked bum cheeks and pushes me up. Silver's standing on the edge of the pool. He drags me out from the water and onto the mosaic tiles.

Madame Pythia is next to me. 'You need to trust,' she says.

I nod. I know she's right. I know that it's important that I prove to Madame Pythia that I can do my job, that I trust in both her and in the water. I roll so that I'm sitting up, I'm not at all graceful, then I shuffle to the edge of the pool and lower myself into the water again.

I hold onto the side. I turn, I look at Martin Savage. He's still in the water. He's still naked. He smiles.

'Lie back and float,' Madame Pythia says. I nod, then I lie back and push my feet off the wall of the swimming pool. I feel Martin's hands under my back, I try not to think about his touching me, instead I trust, instead I ignore his fingers stroking and prodding. I float, and I float some more.

And that's when something changes. I swear that I feel the air changing, I feel the pain and the upset fading and fading some more. I relax, I mean I proper relax, I let the water guide me and I smile a proper smile.

And at that very moment, I feel like nothing bad exists in the world and I feel the happiest I've ever felt.

Clever as Well as Pretty:

And when Martin comes to my desk later, he hands me an iced bun and a can of Diet Coke.

'Sorry, pet,' he says. 'It was mad in there, hope we didn't scare you. Me and Silver were trying to help.' And he smiles and I think he means it, so I smile back.

'Thanks,' I say, taking the gifts from him. The last thing I need is awkward stuff at my place of work. I like that he's being kind.

'It's this place,' he says, holding his arms out wide, 'it brings out the weird in all of us.' Then he laughs.

I laugh too.

'I feel so much better,' I say.

'It's the water, pet,' Martin says and then he sits down on the edge of my desk. 'Is there anything you've seen so far that's not made sense?' he asks. His voice is all gentle and caring and nice.

I think for a minute or two. 'I don't understand how you learned how to do everything,' I say. 'I mean, it's like magic.' I sound silly. Martin laughs.

'I was born this way, pet. I was picked on for being different, I never fit in no place . . .' His voice trails off. 'Bit like you,' he says. He leans over and strokes my shoulder. I nod but I don't really understand what he's saying.

'You got any friends?' he asks.

I shake my head. 'No time, with school and the kids.'

'Well, let's us be friends,' he says and he smiles. He moves a little bit closer, his leg touches mine. 'So what you up to?' he asks, pointing at the book on my desk.

'Just reading,' I say.

'You like books?' he asks and I nod. He leans across me, his chest in my face. I breathe in. He picks up my book and looks at the title. 'Clever as well as pretty,' he says.

I feel myself blushing. I try to stop the red but I can't.

'So, we're friends?' he asks, putting down my book. I don't know what to say, I nod. 'Good,' he says, 'because I'd hate you not to like me.' And then he stands up, goes outside and has a ciggie. I watch him, he's all smiles and he waves at me as he collects his next appointment and takes her to the Males 2nd Class pool.

And that's when I get to figuring that I've been silly and really Martin's nice and mainly he just has to put on an act for all the women who come here just to see him. He's popular, and I should feel happy that he wants to be my friend.

Three-Day Illness:

No one knows how old Madame Pythia is. Her forehead's covered in lines. Mum says it's from all the scowling she does, but I think that's just Mum being bitter. She doesn't really like women much, especially the ones with money.

It's not long before I start to understand how all the water-healing works and why Madame Pythia's the way that she is. It's all 'cause Madame Pythia believes that she's the jug (or something like that) for all those who've sinned. She says she's some kind of a working class Messiah, a prophet, and a massive absorber of all that surrounds her. She says that's why it's her penance, and that every third weekend of the month Madame Pythia gets to be ill for three whole days.

Every third weekend of the month sees The Oracle shut down to darkness. Locals know not to attempt an appointment. Anyone who approaches the bathhouse during those days is said to bring about a curse and 'the death of a loved one will be inevitable'. There's even a sign saying just that that's pinned to each of the three wooden doors for those three days. Silver told me that it was known, that it had once happened to the great-grandfather of Edna Williams. And that's why for those three days of every month Martin Savage and Silver get to escape to their own lives, they're free to be and do whatever they wish. It's not like that for me. It's in my job description that I'm to stay over in The Oracle for them days to nurse Madame Pythia back to her proper strength.

Yesterday, Madame Pythia said, 'My three-day illness is my penance for the spilling of secrets and my absorbing it through my healing hands.' That's when she raised her palms up towards the ceiling and I sort of nodded, not really sure what she was going on about. She was using words like 'cleansed' and 'purged' and I didn't have a clue what she was meaning. That's the problem with working here, it's sometimes like they're talking foreign and I'm not sure what the right response should be. Madame Pythia's told me not to worry about anything and that everything I see and hear is perfectly natural, that everything happens as it should. She says that all the healing and the taking on of other people's problems has to come out of her in one way or another.

But now I'm here, in The Oracle with her and I'm freaking out. The thing is, I'm now the person who has to watch her floating naked in the Males 1st Class pool, making sure that she doesn't drown. The responsibility's doing my head in. What if I go for a wee and that's when she drowns? And I'm not sure how I feel about watching her floating about in the pool with her titties out. She's not like my mum, she doesn't have no saggy belly and her titties point up to the ceiling even when she's lying down.

Mum says that Madame Pythia is off her head and it's pretty obvious that she suffers from migraines when it's her lady time of the month. 'Course I don't say anything like that to Madame Pythia, I mean, that woman's probably the scariest person in the world.

So instead I'm stuck here, in The Oracle, for the next three days, cleaning up sick from the pool and trying not to hurl my guts up. For the next three days I'll be trapped in the dark and Silver's told me that I'm not to be making any noise and not to even say one word out loud. He reckons that even the smallest noise will set Madame Pythia off into a bad place. Silver said that the more Madame Pythia floats undisturbed, then the less cleaning up I'd have to do. He's said I should try and sleep on the wooden folding seats in the changing cubicles by the pool, but maybe keep the stripy curtains open. He's said that at some point Madame Pythia'll climb out and lie on the mosaic tiles and that's when I should try and catch myself an hour's rest. But what if I sleep too much and she rolls in the pool and drowns and everyone says I killed her and they put me in one of them women's prisons? I'm going to try not to sleep for three days. I got myself some ProPlus.

The job itself, the working in The Oracle, hasn't interfered much with my schoolwork. But today, 'cause I'm having to be here all day, Mum's phoned the school and said that I'm sick. I get paid for every hour I'm here. Mum cares more about the money I'm paid than my schoolwork, and the school don't care because they expect it of my sort. Me, well I want an easy life, but mainly I'm hoping that I can get into college and prove them all wrong. I want to learn more about English, 'cause I have all these thousands of stories running around my head and I've been writing them down in a pink notebook that Silver bought me last week. Most girls my age are all about *Sugar* and *Just 17,* but I'm not. I'm not wanting to marry Mark Owen and I'm not interested in his favourite colour. I'm all about books that have stories that have been here forever, I'm all about words and fainting women. Madame Pythia has a million books upstairs in her flat. She's said that I can borrow them whenever I want. Mum doesn't get me, probably because she has my brothers to look after and they're right little buggers and Mum had left school by the time she was my age. I mean she's not that old now, she's only twenty-nine, but you'd never think it looking at her. I think that 'cause my mum'd been pregnant with me and had to drop out of school, well I guess it was my fault that Mum's turned out like she has. I mean she could have killed me in her belly or given me away, but she didn't. Mum gave up everything just for me.

So, I do what I have to do to make her happy. And that's why I'm here cleaning up sick and trying not to hurl and that's why I'm letting my mum have every penny that I earn.

Madame Pythia and Ada Harvey:

As the weeks go by I'm starting to get into a routine, knowing who to expect on what days and having my favourite clients, clients I proper look forward to seeing. There's this woman who comes here to The Oracle every Monday evening. She has a block booking of the six o'clock slot to see Madame Pythia. She's called Ada Harvey. She's probably thirty but she's got what Mum would call 'an old face'. I think that's because she was ill a few years ago and is still recovering. Ada knows my name and she's really kind. If she's baked on the Sunday afternoon, she'll bring me a scone or a fairy bun wrapped in a piece of kitchen roll, with a bit of sello-tape wrapped around it to keep it fresh and clean. Sometimes she asks me to go in with her when she sees Madame Pythia, but Madame Pythia won't let me. She says it's no good for me to learn the ways of the water-healers. She says that I don't have no gift and that I won't be around long enough to care how it works. That's fine with me, I mean I'm getting a bit fed up of all the flashes of titties and willies I get to see around here. I think it's put me off for life.

Ada Harvey's just come in.

'Laurel, you know how I've been having trouble with the hubbie since that last family heal?' she says.

I nod but I didn't know, not really.

'Well I was making my scones and I ended up flabbergasted,' she says and hands me a scone wrapped in kitchen roll with pictures of cats on skateboards on it. I look from the cartoon images, up to her. She continues, 'He's only gone and suggested that we should come to The Oracle as a couple, try again. I think he's intrigued.'

'A lot of people are,' I say. 'Thanks for my scone,' I say.

'To be honest, I think he's worried that he could have done more to save his mam. She died from breast cancer fifteen years ago,' Ada Harvey says.

Then the door to the Males 1st Class pool swings open. Mrs Winter comes out. She's sobbing. She doesn't even look at us, she just carries on sobbing and walking proper slowly out through the main entrance and down the steps to the seafront.

'Looks like she had a good session,' Ada Harvey says, pointing after Mrs Winter. 'You know we had that family healing a while back?' Ada asks. I shake my head. 'Must have been before your time.'

'Was it all that you expected it to be?' I ask, not really knowing the right words to use.

'Oh Laurel, it went okay, just okay. The hubbie was a little disappointed. I think he expected to see some phenomenon, like Madame Pythia walking on water or something,' Ada Harvey says and then laughs. I laugh too. 'Do you know how it all works?' Ada Harvey asks. I shake my head. 'Well,' she says, 'we all sat around the pool, with our feet in the water, while Madame Pythia chatted. She assured him that his mam was always with him, that she was no longer in pain and that she was clutching her right breast. She tried to explain that at his mam's level of purification, that she can be in seven places at once. At this the hubbie laughed. So, Madame Pythia told him how recently he'd had trouble with the volume on his car stereo. She told him that it was his mam who'd turned it down. The hubbie went rather pale. I remembered as well how the volume of music in his car kept reducing, to a normal level. I mean the hubbie likes to play his music so loud when he drives, but each time he fiddled the volume to high it'd go straight back down quiet. Of course, he assumed that there was something wrong with his stereo. He even took the car to the garage. It was a newish car, a newish stereo and the garage could find no fault. And still, the volume would turn down. So Madame Pythia tells the hubbie how his mam hates loud music.' Ada Harvey pauses.

I've unravelled the kitchen roll from my scone while she's been talking. Now I'm lifting it to my mouth. 'She's good like a witch, isn't she?' I say.

'Exactly like a witch,' Ada Harvey says and laughs. 'Madame Pythia told us that our son was specially gifted. Of course I smiled. The hubbie said something about how she was playing with my ego and with my emotions. She told us of how in a previous life, he was actually my sister. Then Madame Pythia told the hubbie to strip naked and get in the pool. While he did she described his character perfectly.' Again Ada Harvey laughs, then pauses, watching me devouring the scone.

'Are you hungry Laurel?' she asks.

I nod.

'Do they not feed you here?' she asks, looking me up and down. 'I'll bring you more next week,' she says, placing her hand on my arm. 'Madame Pythia said how the hubbie was moody and stubborn. She explained that this was because he carried the spirit of a policeman who had died young, who had not accepted his physical death. She told him how, although this spirit was largely positive, he was guiding the hubbie down certain paths, that it was the spirit's inability to accept his death that was causing the moods, the stubbornness and resentment within the hubbie. She said that's why he needed to let the water heal him.'

'And your husband is a policeman too?' I ask.

'Yes, Laurel, the spirit must have guided him into that profession.' Ada Harvey laughs and then continues. 'Then, Madame Pythia asked if we would like to see the spirits that were with us. My husband shouted yes, with perhaps too much enthusiasm. And so the spirits appeared in the water. I swear I saw their faces popping up – one, then another and then another. But my husband was blocked and could not allow his eyes to see. He saw nothing and that's what's making him angry. He thinks I'm making it all up.'

'Madame Pythia told me that there are some who are blind,' I say. Then the door swings open and Madame Pythia stands tall in her violet dress.

Madame Pythia shouts, 'Laurel, show Ada Harvey in.'

Blinking:

'Course I'm not even sure what Madame Pythia's real name is, I mean she must have a first name, I mean no parent'd be that cruel and name a child 'Madame'. I think I heard Silver call her Veronica or maybe it was Sally. I didn't quite catch it, but what I do know is that Madame Pythia delivers her oracles in a proper mental state. If Silver told me she'd been popping an E or seven, I'd believe him. I mean I've watched her from the viewing gallery and sometimes she even sounds like she's talking foreign.

Ada Harvey's left and today, right now, I'm seeing stuff that's making my stomach do hula-hoops. I mean I had a feeling it would when Silver said that I had to cancel his last appointment 'cause him and Madame Pythia were doing a healing together. I mean in all the time I've been here nowt like that's happened before, so my stomach did hula-hoops even before I was seeing what I'm seeing now.

I've sneaked into the Males 1st Class pool. I mean I waited until they'd started their healing, 'cause I know how they get all into it and they don't know what's going on about them. I'm trying to be invisible right next to the changing cubicles and I reckon it's working, 'cause no one's shouted at me to bugger off yet. Madame Pythia, Silver and some lass I've not seen before are starkers, I mean they're fully naked in the water.

But none of that even matters. 'Cause the shape of Silver's face has just changed.

I mean it's altered, I swear he's stopped being Silver and, apparently, instead he's a bloke called Simon who the lass in the water once shagged in a former life. I'm thinking this is like some dodgy remake of *Ghost* and trying not to freak.

A few minutes ago Madame Pythia was giving it all about showing the way to 'reverting the body of his spirit from a former life' and then Silver's face stopped being Silver's face. The lass who was being healed, her and Silver were treading water next to each other in the middle of the pool. Next thing, the lass let out the biggest scream ever and swam through the water to hug Silver. Silver hugged her back and then they snogged, with tongues, proper snogging. Madame Pythia had to pull them apart. That's when I started giggling, 'cause that's what I sometimes do when I'm freaked out. And that's why I'm blinking now and blinking some more to make sure that it's not my eyes playing tricks.

I mean I'm tired, it's been a long shift, it's the last appointment of the day, but none of my blinking's making any difference. And now a proper beautiful white light's surrounding Madame Pythia. Again, I'm blinking and, again, I'm blinking a bit more. I even use my fingers to stretch my eyes wide open. Maybe I'm confused or maybe I'm coming down with chicken pox. I know I'm not though, least I don't think I am. I wonder if it's the vapours off the water, I wonder if they mess with your head and make you see stuff that can't possibly be real. None of this makes sense to me.

'Cause now Madame Pythia's face is changing too. Ada Harvey said Madame Pythia could do that, she said how sometimes Madame Pythia allowed several spirits to 'manifest on her ugly face'. Ada said that one of the spirits she'd seen was her grandmother who'd passed when Ada was a little lass. But this is the first time I'm seeing it with my own eyes. I'm shaking, I'm so confused. I mean it's crazy, but I don't think I ever thought it was real. I mean, if I'm honest, I thought the folk who came here were all nutters, that they saw and heard what they needed to see and hear to make their lives better. But now, I mean right now, I'm not sure what's real and what's not no more.

The other day I asked Madame Pythia why so many people came to The Oracle and she said, 'After a long period of spiritual sleep and materialism, humans are finally awakening and opening their minds to new experiences.' And then, 'Humans are beginning to realise what I have known since birth, that materialism is not the answer.' I remember nodding my head, not really listening 'cause she was going on a bit. I remember thinking she was off her face and wondering why they charged so much for each session, if it wasn't about the money.

But that was all before I realised she could do proper freaky shit with her face. My head's all over the place now and that's when I hear the lass speaking.

'I have been told that there are dark demons smothering me,' she says.

'Who spoke such words to you?' Madame Pythia shouts across the pool. They've swam apart a bit while I've been freaking out.

'A friend,' the lass says.

'A friend! A friend! What rot! You should choose your friends with more care and consideration, my dear!'

I watch as Madame Pythia swims to the lass, lifts her hands and places them on the lass's face. Madame Pythia then closes her eyes and doesn't speak a word. I'm looking at the lass, she looks scared. I wish I could help her, but then I remember that she's paying for this mental stuff.

'Open your eyes,' Silver says, even though his face isn't his face still and even though he's now clutching the edge of the pool opposite me. And that's when Madame Pythia opens her eyes and turns her head to stare at Silver. She stares for a good few minutes, still with her hands on the lass's face and by this stage the lass's sobbing like our Sammy does when he's had a nightmare.

Madame Pythia turns back to her.

'I can see clearly, my dear.'

'But I fear that dark demons are there,' the lass says. She's still crying but at least the sobbing has stopped now.

'My dear, I will speak only the truth to you. I can see that there are spirits that are dark and that they stay close to you.'

That's when the lass gasps. And that's when I gasp too. Silver stares at me, but it's like his eyes don't recognise who I am. He doesn't speak.

Madame Pythia continues, 'Do not have fear, my dear. I can tell you that those spirits are aching, in anguish, in such deep misery. It is true that they are near to you, that they see your energy, but still they cannot touch you. They cannot become you. I can see that you do not recognise the power that you hold within yourself.'

That's when the lass falls below the water and that's when Silver turns back to being Silver, lets go of the edge of the pool and dives under the water to rescue her. He pulls her back above the surface and over to the side of the pool. She's all spluttering but that doesn't stop Madame Pythia from continuing with her speech.

'They cannot climb onto you,' she shouts, she's treading water and raising both of her arms out of the pool and up towards the ceiling. 'It is true that they seek to scratch your surface, yet beneath this fragile outer layer there is a vast reservoir of light. Close your eyes, relax, try to draw upon it.'

Silver's holding the lass with one arm and clinging to the edge of the pool with his other hand. The lass leans her head back, onto him, then she lets her legs lift up into the water. She's floating, she looks calm.

'Even if you cannot look into this light within my presence, know that this reservoir will be there to guide you when you are open to accepting that you are deserving of happiness, of goodness.'

Madame Pythia pauses, she locks eyes with the lass and that's when Madame Pythia declares, 'It is time, we must end this session', and she swims to the side of the pool.

And that's when I run to the doors, swing them open and run to my desk. I know I've been seen and that I'll probably get a bollocking later, but it was worth it.

His Love Story:

Next day I'm at my desk, struggling to complete a piece of GCSE coursework. I'm too close to the deadline and that's making me panic even more. It's English language, it's a love story, and mainly I'm struggling 'cause I don't really think I believe in love. I mean, it's not like my mum has found her happily-ever-after and it's not like any of the women who come here are celebrating amazing marriages. Everyone moans about their husbands and their partners and their kids. I don't think I know anyone who's in love, I mean not like I read about in all Madame Pythia's books. And that's why I'm struggling.

That's when Martin comes up to the desk, he's on a fifteen-minute break before his drop-in sessions start. As usual he sits, then shuffles closer and rests a hand on my shoulder. My stomach hula-hoops and I try to move my chair back a bit without him noticing.

'What you up to?' he asks.

'Coursework,' I say. 'Got to write about love, like I know anything about love.'

'What do you want to know? I'm a bit of an expert,' he asks, he winks.

I look at him, I blush because his eyes are that strong and

powerful and scary. 'Everything,' I say. 'Don't reckon I believe in it,' I say.

'Love exists,' Martin says. 'I once knew a woman,' he says. 'She was one of my first-ever clients. Gwendolyn Price was her name. She came here for treatment but me and her, well she was my fit. I mean she fitted onto me and I fitted into her and it was different. I know that's lame and all pathetic and I know that my wife'd have a paddy at me daring to say that me, that the father of her kids, was with the wrong lass. But Gwendolyn was the woman I should have married.'

I don't say anything. I pick up my pencil and start making notes. Martin's still perching on the edge of my desk, but he's taken his hand off my shoulder.

'Mainly at night when I was lying in bed, when I'd just shagged my wife, well I'd be thinking about Gwendolyn. And I'd be thinking about when I could next be with her. I still loved my wife, but it was clear I wasn't in love with her. Sometimes I even hated her because she could be a right nasty bitch to me and the kids. But mainly we just ended up shagging because that's what married folk do and if I did then she'd not be suspecting that I was at it with some person else,' he says, then he laughs. I laugh too, even though I don't think he's funny. 'What do you think about that?'

'I don't know,' I say. I don't. I mean I look at Martin and I see someone who's old, he's like the age my dad probably is. I don't really understand what he's trying to tell me. 'I don't get it. How do you do that? How can you love, but not be in love?' I ask.

'Love's not that black and white, pet,' he says. 'I wanted to leave the wife, but it was my kids that kept me and the wife together. I thought that the responsibility I felt towards my kids was more important than the love I felt for Gwendolyn. I reckon that me and the wife, that having kids was the reason why everything started going wrong between us, but we were good parents. Being with Gwendolyn was my only bit of me-time, the only time I could have some fun, away from dull-as-fuck routine,' he says.

'So what happened?' I ask, ready with my pencil.

'I couldn't leave my kids, financial and emotional shit, Gwendolyn got fed up of not having all of me. We ended after a year and I reckon my heart broke,' he says.

'I'm sorry,' I say, 'cause I am. He looks sad.

'I still think about her every day,' he says and he sighs. I've not seen him sad before, I feel sad too.

'I reckon that you can fall in and out of love all through your life, but there's only one person who really fits. And that love, that love trumps all other love. The problem is, that like everything in life, you can blink and you'll miss your moment,' he says, and then he's laughing again.

I laugh too.

'So Gwendolyn was my first-and-only real affair. And, of course, after losing Gwendolyn,' he says, 'that's when I started resenting my life. I decided I had nothing to lose and now I shag anything with a pulse. If I can't be with Gwendolyn then I don't give a fuck about anything else.'

That's when I look up at him and he winks and gets down from the edge of the table.

'People have affairs,' he says, walking towards the main door. 'Of course they do. And I do my duty as a husband, I'm there for my wife and I'm there for my kiddies. And I love every one of the women I've shagged, almost as much as they've loved my cock inside them. Everyone's happy and everyone's getting a piece of me. But it's never been like it was with Gwendolyn. I'm just a giving kind of bloke. I shag women and I give them a love that lasts for anything from five to thirty minutes.' He laughs again, I don't really understand his joke. 'What I can do with my cock . . .'

He doesn't finish his sentence and I'm really not sure what he's trying to tell me about love. I'm feeling even more confused.

But a bit later, I'm just coming out the toilet after having a wee and he's waiting. At first I'm wondering why he's waiting to go in the girl's toilet but then I get to realising that he's waiting to see me.

'So when you going to let me take you out?' he asks.

'Out?' I ask.

'On a date,' he says, and I laugh. 'What's funny?' he asks and I think I might have upset his feelings.

'Soz,' I say, I blush.

'How about the pictures?' he asks.

I shake my head, I don't look at him, I look down at the mosaic tiles. 'My mum wouldn't let me,' I say. And that's when he walks away.

'I'm in love with you, Laurel,' he shouts over his shoulder, he laughs as he turns the corner. 'Think of it as research for your coursework,' he says.

And I'm left wondering what that even means.

A Palm Reading:

'Course, I'd known that Silver reads palms. I've been working six weeks now and I know pretty much everything that goes on. I'm sitting on the stone steps outside the Males 1st Class entrance, reading and loving that it's a suntrap. I've got another one of my little dresses on, Mum treated me, buying it from Miss Selfridges instead of Mark One. It's got tiny yellow-and-blue flowers on it. I've got it hitched up into my knickers. I'm stretching out my legs across the steps and I've even taken off my DMs. I'm happy. I hear him whistling. Silver comes and sits next to me.

'Show me your palm,' he says and I do. I mean I don't even think twice about it. I like Silver, he's got kind eyes and he's bought me a tube of Smarties from the shops every day for the last two weeks. I'm saving the lids, trying to spell out 'Laurel', but I've not got 'r' or 'u' yet and I've only got one 'l'. I slide my hand off my open book and hold it up to his face. Silver smiles.

Silver lifts my palm up close to his eyes. He tilts my palm this way and that way and bends my fingers one by one. He runs his chubby man-fingers over the lines.

'Oh,' he says.

'What?' I ask.

I look at Silver, tears are already falling from his eyes.

37

'What?' I ask.

'Run for your life,' Silver says, letting go of my palm with a deep sob. He steadies himself on the metal railing, trying to get to his feet.

'Silver, tell me,' I say. I'm terrified.

'I can't, pet,' he says. 'It isn't what I do. Things happen as they should.' Then he walks back through the open wooden doors and into The Oracle. I hear him sobbing.

'Silver,' I shout, dropping my book and getting to my feet. The steps are hot.

'I wouldn't bother,' Martin Savage says. I hadn't seen him coming. I pull at my dress, to make sure that it's not still tucked in my knickers. He's at the bottom of the stone steps, dragging on a rolled ciggie. 'He'll not tell you if it's bad.'

'Will you?' I ask.

'Don't know if I should, what with you not letting me take you out,' he says.

'Please,' I say.

'Okay,' he says, and then, 'But you'll owe me one.'

He climbs the steps to beside me.

'Sit down, Laurel,' he says. I do. I don't want to owe him, but I'm that desperate.

'Give me your palm,' he says. I do.

'How old are you again, Laurel?' he asks.

'Nearly fifteen,' I say.

'You're pretty,' he says, stroking his index finger up my fingers and down to the base of my palm. It tickles, I giggle even though I don't want to giggle. Then he brings my palm up to his mouth and kisses it with his lips. He makes me want to be sick, I don't like his kisses. 'Ask Madame Pythia,' he says.

'Ask her what?' I say.

'To read your palm, I do tarot.' He laughs, a low and dirty laugh.

38

He lets go of my palm and leans towards me and kisses my cheek. 'You owe me one, you promised. Nice girls don't break their promises,' he says.

He smells of ciggies and stale beer and he makes my insides hula-hoop. I've seen what he likes to do. A couple of nights ago I sneaked up onto the viewing gallery and sat on the back row, on one of them fold-down seats. I was quiet, proper quiet and I watched just what he does to heal the women. I wanted to understand all that stuff he'd said about love. And that's why I know that Martin Savage's dirty, I mean he does proper dirty things. The noises he made and the mess they made. If that's what love is, then I don't want any of it. And I certainly don't want him loving mc.

But Martin Savage is used to having women falling at his feet. I mean I've seen them all at The Oracle. They'll be queuing down the steps leading up to the Males 2nd Class pool. Some days the queue goes all the way down and onto the beach. He's the only one of the water-healers who does a drop-in session every night. I've watched when Martin'll come swaggering along the sand and the women'll turn into quivering wrecks, dying to take their clothes off and let him swim naked with them in the Males 2nd Class pool. I overheard one of the women saying that after one of her friends had let Martin Savage do things to her in the pool, then she'd been able to have babies. She reckoned that Martin Savage could heal insides and because word's spread now every woman in the world's wanting to have a bit of him. It isn't like that with me. I mean I don't get why all the women are falling at his feet, and I know that there are some women who'd happily swim to him sitting naked on the edge of the pool and suck on his willy, while he's huffing and puffing for Wales and trying to say words to heal them.

So when he kisses me on the cheek, I mean I don't know how

to react. It's not like I fancy him. I mean he's old enough to be my dad and I've seen where his lips have been. I mean Martin Savage's probably the kind of bloke Mum would have gone for. He's married, he's got kids and he's a bad bad man. I need him not to love me.

I turn to look at Martin and he moves in to kiss me on the lips. I pull my head back and bang it on the metal rail.

'My head,' I say. It hurts like hell.

Martin Savage gets up, and walks into The Oracle. 'You promised, you owe me, prick-tease,' he says.

He Wants a Virgin:

Later, I was sitting at my desk when he came over and sat on the edge as usual, bending in right close to look at his appointments in the book.

'I haven't had a virgin for a couple of years,' he said. I looked at him, he stared at me.

At first I thought I'd heard him wrong and so I didn't say a word back to him. And that's when he said, 'You'd better be a virgin. I don't want to be wasting my time on you. No one likes a filthy whore.'

'I am,' I said and I blushed again.

'You're a prick-tease, that's what you are. We had a deal, you owe me,' he said, before pushing the appointment book onto the floor and ordering me to pick it up. I didn't at first, I was looking around to see if anyone was watching. They weren't. And that's when he shouted. 'Pick the fucker up.'

I bent to pick up the book.

'And the toilets in my changing rooms need cleaning,' he said, before walking off.

That was a couple of hours ago and I've still not plucked up the courage to go into his changing rooms. I don't want to be near him, I don't even want to be here in The Oracle. I told Mum last night, told her about how weird Martin was and how he made me feel and Mum said that I should just grin and bear it. And then she said that I should stop my moaning and be grateful that I had a job and that we needed the money, and if I gave up then she'd have to think twice about whether or not I could go to college.

So I go to have a look in the Males 2nd Class changing rooms. I push the door open and shout a 'hello' but no one replies. I walk around, looking and looking some more, but it all seems to be pretty clean. I mean I know Maggie, the cleaner, was in this morning. I mean she comes in every morning. There's no towels lying around, the floor isn't dirty, there's not even any water on the floor. I'm walking towards the toilet and that's when I realise that he's in the changing rooms too.

'Time you let me suck on those little titties of yours,' he says. I turn. He's standing in front of the door so there's no way I can get out. 'Undo your dress, time to pay up,' he says.

'I just came to check—' I say, but he interrupts with, 'We both know why you came here.'

'You told me to,' I say.

'You're not stupid. Take your dress off and stop playing games,' he says. 'Do as I say or you'll get the sack,' he says. 'And I'll make sure no one round here gives you a job,' he says.

I start walking towards him, hoping to get around him, hoping for a miracle, a something to make this better. He grabs my arm.

'Get off,' I say, trying to wriggle away, but that makes him grip harder and pull me in closer.

'I'm going to taste you,' he says. 'That's what lovers do.'

I feel sick, I'm crying, I want him to stop, I want to be back at my desk, with my book, with the clients, with the appointment book. And that's when he lets go of my arm and that's when he opens the door out of the changing room.

'Off you go, prick-tease,' he says and he slaps my arse as I walk past.

I'm still crying when I get to the desk. Silver's there, he's watching me, but when my eyes meet his he turns away.

'Silver,' I say, 'what shall I do?'

'Run for your life,' Silver whispers, but he carries on walking.

An Arrow Tipped with Lead:

Next day's here and Silver's still ignoring me, like actually not even coming near me, and sending his last clients to ask me questions for him. I don't know what to do. I mean, I didn't sleep proper last night, 'cause I kept thinking about all the proper bad things that could happen to me. And I kept thinking about what Martin Savage could have done to me in them changing rooms. I ended up really freaking myself out and making my heart beat funny like I'd been sprinting in a race or something. I tried to talk to Mum this morning, but she said I was just being silly and Silver was probably having a bad day. She even said that Martin'd be a good man to 'pop my cherry' as he'd know what he was doing. She'd laughed, like I was being silly for being so scared. I told her I didn't want to go into work and she got cross. I know not to push it with her, I know she's thinking I'm just a stupid little girl but I'm not. I know Silver, he's a kind man, he wouldn't be being like he's being unless there was bad stuff he didn't want to say.

I had to talk to him, I had to find out what he meant, so I waited until his last client left and I walked into the Females pool. But Silver was having none of it. He barged past me and out the main door.

'Course, Martin Savage's finding it all hilarious. Just now he

45

said that if I showed him my titties he'd talk to Silver for me. And now, I mean I know he's watching me now. 'Cause I've just run off and I'm chasing Silver down the steps, along the seafront and onto the beach. My DMs are rubbish to run in and I'm having to push my dress to my thighs to stop it from flying up and showing everyone my knickers. I can hear Martin Savage's dirty laugh behind me and that's when Silver stops walking, turns to me and puts his fingers in his ears.

And that's when he shouts at me, 'Bugger off, Laurel!'

I know I have to, I don't want to be upsetting Silver, I think he's a sort-of friend and I don't have many of them, so I stop and turn back to The Oracle.

I can see him, that Martin Savage, as I walk back. He's like a tiny black fly in front of the huge bumblebee building. I walk slow, much slower than I should, considering there's a bit of a queue snaking out from the Males 1st Class entrance and when Madame Pythia finds out that I ran off she'll have a proper fit.

I'm getting closer to Martin and I can see his nasty face. I don't like him, not one little bit. He's a cheating ball of slime, I've seen what he does to the women who come here to be healed. They trust him and he's proper dirty. But the more I give him the evils and the more I refuse to speak to him, the more he seems to like it. I know he thinks I'm playing hard to get, but I'm not. I hate him.

I walk past Martin Savage and the few women who've formed a queue for appointments, but just before I get to the steps, he jumps forward and goes to put an arm around me.

'GET OFF!' I shout. I think I hear one of the queuing women tut.

'Laurel,' he says, in a sickly sweet voice, 'what's wrong, pet? Has Silver upset you?'

'FUCK OFF!' I shout, barging past him and knocking shoulders with at least two women in the queue.

'Silly bitch,' one of them says.

'Got the manners of her mam,' another says.

I keep walking through the entrance and that's when I hear Martin Savage saying, 'Now, now ladies, leave the poor lass alone. I'll sort her out later, make sure she's okay. I reckon she just needs some Martin-loving.' Then he laughs.

And although the words he's saying are sounding all nice and kind, there's something inside of me that's screaming for me to run for my life.

Her Name is Madora Argon:

But there's no time for dwelling, I've work to do. I mean, it's not like I've got a choice, I don't want Madame Pythia having a go, but my head's all over the place. I'm trying so hard not to stand up from my desk and throw the biggest strop ever. I need Silver to help me, I need to try and talk to him later.

So, for now, I'm sitting at my desk, my bare toes on the cold mosaic floor, and trying to lose myself in a book. That's when I feel a young lass's eyes staring at me. I look up and I blush, 'cause I reckon she's been standing there for ages and I haven't even realised.

I put my book down on my desk. 'I'm after an appointment?' she says.

'For when?' I ask. I flick the pages of the appointment book forward to when there's some free slots.

'Today?' she asks. I can hear a quiver in her voice.

I shake my head, 'cause I know how busy we are, and that's when I glance up at her and that's when I catch a look in her eyes. I've been working here long enough to know when people are desperate, to know when it's proper important that they see a healer. This lass needs help, her eyes are pleading with me to help her.

'They're all booked up, Martin Savage has a drop-in later,' I say, then, quickly, 'but Silver's always good at squeezing in an extra session. If you don't mind waiting?'

'I really wanted to see Madame Pythia,' she says, looking down at the mosaic tiles. 'I've heard she's the best.' She's not crying but I reckon she's not far off. She's pulling her red hair into a ponytail and looking anywhere but at me. I'm staring at her face, her skin's white like posh china. She scares me, she's proper fragile.

'She's booked up for weeks,' I say, I'm still staring at her, she's still looking at the mosaic floor. 'But Silver's proper good.'

She nods and her face does an angry twist. I've seen the look before, it's like the lasses blame me for them not thinking ahead and booking appointments, but there's something else there too. There's more to her angry twist than her just being cross with me. This lass is proper desperate.

'What's your name?' I ask. 'To write in my book,' I say, holding my pencil over Silver's page.

'Madora Argon. But Maddie, I'm called Maddie,' she says and her eyes meet mine. She smiles but her eyes don't.

'Why don't you wait outside in the sunshine? I'll ask Silver when he's likely to fit you in and let you know,' I say.

She nods again, turns and walks out the main entrance, she's dragging her feet and it's like she's no energy left and it's like she's two hundred years old. I want to tell her that it'll all be okay, but I don't know if it will be. I can tell she's broken, I'm guessing there's a man involved and then I think about Martin Savage and I feel sick again.

And that's when Silver comes to the desk and grabs the appointment book. He's standing, looking at his appointments, and I'm trying my hardest to explain about Maddie before he walks away. I'm not even sure he's listening. But then, just when I'm almost finished explaining, Silver throws the book on the floor, walks towards the main entrance and out to where Maddie's sitting on the steps. I wish I knew what I'd done to make him hate me. I thought he was my friend.

The Curse:

But mainly, for the last few days, I've been trying to talk to Silver and trying to avoid Martin Savage, but it's been pretty much impossible. Madame Pythia's already given me a warning for hiding in the Males 1st Class changing rooms and another for not being at my desk in reception. She's not being mean, her words always sound sad. I'm sure she was crying when she was looking at me earlier.

Today my black hair's all flung loose over my shoulders. I think it looks pretty. I'm not doing it for Martin Savage, it's just 'cause I've had it up for a couple of days 'cause our Bill brought back nits from school and it pulls on my scalp when I wear it up too much.

I'm sitting on the steps outside Males 1st Class, I'm not reading or anything 'cause I'm feeling sick with all the hula-hooping in my belly. That feeling's with me all the time now, like I'm waiting for that bad thing to happen. It's not like I can ask Silver to tell me what he saw, no chance at all, 'cause he's proper ignoring me and still not even buying me Smarties from the shop.

There's a couple of people waiting to see Madame Pythia but they're over talking to someone in Silver's queue, outside Females.

'Course I don't hear him sneaking up. He's good at creeping.

'You thought 'bout tying your hair up nice,' he says.

I can feel his fingers doing spidery steps running down my arm, up and down and up and down. I don't move.

'Show me your titties,' he says. I don't look at him.

'Prick-tease,' he says. I don't look at him.

'Bet some lad's giving you one,' he says. I don't look at him.

'I declare that you're sacred to me,' he says. I don't look at him.

'And if you so much as look at any other bugger, I'll rip your hair out and stuff it in your mouth,' he says. I don't look at him.

'You know you love me really,' he says. I don't look at him.

'I mean, what you scared of?' he says. I don't look at him.

'I'm Lord of The Oracle,' he says. 'There ain't nowt in the now or in your future that I don't know.'

I can feel sick coming up my throat and I'm gulping and gulping to push it back down. I want him to go away, I want to scream at him to fuck off back to all them women who want him. There's so many who throw themselves at him, so why won't he leave me be?

'You'd better still be a virgin, this had better all been worth it,' he says, again. And that's when I look at him.

'Fuck off, old man,' I say.

I know I shouldn't have said it, but it's like the words escaped before I had the chance to stop my brain from making them.

'I'd rather fuck you,' he says and he sits down next to me. His thigh brushes against mine. He's calm, too calm. I try to turn my body away, he shuffles closer.

'Over my dead body,' I say. I feel his hand on my thigh.

He laughs. 'Soon,' he says, and then, 'It's your destiny.'

And that's when I turn to look at him. I don't remove his hand from my thigh, I don't scream and I don't shout. There's something in his voice that makes me listen, that makes me know that what he's about to say matters. He's that close to my face I can smell his ciggie breath. It's like I've got no more fight, like all the strength in me's gone. I can't stop him, he's just too strong, he's too focused. He's never going to stop. Martin Savage has got the advantage, he knows what happens next.

'Why don't you just kill me?' I say, I almost whisper. I mean it. I wish he would.

'No point,' he says, and then, 'You're going to die within the year anyway.'

'What?' I say. My eyes are on his face, he's smiling a proper smile.

'Dead,' he says. 'Silver told me. Within a year. Your life's over.'

He says those words and I listen. I'm sure I'm holding my breath. I think I'm shaking. And that's when something changes in me, something hardens, something makes sense. I mean, I think about Silver and I think about all those lines on my palm that told them secrets. I know that Martin Savage is evil but I also know that he's telling the truth, that it's been foretold. That's why Silver's been avoiding me, that's why I've been feeling full of hula-hoops. That's why all my hopes and dreams for my future are pointless. I'm never going to escape, I'm never going to be allowed to have better than this.

I know I'm crying. I can hear Martin Savage laughing. I can't fight him any longer, he's broken me, his fingers have moved up my thigh and are fiddling with the elastic on my knickers.

And that's when I look into his eyes. He can see the change in me too.

'That's right, my shagging you was foretold,' he says.

'It's written in your palm,' he says.

'Get up,' he says, removing his fingers from me and standing up tall. 'Go into my changing room.'

I keep looking at him, I keep looking into his eyes, I see his disgust, I see what he really thinks of me. I know that I've no choice, I know that I'm playing a role. I guess this is what destiny feels like. As I'm getting up, I see that he's unzipping his jeans.

'They all give in eventually, Laurel,' he says. 'Let me show you love,' he says, licking his lips. 'Let me show you what it means to be loved,' he says to me, and then, 'Before you're dead and buried.'

Arthur

EARTH: (*Water. Air. Fire.*)

Reference No: 10-003760
Name: Charlotte (Charlie) Cornelius
Missing Since: 05-Feb-1998

Not only do I have a boner but I'm running out the yard with my pants around my arse and it's raining on my cock.

'You twats!' I'm shouting, but I know they're not listening.

My cock rocks in the wind as I run, but I don't stop and zip up my trousers until I get around the corner, just outside the post office on the main road.

The sky's all grey, mainly 'cause it's been raining forever, and I'm just letting myself get soaking. I'm a proper bell-end. I mean, what was I thinking? Estelle Jarvis is fit, there was no way she'd ever be interested in me. I mean just 'cause she liked all my profile pictures on Facebook. Like she'd ever want to suck my cock. No. That twat Tommy Clarke organised it all and by now my cock'll be all over Facebook.

Why do that? Why put my cock all over Facebook? I look up to the sky, like there's someone there, like anyone gives a fuck 'bout me. The rain falls in my eye and it stings like fuck. I mean I thought rain was supposed to be good for you, not this bastard, not this twatting northern rain. It pours from the skies non-stop, largest recorded rainfall forever, and now the bastard's practically blinded me.

I reckon that 'bout sums up my day.

It all started last night. Estelle Jarvis was all over my Facebook wall.

1. Would I get drunk with you? **yepp**
2. Hug, kiss, or more? **kiss**
3. Do I trust you? **yepp**
4. Share bed or on the floor? **bed lol ;)**
5. Friend, best friend, or good friends? **good friend**
6. Love, like, hate you? **love**
7. Good-looking, gorgeous, pretty, ugly, alright, fit? **gaaawjuss**
8. Would I go out with you? **yepp**
9. Rate (personality)? **10**
10. Rate (looks)? **10**
12. What's your name in my phone? **Arthur B**
13. Would I give you my number? **u ave it**
14. How did we meet? **in school**

I didn't have her number and I was trying to pluck up courage to inbox and ask for it but every sentence I wrote sounded gay. Then she posted 'inbox me I've gotta talk' on my wall and I did. I inboxed Estelle Jarvis, THE Estelle Jarvis who's at the top of the year-eleven tree.

I reckon the other lads from my year were proper wanting to know what was going on, 'cause they were all over my Facebook wall with 'inbox matee?' and I was all 'I will iab', but I didn't, mainly 'cause me and Estelle Jarvis were on chat. That's when she said that she wanted to meet me after school, around the back of the Sixth Form Centre. She said that she wanted to suck my cock and I probs shouldn't have gone along, but I reckoned it was a chance to get me a nice girlfriend who'd maybes have sex with me.

'Course I got to behind the Sixth Form Centre and she was already there. Seriously she was unzipping my trousers before I'd even said a word and my cock was playing along 'cause that's what cocks do. Then she had my cock out my pants and she pulled my pants down over my arse. That's when she stepped back and she was having a right look. I pushed it out a bit and prayed to God that it wouldn't go floppy.

And that's when it all went tits up.

'Alrite gay?' he said. 'You hoping for stinky fingers?'

And that's when I realised there was probs eight or nine of the bastards, all with their phones out, all taking photos of my cock. And that's when I legged it out through the yard, with my pants around my arse and the rain falling on my boner.

I'm maybes thinking that I might have overreacted and I should have laughed while I put my cock away, that maybes me having a boner would've stopped Tommy twatting Clarke from saying I was gay. And I'm maybes thinking that the twats that took them photos are complete dicks and one step away from lager-drinking ASBO yobs.

They've really upped their game this time. I mean this is a hundred times worse than the shit they kick out of me every twatting time they see me. I mean my legging it with my pants around my arse has probs made everything a million times worse. I mean whoever said your school days are the best in your life, well they were talking utter bollocks.

It's not like I can talk to my dad 'bout all the Facebook stuff.

Everyone at school reckons Dad's gay. I've had many a Facebook-wall post off them saying 'Braxton's dad gobblz cock' and 'Ur dad is queer'. But he's not. Dad's just broken, proper broken.

Two years ago I came home from school to find my mum sitting at the bottom of the stairs crying. I thought maybes my dad'd died. He hadn't. He was at work and Mum was gearing herself up to pissing off out of our lives.

Mum told me that she'd got back in touch with some bloke she'd known at university. She'd found him on twatting Facebook and at first it was all 'bout inboxing. Then she'd met up with him for a pint. She'd driven all the way to Leeds just so as they could meet up in a pub they once knew. Mum said it like I'd be impressed that she'd once been in a pub. Mum said it'd been going on for two years. Two fucking years and my dad didn't have a clue. At first I wondered why Mum was telling me all the stuff. I mean I didn't want her getting all menstrual 'bout life and then, Jesus Christ, she made me a bit sick in my mouth when she started going on 'bout how she was still young and needed sex. She didn't say it exactly like that, but that was the gist of it.

The fact was that Dad wasn't giving her any and Mum wanted some.

Mum said that she reckoned she deserved more than the shit life her and Dad were having and that if she didn't leave that very day then she'd probs never leave. Mum said she'd waited until I was fourteen, God bless her consideration, but that now I was fourteen there was little more she could help me with. She made some joke about 'Arthur helping Arthur', 'cause clearly what with me and my dad having the same name, that meant that I was more his than hers. She reckoned she'd done enough raising me and my dad'd be good at the last bits before I left home. I think she said something 'bout expecting me to be left home by the time I was sixteen. Clearly she had high hopes for my future career, even at that early age.

Anyways, that's when Mum stood up off the stairs, I mean she was sobbing so not entirely a heartless slag, but she went upstairs and I followed her into her and Dad's bedroom. Then she packed one bag, with hardly owt. It was mainly some frilly underwear, make-up, some expensive perfume and a couple of photos of me that she liked best. One was from when I was a baby and the other from when I was two, she didn't take owt with her to remind her of how I was then.

I sat on Mum's and Dad's bed and I watched her packing her stuff. All the time I didn't cry and I didn't shout and I certainly didn't speak. I just watched my mum putting the only reminders of her life with us into a bag. Simple. And while she was packing she said that that day was the start of her new life with her new bloke and that he was all set for buying her everything she needed. The bell-end. He was a lecturer and Mum was thinking 'bout going back to study creative twatting writing. She had a novel in her, whatever the fuck that meant. She was going to do all the stuff that having me when she was twenty had stopped her from doing. She said I'd made her tits little and taken away her identity. It was bad enough she was pissing off but saying shit embarrassing stuff like that made it all the worse. She even said that she was looking forward to being a mum again one day.

Then Mum came over to me on the bed and she sat next to me. She put her hand on my knee and gave it a little squeeze. And that was all. No hug, no emotional goodbye. Just my mum standing up, picking up her bag and pissing off down the stairs and out the front door. I was left sitting on Mum's and Dad's bed wondering what the fuck I was going to tell Dad.

And, me being me, I didn't tell Dad for a few hours. I mean I couldn't judge the right time to tell him 'bout Mum pissing off. He came in from work asking me where Mum was and I lied, I said I didn't know. By half ten and after he'd figured she'd gone out without her mobile and left her house keys in the kitchen, Dad was all set for phoning the police. That's when I reckoned I had no choice but to tell him 'bout Mum being a slag.

Dad seemed to take it quite well, that night. That night I reckon he did what any bloke would do after learning their wife had pissed off. He drank most of his single malt and passed out on the sofa. Not forgetting that when I went down in the morning to have my breakfast before school, I found him stinking of piss, lying half on the sofa and half on the floor. But I reckoned that was a normal reaction. I expected a couple of days of wallowing and then me and him'd put the world to rights. 'Cause my dad was ace, proper tough and funny, I expected him to sort all the shit out and make everything better.

I couldn't tell anyone, probs 'cause I knew that the likes of Tommy Clarke would go on 'bout how my mum's new bloke was chewing on her tits. And also I didn't really want anyone to know what a slag Mum was being. I guess in them first few days I reckoned she'd come home. She didn't. Obviously.

After that night of Dad pissing himself, he was all apologetic. He even went out looking for Mum. I told him all I could remember 'bout her new bloke and we even tried logging into Mum's Facebook account, but of course she'd got herself a new password, to go with her new life. She'd even protected her profile so that we couldn't see any of her friends. Got to give my mum credit, she was shit hot on cyber protection.

Anyways Dad didn't give up for quite a bit. He was all for cleaning the house and cooking and being pretty much tops. He was saying stuff 'bout us Arthur Braxtons being made of strong shit, going on 'bout his dad being an Arthur Braxton and how he took no shit from women and how our name was like some sort of badge-of-twatting-honour. It was a laugh, me and my dad against the twatting world. But then I reckon it hit Dad that Mum wasn't coming back and that's when he went all manic.

To start with he got to writing 'cunt' all over my mum's feature wall in the lounge. I reckon it made the feature wall look less wanky, but I didn't tell Dad that. Then he spent days smashing up plates and ornaments. He'd take them out from Mum's cupboards and off Mum's shelves, then go into the centre of the kitchen and hoy them on the floor. I reckon no one'll understand my reasoning but I'd give anything for him to be like that again. It showed he cared and it didn't leave the room stinking of piss. 'Course I didn't like him being like that at the time, God no, not back then. He was a proper nutter. But it was somehow better than now.

After a manic week or so, Dad went all quiet. And that quiet's how he's been since.

Mum never came back. Worse still she never called, she never emailed, she never sent a text and she never even bothered to tell us where she was living. She hasn't even bothered with my two birthdays since. Don't get me wrong, she's not an utterly heartless bitch, she pays money into the bank account every month. Guilt money, I reckon. But it keeps us afloat and social services off our backs. But Dad, well he's not taken my mum disappearing too well. He's managed to tell his mum and his sister to twat off, and even though at first they'd come visiting and trying to make things better. They'd bring around food and bits of shopping, stuff they reckoned we needed like washing-up liquid and talcum powder and bleach for the toilet. But after six months of Dad refusing to speak to them and instead holding up a piece of cardboard with the words 'twat off' written in one of Mum's lipsticks, well they did just that.

My dad's being a bell-end but I get it. I get that Mum broke him, I get that he's got nowt to get bothered 'bout and he's got no one to get washed for. I get it. Instead he spends his days lying on the sofa watching daytime telly or staring at the word 'cunt' on Mum's feature wall. Dad's doctor has him as 'unfit to work'. No shit, Sherlock. And me, well I've spent months trying to make sure that no one ever comes round our house and if they do, they certainly never get to step into this shithole.

'Course, I don't tell anyone 'bout how shit it is in my house.

It's not like I've got any mates to talk to. Tommy Clarke told everyone that the reason my mum pissed off was 'cause my dad's a bender. He said my mum'd caught my dad bumming the milkman, said that's why Mum pissed off, said that's why Dad lost his job. Everyone believed Tommy twatting Clarke. But what am I supposed to do? I don't want to hear them all calling Mum a slag and saying how she's getting boned every night. God, no. And I can't be telling them that Dad's broken and spends his days watching crap daytime telly and pouring stale Walker's crisps into his mouth. So, I keep quiet. I let them think whatever they want. That's 'cause I read an agony-aunt column once and it said how if you fight back you sometimes end up digging yourself into an even bigger hole. So me, well I let the shit-slingers hoy whatever they want at me. Sticks and stones, my dad's no bender.

So I keep my mum's secret and I keep my dad's secrets and instead I put up with daily shit from Tommy twatting Clarke. Well I say daily but I'm proper talented at wagging off school. I mean why would I bother going someplace where I get the shit kicked out of me 'cause Tommy Clarke and his bunch of merry twats've got some gay-bashing thing going on? He reckons Dad's gay, that I've caught being gay off my dad and that I deserve the beating for the both of us. He's even told the lads in my year that if they're friends with me then they'll 'catch being gay' too. Tommy Clarke's proper bright like that. And if I don't leg it fast enough, then I put up with the beatings they give me, simple as that.

So, I go to school when I have to, I keep social services off my back. But every single twatting time I do it ends up with me legging out of school and Tommy Clarke and his merry bunch of twats chasing after me. And all the time I know that none of it would be happening if my mum wasn't such a fucking slag.

But, still, sometimes I dream 'bout Mum. I dream 'bout her coming round one day and letting herself in with a key and 'bout her having bags of shopping from Asda. I swear I can practically taste the custard doughnuts and Jammie Dodgers popping out the top of her carrier bags. And then it's shit all over again when I wake up and realise that my dream was bollocks, that Mum don't give a shit 'bout me and that my life's utter wank. Some days I hate that I wake up.

Mrs Harrison from over the road stopped me the other day and said that she'd seen Mum pushing a pram through the centre of Manchester. She said she was sure it was Mum but that she'd lost a few pounds and got herself a fancy new haircut. She said she'd not seen Mum round our way much recently and wondered if she was all right. I ended up saying something gay like 'my mum's on holiday'. I mean, for fucking out loud, who goes on holiday for two years? I reckon it's perhaps 'bout time I said something honest. So next time someone asks, I'm all for saying that Mum's fucked off with a bell-end and she's not coming back. And that she don't give a twat 'bout me and that she certainly isn't going to want to be having sex with Dad. He stinks of piss and he's fat.

Nice one, Dad. Good work on the parenting front. Nice one, Mum. You utter twat.

I pull my phone out of my pocket. I'm on the seafront now and it's proper freezing. Nowt but crappy black to my left, I can't even see the sea, and the shops are closed; I swear, I must be the only twat stupid enough to be outdoors. Even the seagulls have fucked off out of the rain.

My head's been full of Estelle Jarvis and Tommy twatting Clarke. I must have been walking for hours.

I'm shaking, I don't know if it's 'cause of the cold or my head. The wind's lashing from the sea and onto me, the rain's splashing on my phone's screen and making it impossible to read. I smear it across with the cuff of my blazer and manage to press an icon that takes me to my settings. I tap off it and load Facebook.

And that's when I see a photo of my cock.

'Bastards,' I whisper. 'Twatting bastards.'

I've been tagged. My cock's on Tommy Clarke's wall, so there's no way I can delete it, but 'cause he's tagged me and practically every other person in year eleven, my cock is everywhere. The six inches of my boner is glistening from my phone's screen. Oh God, no. There's already thirty-seven likes and nineteen comments, but I can't bring myself to click on the comments. I know it'll be taken down soon, but that's not the point. The whole fucking world will have seen it by the time Facebook gets to removing it.

That's when I start walking along the seafront. I'm shoving my phone back in my pocket as I walk. The rain's pounding down on my head and the wind's dancing across the Irish Sea. The wind's circling me and making me feel like utter shite, like it's telling me that my life's not worth owt. I stop. I put my shaking hands onto the metal railings and look out to the sea. The cold wind stings my face. I hadn't even realised I was crying. Estelle Jarvis is an utter bitch. I hate her. And Tommy Clarke is an utter twat. But it's me that's the biggest twat in all of this. What the fuck was I thinking? Why the fuck would someone as fit as Estelle Jarvis want to suck my cock? I'm the school fucking freak, why would she be interested in a twat like me?

I've no idea what to do next. I'm freezing, my uniform's fucked, I've no one to turn to, I've nowhere to go. I've fuck all in my life. And somehow the wind's telling me that my life's not going to get any better. And somehow the wind's telling me that this is it, that this is the best my life's ever going to be. And somehow the wind's telling me that all Arthur Braxtons are utter twats.

And that's when I start thinking 'bout ending it all. I mean there, on the seafront, with the heavy sky and the freezing wind, that's when I realise that I've nowt in my life. No mum, no dad who gives a fuck, no mates, beatings at school, and now I'll always be known as 'Cock Boy'. But more than that, I'm thinking that all Arthur Braxtons are fucked up and I don't want to end up like my dad.

I climb up and straddle the railings. I'm all set for jumping down the four metres onto the beach and walking into the sea. There's no need for a note, maybes I'll just update my Facebook status with a 'has had enough'. I get my phone out my pocket, my fingers aren't working properly, it's too cold, I'm too cold. My head's proper fucked. My fingers fumble but I manage to open Facebook, I'm all set. I've had enough of this fucking shit life.

And that's when I hear music.

I'm still clutching my phone in my hand, I'm still freezing my nuts off, but it's like my head and my eyes have gone someplace else. There's music. Sweet music. It's in the air, it's on the wind, it's changed the wind, I swear the music's talking to me, it's proper talking to me. And in that moment it's like Facebook isn't the most important thing in the world, and even thinking that's a bit weird, 'cause a minute ago it was. It's as if walking into the water would be a dickish thing to do, would make me more of a twat than I am. That music, them notes, they're looping up and down, like one of them old-fashioned music hall records that my gran used to play on a Sunday morning. The music is bouncing with the wind. And I can hear singing, but it sounds all muffled and I can't make out the words, but I know that it's in tune, that it's bloody good and that I need to be nearer to it.

I lift my leg, swing it back, I climb down from straddling the railings, back onto the pavement, back onto the seafront. I turn to where the music's coming from. I spin a bit on the spot, trying to get my head to figure out which direction I need to walk. I cross the road, I'm not even sure I look for cars, and then I start running along the pavement. I run left, I stop. I turn, I run right, I stop. I'm running backwards and forwards along the seafront. And then I see a small alley. It's as if the music nods when I see the small alley. I can't explain how or why, but it's as if the music's guiding me. I run.

I run down the alley and then I stop.

I'm around the back of the old swimming baths. The ones we once went to on a school trip. The clock tower on the building strikes six, but it isn't six. There's fences all around the building. There's blue boards nailed to them fences.

I walk around the building, squinting at the blue boards through the crappy rain. On them someone's stuck some demolition notices. I read the 'Keep Out' signs and see that the baths, The Oracle, is going to be turned into something wanky called 'Spa Pleasure Dome'. There's photos of a massive glass building. It's all plummy and aluminium and shiny. I look through the fences at the building.

The Oracle used to be a public swimming baths, then I'm sure my mum said it was run by some weird folk who did mad stuff in the water before the council closed it down. The building's been around over a hundred years and people used to go mad for all the stained-glass and mosaics inside. But that was when people cared 'bout old stuff, they don't seem to care so much these days. It's pissing it down with rain, but still I stop and still I'm staring at the building. The Oracle's been shut for years, I mean before I was born. It's all tired-looking and crumbling, but even I can see that there's something 'bout it that's special. It's got that Gothic feel that I've seen in old horror films, like it's a mansion, all looming, all staring down, like at any moment it'll open up and swallow me whole. I laugh. I think the music laughs a little bit too. I look at the building again. It's like every single brick that was used to make that huge mansion-sized construction was laid in a perfect way, in a pattern that wouldn't fade over time, in a pattern that had meaning and purpose. Them bricks tell a story. But now them bricks don't fit any more, 'cause people want shiny and glass and wanky clean and tidy. I don't get it. I feel the music agreeing with me, like it's nodding again, like it's happy that I understand why it's guided me to this building.

Then I realise the music's louder now that I'm beside the fences and it's clearly coming from inside the building. I think I can see a light on inside, through one of the stained-glass windows, but it could just be the streetlamp reflecting. But none of that matters, nowt matters, except me needing to be inside The Oracle. It's like the music's the most beautiful thing ever and I somehow just know that whatever's inside there is a lot better than me standing out here in the pissing rain thinking 'bout a photo of my cock on Facebook.

My phone's in my pocket now. There's nowt I can do 'bout the photo of my cock. The rain's getting heavier and I'm walking around the perimeter looking for a gap between the blue-boarded fences. I mean there must be a way into The Oracle, the workers must be able to get in somehow.

I'm running now, the rain's making me want to go faster, it's making me want to find shelter. But it's the music, that's what's making me want to get closer to that building. It's like the music's telling me that it's okay to want to be inside. That it would be stupid not to be inside. In fact, possibly, that not being inside is the most stupid thing I could ever do. I mean, even more stupid than thinking that THE Estelle Jarvis would want to suck my cock.

And that's when I see that a part of the fence isn't quite connected to the part next to it.

There's a chain and padlock lying on the floor and it looks like some arse has forgotten to fasten it. I step over the chain and padlock and push open the gap in the fences, just enough for me to squeeze through into The Oracle's yard.

The yard's got huge rusty skips in it. They're probs full of water, what with all the rain we've been having. I swear even by northern standards the rain's being fucking ridiculous. I look around the yard, there's broken pieces of furniture lying on the floor. I reckon I see what was once a chest of drawers, and then I'm walking again and I'm stepping over a rusted metal shopping basket. There's a table with three legs, there's chairs too. Loads of them, wooden and metal. It's like the yard's a dumping ground for owt that's broken, for owt that people can't be arsed with any more, for owt that isn't perfect. Part of me wants to stop and see if there's owt I can pinch, if there's owt I can take back to our house, but then the music seems to speed up a tiny bit and I start running before I even think why.

I climb up some steps leading to a narrow alley between buildings. I know I'm round the back of The Oracle and it feels a bit sneaky, but I don't think I should be going round the front and through one of the three wooden doors. Up some more steps and I'm walking along the narrow alley leading to a backdoor. There are loads of windows round the back. Some of them have rusted bars on them, but mainly they're boarded up with wooden planks.

I'm walking and holding my arms out straight, like I'm Jesus on his cross, I'm running my fingers along the bricks. The rain's spilling over the guttering onto my head, onto my arms. The drainpipe's leading into a grate that's overflowing. I feel like I'm walking in a stream, but really I know it's the alley. The bottom of my school trousers are dragging in the mucky water, but I don't give a fuck. I need to know where that music's coming from.

The wooden back door's not what I expected. I reckon I expected to find something sturdy, possibly with a chain and padlock, something to keep people out. But it's not. The door's half wood and half glass, with the top half being four strips of cheapy glass. I'm all set for breaking the glass when I hear a crunch. I turn towards the sound. I reckon it's like someone's stepped on one of the broken drawers. That's when I think I hear whistling.

I hold my breath, 'cause clearly that'll stop whoever it is from beating me to death with a drawer handle. Well that's my bell-end's logic. I can hear someone splashing as they walk, I can hear that they're whistling and I'm trying my hardest not to shit my pants. That's when my hand goes to the door handle and I try it and that's when the door opens. So fucking easy. But of course the music blasts out and I know that it's pretty fucking obvious to whoever's walking around that I've just opened a door, but I don't really think 'bout that too much. 'Cause the next minute, I'm through that doorway, I'm in The Oracle, I'm on the floor with my back against the wooden part of that door and my knees up right tight against my chest. I'm breathing that hard that I reckon everyone in the building'll be hearing it. Then my right hand's reaching back over my shoulder and turning a key that's been left in the hole.

I try my hardest not to shit my pants when someone turns the door handle. I mean the handle's proper near the right side of my head. And I'm picturing whoever it is out there pressing their face up close against one of the glass panes and trying to see where I am. But I'm safe. I know I'm safe I'm out of the rain, I'm up against a locked door and that music, oh that sweet music. It's like that music will stop owt bad from happening and instead make everything pretty and everything happily ever fucking after.

'Cause that music, it's like it's coming out from the walls of the building and somehow I just know that The Oracle will keep me safe.

I wait for what must be at least half an episode of *Waterloo Road*. The door isn't tried again. I'm looking 'bout the room I'm in but really there's nowt there. It's more a passage leading into dark, but that's okay 'cause that dark's full of that music. And I know that that music's saved me, that that music wants me to be here, that that music is my friend. I don't even get my phone out my pocket the whole time I'm waiting. It's like whatever's on there isn't even a little bit important, like it's not even real. This is my world now. This room, inside The Oracle, here, now. That's when I realise that I'm almost scared to move in case the music stops. So instead I sit with my back against the wooden door and I let the music go up into my arse from the floor. The music becomes part of me and just for them moments, well it's like I've found happy.

My eyes have adjusted to the dark, so I look around, searching for nowt in particular. The room's been stripped of whatever it used to be. There's one single piece of furniture. It looks like tiny drawers with a tin of something on the top. I can't stand up and see what's in them tiny drawers, I can't risk being seen, so instead I keep flicking my eyes around the room, brick walls, concrete floor, a single light bulb hanging from a bare fitting on the ceiling. I could live here, if that music carried on forever, I could stay here forever.

'Course I know I can't really stay there forever, I mean I'm not a complete dick. I know that whoever tried to get in through the door'll be most probs trying another door or two. That's when I decide to crawl across the room on my hands and my knees, 'cause clearly that'll make like I'm invisible. I move my hands and my knees carefully, 'cause I can't see what's on the floor. I swear there's brick and pebble and probs glass shattered all over it. I've already crawled a little distance and my hands are proper killing. I mean I know my school trousers'll be a right mess but I'm thinking that keeping low'll be less chance of me being seen if someone's still looking in through the glass panel. It's only when I get to the doorway, where I've to decide whether to go left or right, that's when I stand up and have a good look around. I turn left and go down a few steps. That's when I reckon I must be under the pools.

The corridor's narrow, the roof's low, it's not far from my head and I'm not even six foot yet. There's pipes every now, every then. They're coming out from the ceiling, must be from the pools above, then they go down to the concrete floor, must be taking the water somewhere. I can hear water. It isn't a drip, it's more a trickle of water, like it's spilling from a tap and into a full sink. I look down and the floor's covered, only a few centimetres, but enough to let my feet splish and splash. I think 'bout needing a piss, then I think 'bout my cock and it being on Facebook. My stomach turns. The music ups a notch, telling me it's okay to feel a bit sick but that it's best I keep moving forward. The air is full of damp, but I'm sure I can smell a fish-and-chips supper. Maybes I'm just hungry. I walk towards the smell, I walk towards the singing. Lights are flickering on across the ceiling as I take my steps and I'm avoiding the pipes and I'm trailing the fingers of my left hand against the bricks of the wall as I hurry. My fingers touch on thin metal pipes that snake along the wall. My fingers flicker along the nobbles and bobbles. Thing is I've no idea what they are but I'm still letting my fingers rest on them. That's when I hear an echo of my splashing feet. Well I think it's an echo. It might not be.

I stop.

The footsteps continue, the whistling is there again, it's all in time with the singing, that proper awesome singing.

I start running. I'm running and running and the water's splashing up my school trousers and up the walls and I'm hoping that I don't fall flat on my face. I'm running, I mean I'm running and dodging pipes and every time a light flickers on over my head, I can see the exit getting nearer and nearer but it's the music getting louder and louder that's guiding my way.

And then I'm there.

And then I'm going up the four steps. And then I'm closing the door behind me and there's a bolt and I'm pulling that along and I'm holding my breath and that's when he starts banging on the other side of the wooden door.

'Open the door, you little bastard,' he shouts.

But I'm not hanging around there no more. No, I've turned around and I can see that I'm in an entrance hall to someplace posh and there's stairs on my left. The walls are tiled, emerald-green glossy tiles stretching from the ceiling alcoves to the floor. I run my fingers over them, they're cold and smooth. Them tiles aren't all the same, there's tiny details on some, flowers, leaves, curves, they might tell a story but I haven't time to listen.

I turn, I walk forward and I push open double doors labelled Males 1st Class pool.

And that's when the music stops.

This place is weird, I mean apart from the music stopping the minute I open the door, I mean it's like I swear I can feel someone watching me. I'm walking forward in tiny steps, I'm a ballet dancer, practically on my toes. I'm hoping Tommy twatting Clarke isn't watching.

I walk over to the pool. I fucking hate the water, never learned how to swim, and I'm wondering why the pool's still full of the stuff even though the baths have been closed for ages. I don't go near the edge of the pool. Knowing my dodgy luck, I'll trip over my shoes and end up drowning. I don't reckon I'll be missed, I mean it'll be weeks before my dad even notices and even then he'll probs not bother telling anyone.

I'm walking around the pool, careful to step over bits and pieces. There's some right odd-looking stuff. Pairs of shoes (work boots, high heels, black school shoes, trainers), there's coloured lids from

Smarties, bits of rope, work tools, rusted wheels, a bike without wheels, even the odd door or two. This place is proper weird.

I get to in front of the changing cubicles and I see a grey plastic sword on the floor. I used to have one like it when I was a kid, think I got it when we was out for the day at Conwy Castle. Mum'd not discovered Facebook then, she was still happy being a mum and wife. I reckon the sword's part of a set, think there'd be a grey shield too. I bend down and pick it up from the floor. It's proper light and straight away I'm seven and I'm a knight.

And that's when I start prancing around, fancying I'm in a battle with Tommy Clarke and I'm all set for slicing open his chest with my sword's mighty blade. I'm giving it all this and all that, jabbing forwards and back, my feet doing jiggy little steps over and on the rubbish, and I reckon that if anyone's watching then they'll think I'm a right wanker.

And that's when I stop my prancing 'bout and that's when I start humming the tune that made me come in here in the first place. I like it here, there's something 'bout this place.

'You're off your head,' I say to myself. I stop walking and I hoy the plastic sword into the pool, then I turn and make my way back to the double doors.

I've pushed open the doors and, as they swing back to close, I turn to the pool. And that's when I'm sure that I see an arm stretching out from the centre of the pool. That's an arm clutching the plastic sword that I've just hoyed in.

'What the fuck,' I say. 'What the fucking fuck was that?'

The double doors stop swinging and close behind me. I look left, I look up. The green tiles cover the banister that sweeps around and up with the stairs, terracotta tiles cover them stairs, but under my feet, here in the entrance hall, are mosaics of leaping fish. I swear one of the fish moves.

And then the music blasts out again, a little louder than before and little bit more awesome and I know that it's calling me from the ceiling down to the floor. But I reckon it's inside me, like I'm not hearing it through my ears, like it's in my head and in my body and pumping its way around with the beat of my heart. I don't think twice. I turn, I'm leaping up the stairs two at a time, running my hand along the smooth green tiles that coat the banister, keeping my eyes on the terracotta tiles that cover them stairs.

And then I'm there, at the top. Even though I leg it out of school whenever I'm there, I'm usually a talentless twat when it comes to running. But that's all changed today, 'cause even though I'm at the top of the stairs practically dying from trying to catch my breath, that singing's louder than ever and my whole body's needing it. It's welcoming me home, it's telling me I don't need to run no more.

That's when I find myself standing up straight and oh, God, no, I'm running into the light.

Well maybes that was a bit dramatic, but right now I'm hiding in a wooden-box room, it's like a fancy VIP area, probs for them Edwardians who didn't want to mix with common folk. It's at the top of the viewing gallery, I can see loads. I'm kneeling on the floor and I'm looking through a broken glass panel. The moon's popped out from behind a cloud, it's shining in through a huge window and over the massive swimming pool below. The wooden-box room that I'm in has two doors, one marked 'in' and one marked 'out', but I'm going through neither of them.

And, oh God no, I've already got a boner.

I can see two lasses. There's a lass sitting on the side of the pool, with a hand swaying in the water. She's not singing, there's no singing now, that stopped the minute I walked into the light. The lass sitting on the side of the pool, right close to the edge, I think she's pouring Smarties into her mouth with the hand that's not in the water and there's a big thick rope over her legs. The sleeves of her jumper are pushed up to her elbows and it looks like she's got tattoos of leaves covering her left arm. She looks young and sad. God no, Rope Lass's not why I've got a boner, no, that'd be weird, it's what's in the pool that's doing it.

'Cause that's where the second lass is. She's in the water. And she's floating on her back, with her brown hair swirling out around her. The moonlight's shining down on her milky-white skin and best of all, she's completely stark bollock naked and I can see that she shaves her pubes and she's got really huge nipples.

I swear to God, I best not move an inch, 'cause my cock's going to burst. But even when I think that, I'm also thinking that it's best I don't move, 'cause the last thing I'd ever want to do is scare Swimming Lass in any way. I can't explain why, I just know that I shouldn't scare her, I just know that I'm meant to be here, now, in The Oracle. I reckon that that lass, Swimming Lass, the one in the water with the swirling brown hair and no pubes, I reckon she's the most beautiful lass I've ever been near.

My knees are stiff. I reckon I've been kneeling here for at least a full episode of *Waterloo Road*. I'm trying to figure out where they were hiding when I was doing my 'prancing like a wanker with the plastic sword' act and I'm trying to figure out how I missed seeing Swimming Lass in the pool. None of it makes sense, I'm a twat. I'd felt someone was watching me but, somehow, I'd missed what was right in front of my eyes.

I mean this box that I'm in is like the ideal place ever to be staring at lasses, well one lass, Swimming Lass, and I can't take my eyes off her. The way she moves through the water, the way the water falls over her perfectly flat, perfectly white, perfectly smooth stomach. It's like I'm in a visual wank-tank, but I'm not even touching my cock, 'cause doing that would be wrong, 'cause this lass, she's worth so much more than that. I reckon I've hardly breathed the entire time I've been here, watching. Instead I've looked at her looping and spinning and swirling through the water.

But soon I start to feel a bit uncomfortable, like I know I'm pushing my luck still being here, so I make up my mind that I need to move out of the box. I need to go outside and wait for Swimming Lass to come out. 'Cause there's no question, I mean it's a no-brainer, I need to know who she is.

But of course, there's so many different ways out of The Oracle and I've no idea where Swimming Lass is going to be coming out. So instead I'm sitting on someone's front wall on the opposite side of the road, the one that runs parallel to the seafront. The houses are all terraces, two rooms up, two rooms down, with no front garden, just a dwarf wall to separate off each plot. I don't reckon anyone lives in this house, 'cause the front door and the front window are boarded up and the upstairs windows are broken. But you never know. I mean one of our windows is broken too and we've no house insurance so there's no chance we'll ever have the spare cash to fix it. I reckon most of the people in this street ain't got much money, like me and Dad, but I reckon they've probs not had their mums fuck off with some bloke she 'reconnected' with on Facebook. Fucking Facebook.

I look around the street a bit. The streetlamps are shining. None of the houses have driveways and this side of the road's got double yellows on it, so there's no place to be parking cars. It's quiet, a bit too quiet for my liking, but I reckon I've got some of the angles covered and I'm flicking my eyes from left to right and back again. I've been here ages.

At least I've had a right good look at The Oracle. I can see the back and the side from here. It's proper huge. It's like ten of these

terraced houses all squashed together but not with the crappy
bricks and cladding that some of these houses have. The Oracle's
all perfectly chosen bricks, patterns and shades of browns and
yellows, and I reckon all the windows have stained glass, but I
can't be making out the pictures. I know there's a light at the front,
under the clock tower, it shines onto the clock. It's the wrong time,
but that doesn't matter to me. I'll maybes walk around the front
the next time the clock chimes, have a good look. I mean The
Oracle's just a huge Gothic mansion of a building, and probs most
people walk past it and don't even notice just how beautiful it is.
I mean, they can't have, if it's going to be knocked down and
replaced with some wanky glass thing. I mean, it's not like anyone'll
just walk past a fuck-off huge glass-and-aluminium monster and
not notice it.

Fucking rain. I swear it's never going to stop, I swear we're
practically living underwater. I'm sopping wet and I'm pissed off.
I mean I can still hear singing, or I think I can. I'm wondering if
I imagined the whole thing. I mean I've seen what happened to
Dad after Mum left. Maybes the shock of my cock being all over
Facebook has knocked me over the edge. Maybes I'm proper
broken too, like Dad. Maybes all the Estelle Jarvis bollocks has
made me start imagining naked lasses in swimming pools and
soon it'll be me and my dad on the sofa watching crap daytime
TV and scrapping over the last bag of crisps.

But I'm sure I did see her. I mean I can't be that much of a
nutter already. I mean it took Dad weeks before he flipped. But
she's not come out, that Swimming Lass is nowhere to be seen. I
mean how long can one person stay swimming? I mean she must
be out of there now, she must be needing to go home at some
point.

I wait and then I wait some more.

I get my phone out my pocket and I switch it back on. It don't take long before there's a million notifications flashing across my screen. I see the word 'cock' a million times. I daren't go and look to see if the photo's still there. I mean, is there a record for the number of likes one wall-post can get? If there is then I reckon my cock's photo'll be giving it a run for its money.

I look at the time and it's already 1.27 a.m. I'd like to think that my dad'll be wondering where I am or even a bit worried or that my tea'll be sitting on the table cold and someone'll have filed a missing-persons report, or something. But I know none of that's true. The truth is that Dad won't even have noticed I didn't come home. He's not living in the same world as me, he's like one tablet away from an overdose.

It's 'bout now that I start thinking that maybes I've missed Swimming Lass leaving. I mean she looked 'bout the same age as me, but the lass beside the pool, Rope Lass, the sad one with the rope, I reckon she was maybes her little sister and it's way past her bedtime, especially with school tomorrow.

I pull my blazer a bit tighter round me. It's wet, so the pulling's pointless. There's no way I can wear it to school tomorrow but that's not a problem as I'm not going in. I'll fake another letter, saying I had the splats or something. There's no way I'm putting myself through that shit. I reckon I might come back to The Oracle instead, have a proper look around.

I start walking down the road, then back down the alley that leads to the seafront. I glance at a faded 'Missing Person' poster tied to the lamppost, I shiver. The rain's pelting on my head and there are scattered puddles all over the pavement. I'm just 'bout to cross the road onto the seafront and even though there's hardly any cars 'bout I still find myself looking left and right, and that's when I see him. I mean I even think he's whistling. I mean he's fat and he's trying to hide behind a lamppost, so I can still make him out. And, I don't know how but, I know that he's the bloke who was following me when I was trying to get in The Oracle.

And that's when I start running, again.

It's gone ten before I wake up and of course Dad's not bothered to try and wake me. I know it's only a matter of time before school rings to see where I am, so I ring in from my mobile. They've a system where you leave a message, saying your kid's form and the 'nature of the illness'. So I put on my best fake parent voice ready to say that 'Arthur Braxton's got the splats'. I reckon they'll fall for it again, especially if I take in a letter and get Dad to sign it. I mean if they ever investigated and sent social services to our house there'd be no question 'bout how I could be ill so much. This place is a filthy shithole.

I don't bother with breakfast, 'cause there's nowt in, so I call at the corner shop on the way and I get myself a can of Red Bull and a packet of Pickled Onion Monster Munch and I make my way back to The Oracle.

It's raining, what a fucking surprise. I'm wearing my jeans and a hoodie, I don't even own a coat, we've not got the money for the kind of coat that'd be seen as okay in school, so I'm pretty sure I'll be soaking by the time I get there. I try dodging the rain by walking close to walls or ducking under some of them huge trees on the side of the main road. I mean I even stop in bus shelters a couple of times, but the rain's pelting and it seems to me that there's one continuous puddle all over the pavement. There was something on the radio 'bout it being the most-recorded rainfall since records began. No shit, Sherlock. I reckon I should be building myself an ark. Bet Mum's new bloke's built her an ark out of his pubes or something. I shake my head, sometimes it works, sometimes it makes them kinds of thoughts 'bout Mum piss off.

I get to The Oracle and I'm not the only one to have thought to visit. The fencing's been opened a bit and there's work vehicles and even two posh black cars in the grounds. There's men running around with high-vis jackets on and them yellow plastic hats and it's all bustling and busy. I can't hear any music, but with the racket of cars and trucks and men shouting and doors slamming, it's a completely different feel to last night.

I walk up to the open fence and have a proper look at the signs that are nailed to it. 'COMING SOON', it reads in silver metallic letters, 'Spa Pleasure Dome'. There's a huge American flag covering half of the illustration and peeping out from under it is a photo of a shiny aluminium-and-glass-dome building. Along the bottom are the words 'AN EXCLUSIVE RANGE OF WORLD-CLASS BEAUTY SERVICES COMING SOON!'. The posters are on every fence panel and what's 'coming soon' couldn't be further from the rundown building in front of me.

'Shame, ain't it?'

I turn and there's a woman standing next to me. She looks a bit like I reckon Mrs Santa'd look. She's fat, dressed head to toe in red and wearing one of them plastic rain bonnets that my gran used to buy from the hairdresser after she'd had her hair done.

'What is?' I ask.

'Them knocking down The Oracle to build that "Spa Pleasure Dome"', she says and then she scuttles away all fast and wibbly.

And while I watch her wobbling away, that's when I realise, that's when I figure out that if they knock down The Oracle, then I've no idea how I'll get to see that Swimming Lass again. And, before I've even realised, there's something in me that's making me feel that not seeing that Swimming Lass again and not being in The Oracle again, well them'd be the worst things ever. Even worse than Mum going away.

I nip into the grounds of The Oracle. I mean, it's not like there's any big security guard there to stop me. All the people working there are running back and forth across the car park and between the three buildings, trying to escape the rain and not paying attention to much else.

There's the main building, where the three swimming pools are, but then there's a couple of other smaller buildings too, but I'm not sure what's in them. I came here once on a school trip when I was in primary school and I reckon one of the buildings used to be where they did washing in the olden days. I wish I'd paid more attention. There's the main building to my right, with steps and a narrow alley running between its back and the side of the other building that's straight ahead. That one's shaped a bit like a church but without a spire and all the windows are stained glass and pretty. Then there's one more building, to my left, it's shaped a bit like a greenhouse but it's made from bricks instead of glass. All the bricks form patterns that match across all three buildings; they're red and yellow and orange and it's clear that someone's taken ages to make sure that each and every brick's in the right place.

Anyways, I'm dodging workers and manage to hide behind a skip when I see a couple of posh-looking businessmen standing still, under huge black umbrellas. They're probs American.

'Jesus. Looks like there's no end in sight for this rain,' one says.

'Workmen saying it's put at least another month on the schedule,' the other says.

'And that's before Building Regs can approve the plans,' the first one says.

'Fucking shambles,' the other one says and they carry on walking to their huge black cars. I've seen cars like that before, they were on *X Factor* the other year. It was something like the auditions' round and each of the judges pulled up in front of the venue in a huge fuck-off black car each. There was no need, they could have all come in one car, but it's like that kind of car with just one person in it can make any twat feel important.

I wait until I hear the car doors slam shut, the cars start, and the cars drive off, before I stand up again. The rain's soaked my back from my crouching behind the skip and my hoodie's proper dripping water. This rain's like nowt I've ever seen before. It's proper huge drops; it's proper 'get the fuck out the rain' rain.

The car park isn't that big and it used to be that cars could park right up close to the building. After the American suits leave, there are mainly just workers running around and between the buildings, their heads are down and they're dodging the rain. I don't think there's much chance of seeing the lass today, but I want to be inside The Oracle. I mean owt's got to be better than being at school or being out in the rain and maybes if I explore the building a bit, then I might find a clue to who she is. And, maybes, if I'm honest, I'm wanting a clue that she exists and I'm not turning into a mental like Dad.

I go in the same door I went in last night and I head the same way I went last night. Before I know it, I'm in the hallway and heading up them terracotta-tiled stairs to that wooden box that was the entrance to the viewing gallery. I don't see any workers inside this part of the building. I reckon they must all be outside or under the pools or something, 'cause there's definitely not any up here. And then I'm looking through the broken glass window and down onto the pool.

That's when the sad lass, Rope Lass, steps out of the shadows, carrying her rope. Her hair's wild, tatty down her back. And she's tiny, skinny, a little lass body all covered in clothes that make her look poor. Her eyebrows are black, her hair's black too, but her lips are proper bright red. I don't reckon she wears lipstick. Rope Lass looks up to the wooden box and her face changes a little bit. I know that she's full of unhappy but maybes she just smiled, a sad person's smile. I look at her eyes. I mean I can't see them like proper close up but still I just know. I swear I just know that they're intense, that they scream out pain, that they scream out sadness and loss. I can't help but wish I could make her better, that we were mates. I duck down a little bit more, I mean I doubt there's a way she could have seen that I was here. I crawled in on my knees and everything.

Still she's walking around the pool, carrying that rope and hoying what look like lids from them old tubes of Smarties to make a trail behind her. I'm thinking that she's probs a nutter, but also that she's bunking off school like me so maybes she's got problems at school too. I don't reckon she goes to the same school as me, I mean I don't know for sure, mainly 'cause she's not the kind of lass anyone'd notice. She's just sad and doesn't really look like owt or anyone. And the minute I think that, I'm feeling like a twat, 'cause she's the kind of lass that the likes of Tommy Clarke and Estelle Jarvis would give utter shit to. Rope Lass is like me. So I watch her walking around the pool. Every now and then she looks up towards me and I can see that her bright-red lips are moving, like she's talking to someone, but there's no sound coming out.

I must have been watching her for at least an episode of *Waterloo Road*, my knees are stiff and I'm wanting to take my hoodie off 'cause it's soaking wet. I start to pull it off, trying not to make too much of a show of it, even though it's a bit small and a bit tight round my head. And then, when it's off and lying on the floor next to me, when I get to look out through the broken glass panel again, I see her.

Yes, HER. The lass from last night, naked Swimming Lass. I think I hold my breath. I swear I'm terrified to move my head, let alone any other part of my body. I let my eyes follow her as she swims up and down and around the pool. I swear she must be in training for the next Olympics or something. I think I remember someone saying, back when I came here on that boring school trip, I reckon there was something said 'bout one of the pools being Olympic-sized, something 'bout it being one of the first in the country. I could kick myself now for being such a twat and not having listened carefully. I mean, that could have been my way in, I could have opened with some spiel or other 'bout the pool size, made myself sound clever. God, I'm a twat.

Even though my knees are stiff and aching, I'm still not moving. Instead I'm watching her, the Swimming Lass. I like it best when she floats on her back. Her brown hair fans out and frames her face. Her nipples are proper big and dark and she's proper hairless. I thought all lasses had pubes, but maybes she shaves them off to help with her swimming's speed or something. She looks so at ease, as she flips onto her belly, pushes her arse up to the air and arches into the water. Everything 'bout her's perfect. The way she glides, the way she spins her body over the surface, like she's Jesus fucking Christ and virtually body-popping her way over the water. It's like she's one with the water, like it gets who she is. I swear I could stay here forever watching her.

That's when I sneeze. And, of course, it's not a fucking dainty sneeze; it's a blasting foghorn of a sneeze that echoes around the entire baths. I hold my breath. I daren't move an inch. That's when Swimming Lass stops her spinning through the water and moves over to the side. That's when the Rope Lass makes her way over to where Swimming Lass is and bends down beside her. I can see them speaking, but I can't hear a word. That's when the sad lass, Rope Lass, points up to the wooden entrance box I'm in. Then she does this waving thing with her hand, like she's beckoning me out. I don't know what to do. I want to step out, I mean my legs are desperate for a stretch, but I'm terrified that I'll step out and

they'll start screaming and accusing me of being a paedo or something. And that's when Rope Lass starts shouting.

'Come out, wet boy,' she shouts and I reckon I've got no choice
but to step out of my hiding box and face the music.

I stand up, my knees are stiff like I'm old and forty. I walk out
through the 'in' door and I stand still, looking down over all the
seats and onto the viewing gallery. The floor's wooden, them
exposed floorboards that posh people like to have in their houses,
but this stuff's all dusty and creaky and no single plank looks the
same. There's blue-and-white police tape stuck to some of them
and on the fancy wooden handrail at the front, probs to point out
possible danger, or maybes someone's fallen over the rail and died.
From here I can look down over the pool, I can look right and
see more of the viewing gallery, or under that there's them changing
cubicles down at the side of the pool. All of the stable doors are
swung open and all of the pink-and-white stripy curtains are
pulled back. This place is huge, like football-stadium huge. The
ceiling's miles away from my head and directly opposite me, right
at the furthest wall, way above the pool and almost touching the
ceiling, is an awesome stained-glass window. I reckon it's all water
lilies and lily pads and in the centre the glass is cut and coloured
into a lass. The lass's got black hair, she's wearing a blue dress,
she's standing on the water and she's got butterfly wings. The
light's shining through her and onto the water in the pool and
down, onto her, the naked Swimming Lass.

Rope Lass is back standing up straight and she waves at me.
She's not smiling, but the waving must mean that they're not
pissed off with me. I look at her tattoos, they can't be tattoos.
They look like a kid's been drawing leaves on her arm in felt tips.
Swimming Lass back-flips under the water and I see her naked
legs flashing through the air. Her toes are pointed and she's like

the most perfect thing in the world. I'd quite like her to wave to me, but she doesn't. I mean she looks up and she smiles and that's why I'm waving like a mental at both her and Rope Lass, but this time they don't wave back to me.

I walk down a couple of steps, to the front row of the viewing gallery. The wooden seats are pieces of wood on a metal frame. All of them are facing up to the ceiling, so I've to pull myself down a bit of wood to sit on. The hinges creak as the wood comes down to rest on the metal bar. The wood's rough and tiny splinters stick out my fingers when I look to see what's hurting. I take my time sitting down, mainly 'cause I'm not sure the wood and the metal can take the weight of my arse. But it does. And soon I'm there, sitting, watching, with my boner fit to burst.

'You got any popcorn, lad?'

I turn my head quickly, so quickly that I'm nearly sick. I don't know how I never even noticed but there's two old blokes sitting on the row of fold-down chairs behind me. I swear, I must have been watching the naked lass, Swimming Lass, and concentrating on her and nowt else, 'cause I never even heard them coming in.

'You old fool,' the second old man says.

'Indigestion, popcorn cures my indigestion,' the first old man says to the second old man, then they both laugh like they're off their heads.

I look at them. They're both little and grey, all grey I mean. They're wearing matching grey suits, with grey ties and grey shirts and I reckon they might be twins. I mean they're definitely brothers. And their faces are the same, I mean exactly the same, pure white, no lines, no marks, no hair, I mean no eyebrows even. And I know they're old, their bodies are round like old men, but their faces don't show that old. It's like they've been carved from plastic, like their faces are all pointy and shiny and identical and freaky as fuck.

'I'm just going, I'm sorry—' I start saying. I stand up and the wooden seat springs back up. The two old men stop their laughing.

Bang! The wooden seat is back vertical.

'Did you see that?' the first man says to the second old man. The noise hasn't bothered them. He points down to the pool. I turn around quickly, expecting to see Swimming Lass. But there's nowt there, naked Swimming Lass and her sad friend, Rope Lass, have gone. I lean forward, over the fancy wooden handrail and look all over, but they're nowhere to be seen. I turn back to the old blokes, wanting to ask them what they were pointing at in the pool. They're looking at me, both of them and they're smiling. They've got the same freaky toothless smile. I shiver.

'Here, catch,' the second old man says. Then he stands up, all shaky and old-man-like and he hoys a white lifesaving ring into the air. It spins up and up and then travels over the edge of the viewing gallery and down into the pool.

'Shot,' the first old man says, still sitting down, but he lifts his arm into the air and does a football fist.

'Result,' the second old man says, undoing his tie and swinging it around in the air. The two of them start their laughing again and I'm unsure what I'm supposed to do, say, or owt.

I swear I don't really know how to react, so I step out and I'm 'bout to walk up the stairs towards the wooden-box room and away from the viewing gallery. They're off their heads, I reckon. I let my eyes have a little glance sideways as I walk past them. Oh God, no, they might even be holding hands. Oh for fuck's sake, I'm thinking, just my luck to have a couple of paedos after me.

'Are you leaving?' the first old man shouts after me.

'Yeah, got school,' I say but I don't stop.

'Good, good,' the second old man says.

'Yes, see you soon, young Arthur,' the first man says.

'Hurry back, Master Arthur Braxton, the third,' the second old man says.

'Named after his father,' the first old man says.

'And his father's father,' the second old man says.

And that's when I go a bit quicker and I hurry through the 'out' door and down the stairs. I'm trying not to think 'bout how they might know my name.

'Course, I don't want to go home. I mean I can go home, my dad don't give a fuck where I'm at, but I don't want to. I want to see Swimming Lass, I want to warn her 'bout the paedos. I reckon I'll scout around outside for a better position, one that covers all the exits, and I'll wait for her. I mean she's there so early, she's bound to be leaving soon, she must be getting changed. I mean she must have to go to school at some point, even if she's in training for the Olympics. I think that, then it's like her tits flash inside my head and straight away my cock's reacting with a boner that's trying to burst out my pants. I try to think 'bout something else, 'cause me having a boner's not really what I want when I'm trying to impress her. So I get to thinking 'bout the feature wall in my front room and my dad lying on the sofa and how much he stinks of cheese-and-onion crisps and before I know it my boner's gone and I'm focusing on where best to stand.

I find a top position; it's on a corner, between the seafront and that road where I sat the other night. I can flick my eyes right and left and cover all the exits if I keep myself focused. I quite like where I'm standing. The terraced houses look nice in the light. I wish Dad would think 'bout moving out of our shit heap of a house, it might be all right moving here. I'm concentrating hard, it's not dark yet, I mean it's probs lunchtime but there's no way I'm going off looking for food. I want to see Swimming Lass and this is my best chance of meeting her.

I wait and then I wait some more. I get my phone out my pocket and I switch it on. The second I do that I'm regretting it, 'cause straight away there's fifty million notifications flashing across my screen. I watch as the word 'cock' appears fifty million times and every time I think oh God no. My cock's still on Facebook. I reckon everyone in the world will have seen my cock by now and that's not really how I wanted to be known. I wonder if Swimming Lass has seen it. I mean she looks close to my age, we're from the same area, so the chances are we've got a few friends in common on Facebook. I make a mental note to tell her I'm called something else and to definitely not try to friend her until all the cock-tagging has stopped and the blokes at Facebook have taken the photo down.

Oh God, my life is an utter twat.

'Course it's still raining. I mean, why wouldn't it be? The pavement's still covered in puddles and the rain's pelting on my head. I pull my hoodie up but it makes no difference. This rain's a determined fucker and it's getting on my hair and into my head whether I like it or not.

I reckon I've been here at least two episodes of *Waterloo Road*. I'm walking up and down, to keep my legs from snapping off. They're that cold and I swear the rain's in my bones. That naked Swimming Lass must proper love the swimming pool, I mean she must have gone back in the water, 'cause she's been in there hours. The swimming pool does nowt for me, I mean I've never even thought 'bout learning to swim. I can't have missed her again, can I? I'm starting to think I might have missed her again. I'm starting to wonder what the fuck's going on.

I'm still looking left and right and that's when I see him. It's that same bloke from the other night. He's fat and old, he's trying to hide behind a lamppost again and he's whistling. I mean it ain't even dark like it was the other night, so he can't possibly think that if he stands still he'll blend into the rain and the scenery. I mean he's a talentless twat at hide-and-seek. But even that thought ain't making me laugh, 'cause there's something 'bout him and there's something 'bout them old blokes in the viewing gallery knowing my name and it's all a bit too much.

And that's why I start running, again.

But then I'm back.

I mean The Oracle's got like this magic magnetic force thing going on and even though I only ran from here like five hours or so ago, I'm back.

I'm here, I'm standing outside again and it's raining again. God, I don't think it'll ever stop. I'm going past feeling cold and I've gone past knowing what it's like not to be wearing wet clothes. But I don't give a fuck, 'cause all I can think 'bout is that music. I can hear that music again. That music from inside The Oracle's in my body. It's like it's pumping against my skin from the inside, trying to get out but happy being in there. I feel like I could be safe, I feel like I could be happy, I feel like I need to be back in The Oracle.

I'm standing outside the fences, the ones going around the building. I've waited until the workmen all knocked off. I'm walking round the fence, looking at the blue boards nailed to them and trying to figure out how to get in. The sight of 'Spa Pleasure Dome' and all its glass and aluminium and shiny makes me feel a bit sick. I don't know why, but inside me that feeling that knocking down The Oracle'll be wrong has grown stronger, much stronger. And when I think 'bout that, the music starts again, like that singing is agreeing with me, like it's saying that it feels that way too. Like it's telling me that I belong in The Oracle with them, that they'll keep me safe and make everything better. I reckon I'm losing the plot.

I look up to the stained-glass window, the one that had a light shining from it last time, but I can't see no lights on today. It's grey as fuck out here, so I reckon that there's no one in there, but still I want to be in. I'm all for waiting inside for Swimming Lass. The rain starts pelting down heavier, like it's pissed off with me for hanging around the fence and not being proper in my decision to go inside.

'Right, right, you fucker,' I say to the sky, then I'm next to that chain and padlock lying on the floor again. I swear, it's like they want people to break in. I push open the gap, just enough for me to squeeze through and run over the yard. I glance in a rusty skip and see some water-covered furniture, but I don't stop. I'm running in time with the singing and she's speeding up, like she knows I'm coming and like she's happy that I am. I leap over puddles, I dodge bits of wood and then I'm climbing up some steps and practically leaping along the narrow alley leading to the backdoor.

I reach the backdoor and try the door handle again and of course the door opens.

I waste no time, this time. I feel my way along the walls and I let my eyes get used to the dark. I know I just need to get to the end of the passage and then I'll see some light. I'm hurrying now. I want out of the dark. I turn left and go down a few steps. That's when I reckon I must be under the pools again. My eyes have adjusted and I can see that the corridor's narrow. There's pipes every now, every then, going up to the ceiling and down to the floor. Lights are flickering on across the ceiling as I take my steps and those steps are plopping into the now deeper water on the floor. The sound of me in the water's adding a base line to the singing. I like it. I'm smiling, I'm feeling happy. I swear, this is what it feels like to be happy.

I'm running now, I mean I'm running 'cause I can see the exit getting nearer and nearer and all the time my footsteps in the water are making music. Every now and then I jump in the air and land with two feet or I stop and do like a mad water tap-dance mixed with an Irish jig. This isn't me, this kind of happy isn't me. But I twatting well like it. I like how that music is making me feel, I like how safe I feel, I like that I belong someplace, this place, this is home.

And then I'm there.

And then I'm going up the four steps. And then I'm closing the door and there's the bolt and I'm pulling that along and I'm stopping. I'm bending forward and I'm catching my breath and then I'm laughing. I'm laughing like I've never laughed before. I'm laughing like I mean it.

I turn around and get a good look at the entrance hall. It's proper posh, the mosaics on the floor must have taken some twat ages to make, the vibrant green tiles look like they're polished daily. But this time, I'm not for climbing the stairs and running my hand over the green-tiled banister. This time, I turn and walk towards the door that leads into the Males 1st Class pool.

I push the doors and they swing back. They creak and the moment I step forward onto the spotted mosaic floor, the music changes. I look to the pool and I see the music. It's in the bubbles that erupt from the centre of the water. The sound's like one of the functions on a dodgy synthesizer, the music's swirling, it's popping out with the bubbles. The sound's nowt like what it was when I was outside, it's calmer, it's soothing.

I stand still and I reckon I let out my breath. The door keeps swinging backwards and forwards behind me. Fuck knows why I've been holding my breath or what I expected to see in here, but Swimming Lass isn't there. I turn and walk down the side of the pool. The old changing cubicles look ace. There's a row of them right close to the edge of the pool. The blue paint's all rusty and old, but it's awesome. I think 'bout all the men who've been here before. I think 'bout them nipping inside the changing room so as not to show the world their cocks.

I think 'bout my cock being on Facebook and I feel a bit sick in my stomach.

'Oi! You, BOY!'

I turn when she shouts. That's when I see her in the water and that's when she starts singing again. She's swimming in the pool, floating on her back, her long ginger hair's fanning out behind her. It's proper long. Her nipples are all pink and pointy. But I don't have no boner. I look at her in the centre of the pool and straight away I'm thinking that she's a mermaid. I mean, she's like a mermaid, I reckon, but without a tail, but she's how I think a mermaid should look. I stare at her hair, it's long, much longer than any of the lasses in my school, I reckon it must be almost at her knees when she's standing. She doesn't stay in one place.

I watch her. She's singing, she's Singing Lass, it's the same singing voice that made me come into The Oracle. I think her voice sounds like marshmallows would sound, if they could sing. I wonder where Swimming Lass and Rope Lass are. I wonder if they're watching me right now. I don't want Swimming Lass and her friend to think I fancy this mermaid, 'cause I don't, I proper don't, Singing Lass makes my cock shrink. She makes me feel uncomfortable.

But still, somehow, I can't take my eyes off her, off Singing Lass. She's swimming, she's swimming and singing under and over water. My body's full of her singing. I'm part of the song, she's singing through me. I try but I can't take my fucking eyes off her, with her super shiny skin and ridiculously long and ginger hair. She's freaky as fuck. I swear her lips and eyes are ginger too. And her skin's practically see-through, it's that white. I've no idea how old she is, she might be forty, she might be eighteen. Something tells me she's no age at all, but her body belongs to a woman, a tiny woman.

Singing Lass appears out of the water every now and then, but mainly she's singing underwater and making the music come through the walls and the floor and into me. I wonder if she's got some special kind of microphone at the bottom of the pool, one that's all fitted and fixed to speakers around The Oracle. She must be part of some show or other. Maybes they're travellers. Every now and then she pops up and leaps a perfect twirl in the air like there's a trampoline on the bottom of the pool, then she sings a perfect note, before diving back into the water. At least twice she looks right at me and smiles. Her smile makes my insides turn.

'Come here!' she shouts. She's reaching the side of the pool and I watch as she flips over onto her front and grips the edge with her thin fingers. 'What's your name?' she asks.

I walk towards her. 'Arthur,' I say. 'Arthur Braxton.'

'Hello, Arthur Braxton,' Singing Lass says, her voice all singsong. 'I'm Madora Argon, but they all call me Maddie.' Then she looks down my body and her eyes stop on my cock and she smiles. 'Nice,' she says. Then she hoys herself backwards and dives down into the water. The water barely ripples, instead a tiny swirl appears above where she dived, and a stale smell of sweaty sewers floats towards me.

I watch the swirl and wait for her to come up for air. She doesn't. I mean, she doesn't for ages, I think she might have drowned and suddenly I'm running up and down the side of the pool, jumping over crap, looking for one of them lifesaving rings and then looking back at the water. Crap. Shit. Bollocks. I can't swim, so it's not like I can do the hero thing and dive in after her. I mean, it's not even like I can swim badly. I fucking hate the water I do.

And when I think 'bout how much I fucking hate the water,

well that's when Maddie appears again, all smiley, all fresh and innocent looking, but somehow I know that she isn't any of them things. There's something 'bout her that makes me feel itchy. There's something 'bout her that makes me feel awkward.

She's singing again. She's looping notes in time, as her body twists in and out of the water. I find my eyes fixing on her face. White pearls surround her ginger lips, they spill from her ginger eyes and down her cheeks. The pearls trace a line where tears would've fallen. They're perfectly white against her see-through skin. I wonder why she cried. I wonder if the pearls are stuck to her skin or if they'll fall to the bottom of the pool and become treasure. That's when I figure that I'm wondering weird stuff.

'Are you practising?' I ask her.

'For what?' Maddie sings.

'Some kind of show?' I ask.

'A freak show.' She laughs.

I want to ask why she's naked, but I can't say that word, not to her.

I watch her swimming, she's not singing, just looping in and out of the water. Her body is perfectly white. It's flawless. No marks, no ginger hairs, other than on her head, nowt but white. I reckon it'll be smooth to touch. She's beautiful, but not beautiful like how the other lass, how Swimming Lass, was. Maddie's beautiful like glass.

That's when she sings again, louder this time. I stay very still, I can't move.

She stops. She stares at me.

'Why aren't you moving?' she asks.

I don't speak.

'Why aren't you drowning, like the others?' she asks.

I don't speak. And that's when she sings again, louder, and then she dives below the water. The bubbles pop on the surface with the beat of her vocal. The smell from the popping bubbles makes me a little bit sick in my mouth. I wonder if she's breathing underwater, I wonder how she does it. I mean, Maddie must have amazing lungs. Her voice is enchanting. It takes away time and place and me. Yes, Maddie's singing makes me not want to be me.

I can't help myself. I'm moving towards the pool, I'm stepping towards the fucking water. I'm there, I'm at the edge. Maddie's all smiles, wanting me to step in. I want that too, I don't understand why, I mean I can't swim, I fucking hate the water, but it's like none of that matters.

But then SHE appears. My eyes flick to her. Swimming Lass.

'No. Mine!' she screams.

And it's like Maddie's song doesn't matter any more. Swimming Lass is back. I step backwards, away from the pool's edge.

'Oi! YOU, BOY,' Maddie shouts. 'Why don't you listen to my song?'

I ignore her. I'm looking at Swimming Lass in the water. She's still alive, the paedos didn't get her, it's all good. She's at the far edge of the pool, the opposite edge. She's looking at me and her friend, Rope Lass, is now sitting, cross-legged, on the side of the pool watching me too. Her sad is shooting in through my eyes. I swear she makes me want to weep like a baby.

'You old fool!' I look up to the viewing gallery. It's the old men again, the freaky toothless fucks.

'Popcorn, lad, did you bring me my popcorn?' the first man shouts from the viewing gallery.

'Sorry, I—' I start to say.

'Cures his indigestion,' the second old man says, then they both laugh like they've said the funniest thing in the world.

'You met Delphina?' the first man says to me. He points down to Swimming Lass and her friend.

'Here, catch,' the second old man says. Then he stands up, and he hoys that white lifesaving ring down to me. It lands on the floor, nowhere near where I'm standing.

'Shot,' the first old man says.

'Result,' the second old man says.

'Thanks,' I say.

'Delphina's a keeper,' the first old man shouts down to me.

'A right looker,' the second old man shouts down to me.

'Reckon you're in there,' the first old man shouts, then him and the second old man start with their ridiculous laughing again.

'Oi, BOY.' It's Maddie. But I'm not listening. Instead my feet are walking to the lifesaving ring and then, 'cause I can't stop, me and the white lifesaving ring, we're heading towards her, to Swimming Lass. After all, she's the reason I'm here.

'Hello,' I say.

'Hello,' Swimming Lass says.

'Hello,' Rope Lass says.

'I'm Delphina and this is Laurel,' Swimming Lass says. Laurel stands, with her rope, and runs into one of the changing cubicles.

'Arthur,' I say. 'Arthur Braxton.' I've forgotten to make up a new name. I'm a twat.

'Hello, Arthur Braxton,' Delphina says.

And that's when it all begins.

And that's when I see him, the man who has been following me and hiding behind lampposts and stuff. He's there, in the open doorway, giving me evils and whistling one of them old-person tunes.

Delphina

WATER: *(Earth. Air. Fire.)*

DAY SIX

'Now over to Steve for the latest weather update.'

'Thanks Rich. It's pretty grim out there. Severe weather warnings have been issued for some counties in the northwest of England and Wales, with up to 375mm of rain expected to fall in some areas tomorrow. The Met Office predicted persistent rain and strong winds. BBC Wales weather presenter Sam Brown has said that flooding is a big possibility.'

Setting: *Delphina is in the water of the Males 1st Class pool. She is holding onto the edge of the pool, near to where Arthur is kneeling. He is at the side of the pool, in front of the blue changing cubicles. He is not touching the water. Laurel is inside of one of the blue changing cubicles behind Arthur. The half-stable door is closed and the stripy pink-and-white curtain has been pulled across, but Laurel's bare toes are peeping out. Silver is standing in the open doorway. He is watching them.*

DELPHINA: [*pointing*]. That's Silver, he's a bit like my dad.

ARTHUR: He's been following me, hiding behind lampposts and shit.

DELPHINA: Silver! [*Silver turns and leaves*]

ARTHUR: Should I be worried?

DELPHINA: No, really, Silver looks out for me. He's like my dad but better. He's the one who told me all about Martin Savage.

ARTHUR: Martin Savage?

LAUREL: Martin was one of the three water-healers that gave predictions, told fortunes and spoke truths from inside here. People would come from all around, just to get some time with The Oracle's water-healers.

ARTHUR: [*laughing*] Water-healers, fucking hell, this place is weird.

DELPHINA: My mum used to work the front door here. She'd sit at a desk, nose in a book, making sure that people queued and had money to pay. Silver said my mum was still at school, apparently clever, only fourteen, and earning pocket money through door work. Martin Savage was married, with three kids, but still he and my mum had a bit of each other.

ARTHUR: Where's he now, your dad?

DELPHINA: Rumour is that he trades as a psychic and has a shop called Crystal Zone, but it's no place near here. He ran as far from here as possible. I never met him. Silver says I never will. And if I'm honest, I don't think there's anything I want to say to the man who abandoned me when I needed him most. Silver's been the only man, the only dad I'll ever need.

ARTHUR: My mum buggered off a couple of years back and my dad's worse than useless. I can't remember the last time I heard him speak.

DELPHINA: Who looks after you?

ARTHUR: [*proud voice*] I look after myself. [*Delphina smiles*]

DELPHINA: When I was younger Madame Pythia was still here. She was in charge of The Oracle. Did you know her?

ARTHUR: [*laughing*] Was that her proper name?

DELPHINA: I think so.

ARTHUR: So you live here, in The Oracle?

DELPHINA: I always have. Madame Pythia was the boss, the main water-healer, the one who worked out from this pool. Everyone wanted to be healed by Madame Pythia, Silver says she was a goddess, mysterious, magical. I think he loved her. And even though The Oracle closed soon after I was born, Madame Pythia still lived in the flat upstairs and Silver lived in a caravan out the back, but Martin Savage had done a runner.

ARTHUR: So where's your mum?

DELPHINA: Silver's told me all about her, said how my mum was a good girl. Apparently she came from a broken home, with her mum being a single parent to seven of them. My mum was the eldest and Silver said that she had commitments to them other children. Silver said that I'm lucky to have been born, 'cause my mum could have very easily killed me when I was little and still inside her stomach. But Silver said that my mum had a good heart and wanted to give me a chance at living. Silver said that that's why my mum thought it best three hours after I was born to throw me in the Males 1st Class pool.

ARTHUR: [*raises voice*] She what?

DELPHINA: She threw me in here. To let them water-healers drag me up. My mum did that just before she hanged herself from up there. [*points to blue-and-white police tape at front of the viewing gallery*]

ARTHUR: [*looking up to viewing gallery*] Oh God, no.

DELPHINA: It was Silver who found us both, me in the water and my mum dripping blood and dangling from a rope. There was a note sellotaped to my baby grow and the words were in biro, but could still be read.

LAUREL: [*opens stripy curtain and shouts*] Property of Martin Savage, the words said.

DELPHINA: [*looking at Laurel*] But Martin Savage didn't want anything to do with me. It was Silver who made me better, him and Madame Pythia did everything they could.

ARTHUR: The bastard.

DELPHINA: [*looking at Arthur*] I once asked Silver why, if his name was on me, why Martin Savage hadn't thought to claim me. He told me that Martin Savage wasn't interested in bringing a bastard baby into his happy home.

ARTHUR: [*angrily*] But it was his responsibility.

DELPHINA: Silver said that when my mum found out she was

111

pregnant, she told Martin. Silver had been working that night and said that he could hear them rowing whilst he was doing one of his healings. He said that he had to stop his curing and go and have words with them both. It was then that my mum told Silver that she was having a baby and it was then that Martin told my mum that he wanted nothing to do with her or the baby. It was simple, really. He had his wife and his other kids to put first and he didn't intend on leaving any of them.

ARTHUR: [*whispering*] The bastard.

DELPHINA: Silver told me that it was then that my mum started not wanting me either. I asked Silver how he knew all this and he said that it was all down to his job, down to his palm reading, that he could see into minds and he could see into the deepest and darkest things, even if sometimes he didn't really want to. Silver told me that he'd seen it all weeks before it happened, that he'd told my mum to run, but she hadn't. Silver said that my mum couldn't live with a reminder of Martin not loving her, 'cause Martin was the most important person in the whole wide world to her and having me should have been a perfect comma in their relationship.

ARTHUR: [*laughs*] And you believed him?

DELPHINA: [*laughs*] I knew, I mean, in my heart I knew that Silver was lying to me, but back then I was happy to go along with it. It made my mum sound like a romantic princess. Like some of those storybooks that Silver had read to me when I was little, like my mum and my dad were in love but destined not to be together, like their love was the purest thing to exist. It made it easier for me to deal with.

ARTHUR: [*nods*] I get it.

DELPHINA: Being abandoned by one parent is bad enough, but the other hanging herself after throwing you into a deep pool, well that was just too much for any little child to deal with. So, instead I focused on the beauty of them, on a love that was never allowed to be.

ARTHUR: [*smiling*] You're awesome.

DELPHINA: [*looks embarrassed*] I'm not, not at all. I just don't get why my mum decided to hang herself. I mean why did she take one look at me and decide that this world wasn't for her?

ARTHUR: No one could look at you and think that.

DELPHINA: [*looks embarrassed*] Silver said that my mum always knew she wasn't going to be keeping me and so I was never named. My mum never went out buying them little scratch mittens or bibs or even a first teddy. Instead, three hours after I was born, my mum wrapped me in a blanket, put me in a rusted shopping basket and threw me into here. Then my mum disappeared from this world and left me in the grips of the water. I don't know if Martin Savage ever tried to love me, but I do know that it was Madame Pythia who claimed me as her own during those first few hours of my life. Madame Pythia liked to collect pretty things and Silver said that I was the prettiest thing ever.

ARTHUR: [*smiling*] You are.

DELPHINA: [*smiling*] Madame Pythia had never had time to be having children of her own, so when I was rescued in here, all tiny and screwed up, she named me Delphina and promised to keep me safe.

ARTHUR: But didn't you have any other family? What 'bout your grandma?

DELPHINA: I don't know why my mum's mum never came forward to claim me, I don't even know if she knew I existed. No one talks about all that kind of stuff with me. And that promise Madam Pythia made to me when I was all tiny, well she really didn't keep it for very long.

ARTHUR: That's adults. They mainly talk utter bollocks.

DELPHINA: [*nodding*] Within a couple of days of my mum's hanging,

The Oracle was closed, pending an investigation. My mum's death was noted as suicide and my mum having just had a baby was noted too. But no one came looking for me. I don't really know why, because I was here all the time, so they clearly didn't look very hard, but I reckon Silver and Madame Pythia must have hidden me really well. That was seventeen years ago now.

ARTHUR: You're seventeen?

DELPHINA: [*nodding*] Silver says that the press went after Madame Pythia and The Oracle, he says it was a witch-hunt and one Madame Pythia couldn't make go away. They accused Madame Pythia of witchcraft, of enslaving innocent children, of allowing rape, of running a cult. Silver explained what each of the accusations meant. But, in simple terms, The Oracle never reopened.

ARTHUR: But why'd you never leave?

DELPHINA: At first, Silver said that it was all good. Him and Madame Pythia would take turns in looking after me. He said that Madame Pythia couldn't do enough for me, that she loved me like I was her own flesh and blood. He said that I was her everything, that she shifted all her attention and all of her power into making sure I was healthy, into making sure that I was safe. He's shown me contraptions that they crafted together, water-baskets to keep me close to the water, he's told me of the routines and shifts, of the schedules and strict timetables they followed to nurture, to keep me safe.

ARTHUR: But?

DELPHINA: But then, Silver said, something changed. He said that just after my third birthday Madame Pythia packed her bags and buggered off. Silver's not heard from her since. I don't know what I did wrong. I don't know why she stopped loving me. I'm guessing that I wasn't the daughter she hoped I would be.

ARTHUR: [*whispers*] The twat. Sorry.

DELPHINA: That's why now, it's just me, Laurel and Silver. They're

the most important people in my life. They're two of the few
people I've ever met. I can't remember Madame Pythia at all
and I've never, not ever, left The Oracle.

ARTHUR: [*raising voice*] You've never left here?

DELPHINA: Not ever.

ARTHUR: But why?

DELPHINA: Everything I need is right here.

ARTHUR: [*looks confused*] Everything?

DELPHINA: [*nodding*] Sometimes I wonder what he's like, I mean
my dad. Silver said he was one of the best water-healers he'd
ever worked with. Silver said that Martin's problem was that
he had too much dark in him and that's what made him mess
with my mum and run away from me. Perhaps Martin's never
realised that me not having a mum or a dad means that I'm
not even sure who I really am. Silver keeps in touch with him,
through the spirit world, but he's never been back to see me.
As far as Martin's concerned there's no proof that I'm his and
me, well it's like I don't even exist.

ARTHUR: But you've never left here? You've never been to town?

DELPHINA: No. I've managed to live all my life without ever having
left The Oracle.

ARTHUR: But you must have—

DELPHINA: [*crossly*] I've never been outside.

ARTHUR: What's with all the shoes, over there? Are they yours?

[*Arthur points to the pile of shoes by the side of the pool*]

DELPHINA: They're from—

ARTHUR: Do you have Facebook?

DAY SEVEN

Subject: An email from Clywd County Council to managers of North Wales amateur football league.

Dear all,

Due to excessive rainfall and serious concerns for players' safety, all games scheduled to be played on council-owned pitches have been cancelled until further notice.

Many thanks,

Simon Douglas

Sports Liaison Officer

Setting: *Delphina and Silver are in the Males 1st Class pool. Silver is floating on his back, Delphina is swimming around him. The twins Pollock and Kester are in the viewing gallery, Maddie is swimming and singing in the water, Laurel is sitting on the floor, crossed-legged, in front of the changing cubicles and eating Smarties.*

DELPHINA: Well I guess, you know, it's been seventeen years.

SILVER: No, pet.

DELPHINA: [*splashing water*] You don't even know what I'm going to ask.

SILVER: It's a no, pet.

DELPHINA: I mean for those seventeen years I knew no different. I guess I never really thought that there could be more. I mean I knew of nothing else, my world was The Oracle.

SILVER: It still is.

DELPHINA: But Arthur—

SILVER: He should never have come here, pet. The shoes, the odd bone, he'll put two and two together, pet.

DELPHINA: No one else has.

SILVER: That's because we keep folk away. We both know the folk who come in here don't tend to leave.

119

DELPHINA: But you let him come, you knew he'd come. You say everything has a reason—

SILVER: And it does. Now that lad's life has stepped onto a new path and there's nowt I can do to stop things from happening.

DELPHINA: I've spent all my days mainly swimming and there have been others around to teach me things. I mean you've taught me about books and history, Maddie's taught me everything I need to know about music. [*looks up to viewing gallery*] Pollock and Kester have taught me maths and [*looks to changing cubicles*] young Laurel really does keep me company. But it's nice to have someone new to talk to. And I know I could swim down into the otherworld.

SILVER: That's where you'll go when your hope's all gone, pet. When it's time.

LAUREL: Don't be doing that. Don't be going down to the underground reservoir. They're weird down there.

SILVER: It's where the loose ones—

DELPHINA: And I know you lot are the best friends in the world and I have everything I need. I was happy, but—

SILVER: But now he's come along and we're not enough for you.

DELPHINA: I fell in love the minute I saw him.

SILVER: Bollocks, pet, you're talking bollocks. He's just the first lad you've talked to.

DELPHINA: You're wrong. I feel it in here [*she places her hand over her heart*]. It's like we're one person. I don't have enough words . . .

SILVER: [*tuts loudly*] He's just a lad, one a penny round here.

DELPHINA: NO. He's mine.

[*Silver laughs, but his laughter is not filled with happiness*]

DELPHINA: [*changing the subject away from her love for Arthur*] What's Facebook?

SILVER: [*swimming over to the wooden steps*] It's nothing you need in your life.

120

DELPHINA: Where you going?

SILVER: [*climbing out of pool*] To the bank.

DELPHINA: Why do you need to go to the bank?

SILVER: Not a river bank.

[*Delphina looks confused*]

SILVER: A bank for money.

DELPHINA: You've never mentioned it before.

SILVER: There's never been a need, pet.

DELPHINA: Why do you need money?

SILVER: Stop with the questions.

DELPHINA: I don't understand.

POLLOCK: [*shouting down from the viewing gallery*] You need to tell her what's out there.

KESTER: [*shouting down from the viewing gallery*] There's a whole other world, Delphina. You don't know the half of it.

MADDIE: [*singing*] They speak a different language.

LAUREL: [*whispering*] They'll eat you up.

DAY EIGHT

'The Met Office has issued severe weather warnings with continued heavy rain in North Wales. Yesterday the highest total for *any* twenty-four-hour period, *since* records began, was recorded . . .'

Setting: *Silver is standing in front of the changing cubicles. Laurel is sitting on the mosaic floor close to the pool. She is spelling out words using the lids from her Smarties, from a drawstring bag. Delphina is floating in the Males 1st Class pool.*

SILVER: Come here, Delphina.

[*Delphina swims to the wooden steps of the pool. She pulls herself up to the top step, her legs remain in the water. Silver takes off his flip-flops and moves to sit on the other side of the wooden step. He lowers his calves and his feet into the water. He takes Delphina's hand and turns her palm to his face*]

SILVER: [*sighing*] Oh, Delphina.

LAUREL: [*shouting*] LEAVE her alone.

DELPHINA: It's okay Laurel.

[*Silver glares at Laurel*]

LAUREL: [*crying*] Don't listen to him.

DELPHINA: [*to Laurel*] It's okay, Laurel, really, it's okay. [*to Silver*] Carry on.

SILVER: You must never try to walk out of The Oracle.

DELPHINA: Why?

SILVER: Because you are destined to cause a car crash, to kill five people, most probably before you turn twenty-one. [*pointing to palm*] It is written in your palm. The palm does not lie. You have the power to stop this.

LAUREL: He's talking rubbish, Delphina, we all know you can't walk—

SILVER: [*shouting*] SHUT IT.

[*Laurel runs into one of the changing cubicles. She slams the stable door closed and pulls the stripy curtain across. Her naked toes poke out below the door*]

DELPHINA: Laurel, come out sweetie, it's okay.

[*Silver turns Delphina's hand over, lifts it to his lips and kisses it. Then he lets go of Delphina's hand. Silver twists around, lifts his feet from the water and picks up his flip-flops. He walks into one of the changing cubicles around the pool*]

[*A few moments later Silver comes out of the changing cubicles in his Hawaiian swimming shorts. He runs to the pool. He attempts to dive, but does a belly flop. Delphina laughs. She swims over to him*]

[*Delphina and Silver laugh together. Delphina shows Silver her new tricks that Maddie has taught her. Laurel steps out from the changing rooms. She is sheepish and walks to the furthest corner from the pool, but she is still watching*]

[*Delphina stops. She stays very still. She looks up to the viewing gallery. Arthur is there. He is looking at her. Delphina smiles at Arthur. Arthur smiles at Delphina*]

DELPHINA: [*shouting up to the viewing gallery*] Come down. [*she dives underwater and swims three lengths*]

[*Arthur crashes through the doors. He is out of breath*]

DELPHINA: You didn't visit yesterday.

ARTHUR: I wanted to, but I couldn't get in. Someone'd put the padlock and chain on and there were three security guards patrolling.

DELPHINA: I don't know what you mean.

ARTHUR: [*looking at Silver climbing out from the opposite end of the pool. Silver is pulling himself up by his arms onto the edge of the pool and swinging his legs out of the water*] I mean someone didn't want me to get in.

DELPHINA: [*looking at Silver*] Silver!

[*Silver moves to and sits in one of the alcoves at the far side of the room. Silver is watching Delphina and Arthur*]

ARTHUR: [*nodding his head towards Silver*] I don't think he likes me.

DELPHINA: He's just protecting me. You're the first boy to come here—

ARTHUR: You've never had a boyfriend?

DELPHINA: You're the first boy I've ever spoken to.

ARTHUR: But why me?

DELPHINA: The water goddesses chose you. They let me save you.

ARTHUR: [*laughing*] You're a nutter!

DELPHINA: Silver must know you're supposed to be here, otherwise you'd not be. I mean, he's clearly stopped you a little bit, but if he really wanted to—

[*Delphina is embarrassed, she's never felt such strong emotions. She is overwhelmed with love for Arthur. She lets go of the edge of the pool. Her body drops below the water. She counts to fifty. She remerges*]

ARTHUR: You're good at that.

DELPHINA: What?

ARTHUR: Holding your breath under water.

[*Delphina doesn't speak. She stares at Arthur and smiles*]

ARTHUR: So, are you on Facebook?

DELPHINA: I don't even know what that is.

ARTHUR: [*laughing*] You're funny.

LAUREL: I'm on Facebook. [*Laurel is shouting from the furthest corner of the pool area*]

ARTHUR: Cool, add me.

DELPHINA: [*looking confused*] Are you going to come in?

ARTHUR: Hate water. I can't swim.

DELPHINA: [*laughing*] It's easy. I can teach you.

ARTHUR: It's all right, I'm happy just watching.

LAUREL: I'm happy just watching too.

[*Delphina and Arthur turn to look to the furthest corner of the pool area. Laurel turns so that her back is to them. Arthur and Delphina laugh*]

ARTHUR: How come you're not at school?

DELPHINA: I don't go to school.

ARTHUR: What, you didn't stay on after your GCSEs?

DELPHINA: I've never been to school.

ARTHUR: You're lucky. Are you a gypo or something?

DELPHINA: A gypo?

ARTHUR: A traveller.

DELPHINA: [*looking towards Silver*] Silver teaches me, so do Kester and Pollock. [*Delphina looks up to the viewing gallery, but the twins Kester and Pollock are not there*]

ARTHUR: Kester and Pollock? The paedos?

DELPHINA: They're my friends.

ARTHUR: [*looks embarrassed, so changes the subject*] School's wanky.

DELPHINA: Wanky?

ARTHUR: [*laughing*] God, you're funny! This school year's supposed to be important, got my exams at the end of it but I can't be arsed. Don't even know what I'll do next. I mean there aren't many jobs round here.

[*Delphina nods. Delphina looks confused*]

ARTHUR: Some of the lasses in my year starve themselves.

DELPHINA: What do you mean?

ARTHUR: They don't eat. It's like they're having a competition to see how long they can go without food. They survive on chewie.

DELPHINA: But why?

ARTHUR: [*smiling*] They want to be skinny. They want a perfect body. Like you, I guess. [*Arthur blushes*]

DELPHINA: [*smiling*] What's a perfect body?

ARTHUR: Yours, yours is perfect.

DELPHINA: It's just a shell. [*Delphina spins away from the edge of the pool. Then she floats across the water on her back. Arthur is watching her, she likes that he is watching her*]

ARTHUR: [*squeaky voice*] You're perfect.

DELPHINA: [*flipping onto her front and gliding towards Arthur. She wants him to love her, she wishes she was normal*] I'm not. I'd give anything to be like those girls you talk about.

ARTHUR: I wish they could see you.

DELPHINA: They can't, Arthur, no one must know I'm here.

ARTHUR: Why?

DELPHINA: I'm a secret. I'm supposed to be dead, remember? You have to promise me that you won't tell a soul I'm here. Please, Arthur, please promise me.

ARTHUR: I promise.

DELPHINA: [*eyes fixed on Arthur*] No one can know about me. Promise, me. Cross your heart.

ARTHUR: Cross my heart. [*crosses over his heart with his fingers*] I promised, didn't I?

[*Delphina swims down to the bottom of the pool and back up to the surface. Arthur watches as she resurfaces. Arthur smiles*]

ARTHUR: If you were in my year my mates would all be after you.

DELPHINA: [*laughing*] After me? That sounds bad.

ARTHUR: You're at the top of the tree, Delphina. You've no clue.

DELPHINA: You don't half talk some nonsense, Arthur Braxton.

[*Delphina pushes her hand along the surface of the water. The water splashes onto Arthur. Arthur laughs*]

DELPHINA: [*whispers*] I miss you when you're not here. [*Arthur doesn't hear*]

DAY NINE

'Flintshire, Wrexham, Denbighshire, the Wirral and Greater Manchester are also subject to heavy rain warnings. With this level of rainfall continuing throughout today and conditions expected to worsen, the Met Office said it would be likely to extend its warnings into next week. So, looks like we best get building our arks. And back to the studio . . .'

Setting: *Delphina is holding onto the edge of the Males 1st Class Pool. Arthur is crouching down beside the edge of the pool. Kester and Pollock are in the viewing gallery, looking down on the pool. Laurel is inside one of the changing cubicles beside the pool, the half-stable door is closed, the stripy curtain is open. She is eating Smarties.*

ARTHUR: Where will you swim when the pool's knocked down?

DELPHINA: [*confused*] What do you mean?

ARTHUR: They're knocking down The Oracle, turning it into something wanky called 'Spa Pleasure Dome'.

DELPHINA: But they can't.

LAUREL: [*screaming*] They can't!

KESTER: [*shouting down from the viewing gallery*] What's that, young Arthur?

POLLOCK: [*shouting down from the viewing gallery*] Speak up, young one.

[*Arthur stands up from his crouching position near the edge of the pool*]

ARTHUR: [*loud voice*] How don't you lot know 'bout this? [*Arthur looks from Laurel to Delphina and then up to Kester and Pollock*]

133

There's photos of a massive dome glass building all around the fences outside.

KESTER: [*shouting down from the viewing gallery*] We don't go out much, young Arthur.

ARTHUR: But you must have seen all the workmen—

POLLOCK: [*shouting down from the viewing gallery*] Tell us more.

ARTHUR: 'Spa Pleasure Dome' is going to be all glass and aluminium and shiny.

KESTER: [*shouting down from the viewing gallery*] You're a rambler, lad.

POLLOCK: [*shouting down from the viewing gallery*] Get to the point, lad.

DELPHINA: What do you mean?

ARTHUR: Well this, I mean The Oracle, well I guess they think the building's all tired and crumbling and not really commercial. So they're going to knock it down—

LAUREL: [*Laurel pulls the stripy curtain across. She starts sobbing*] NO.

DELPHINA: They can't do that. This is our home. This is where we live.

ARTHUR: The local folk were working to save the building, I'm sure there's to be a meeting or something, but then there's talk of creating jobs for local people—

DELPHINA: But I've nowhere else to go.

[*Laurel's sobs grow louder*]

ARTHUR: How didn't you know? You must have seen all the workmen round here?

DELPHINA: Not really, the workmen stay away. And Maddie deals with any strangers she brings here, but that's only every two years and . . .

ARTHUR: How?

[*Delphina looks to the bottom of the pool and then over to the pile of shoes. Arthur follows her eye and then asks a question*]

ARTHUR: Who do the shoes belong to?

DELPHINA: [*avoiding the question*] How long do we have?

ARTHUR: Not long. I don't know. I mean, Silver will know more.

DAY TEN

'On a lighter note, Jamie Lenoir from Flint hit the headlines today. The thirty-six-year-old father of two has constructed his very own ark made entirely out of wood donated by his neighbours. His local community have rallied behind him to support his ambitious project and the resulting ark is quite a sight to behold.

"'It's big enough for me, the wife, the kids, two dogs, two cats and my mam's budgies," Mr Lenoir claims . . .'

Setting: *Arthur is sitting on the edge of the pool. His black trousers are rolled up to his knees. His calves are submerged in the water. Delphina is hanging on to the edge of the pool and kicking her legs through the water. Arthur pulls out his iPod, he wants Delphina to hear the music he likes but is worried she will hate it.*

DELPHINA: What's that? [*pointing at Arthur's iPod*]

ARTHUR: My iPod?

DELPHINA: What does it do?

ARTHUR: [*holds out his iPod for Delphina to see, but she doesn't take it from him*] It's got all my music on it, I mainly listen to it when I'm in bed.

DELPHINA: [*Delphina looks and nods but won't touch. She is afraid of water breaking it*] What does it feel like?

ARTHUR: What? [*puts his iPod back in his pocket*]

DELPHINA: Lying on a bed.

ARTHUR: [*laughing*] Random.

DELPHINA: I've always wanted to know. Silver's said 'I'm off to bed' since I've been little. He had one delivered here once. He showed me what a mattress looked like, but I never asked what it felt like, you know, to be in bed.

ARTHUR: You don't have a bed?

DELPHINA: [*pointing at water*] I sleep down here.

ARTHUR: [*Arthur thinks Delphina means that she sleeps on the poolside, not in the water*] He's a tight bastard.

DELPHINA: It's not—

ARTHUR: [*raising voice*] That's child abuse, that is. You can't be expected to sleep on them mosaics.

DELPHINA: It's not what—

ARTHUR: You can ask me owt you want.

[*Delphina smiles*]

[*Delphina lets go of the edge and flips back into the water. She somersaults and then re-emerges to face Arthur*]

DELPHINA: Three words. Tell me about 'bed'. Go on, in three words.

ARTHUR: Okay, so . . . comfortable . . . warm and safe.

DELPHINA: I'd like that, all of that. I'd like to feel warm.

ARTHUR: Have you never felt warm?

DELPHINA: The water feels warm to me. It'd be ace to be covered in something different.

ARTHUR: [*looks confused*] And safe?

DELPHINA: I can't begin to understand what that would feel like. Mainly I feel so exposed, so alone, so scared of shadows. I can't imagine what it'd feel like to be protected . . .

ARTHUR: If we have a baby.

[*Delphina laughs*]

[*Delphina smiles. Arthur smiles*]

ARTHUR: Seriously, if we do. Let's not fuck her up like our mums and dads fucked us up.

DELPHINA: What'd you call her?

ARTHUR: [*answers quickly*] Emily.

DELPHINA: [*Delphina treads water. Delphina smiles*] Emily.

DAY ELEVEN

'Local fire fighters have had a different emergency call-out today. Summoned to Chester Zoo, the fearless fire fighters struggled with high floodwaters to rescue a stranded zebra who had escaped from the safety of its paddock only to become trapped on an island of high ground as the waters quickly rose.

'Armed with just rubber dinghies and paddles, the fire fighters rowed out to the striped crusader and managed to secure him on his very own dinghy, before escorting him to safety.

'After the daring rescue, an unnamed fireman was heard to say, "I've rescued cats from trees, dogs from sewers and even a goat from a kitchen, but this is the first zebra." Another was said to be relieved that all of the elephants and lions were safe.

'A spokesperson at Chester Zoo has confirmed that Kate the Zebra is remarkably calm after her adventure.'

Setting: *Laurel is hiding in one of the changing cubicles beside the pool. Kester and Pollock are watching from the viewing gallery. Silver is attempting to climb down the wooden steps and into the water without Delphina noticing. Delphina does notice. Silver has one foot in the water when Delphina is next to him and speaks.*

DELPHINA: When were you going to tell me?

KESTER: [*shouting from the viewing gallery, down to Delphina*] Speak up, pet.

POLLOCK: [*shouting from the viewing gallery, down to Delphina*] Speak louder, pet.

SILVER: [*holding onto the steps and still with one foot in the water*] Tell you what, pet?

DELPHINA: That they're going to knock down The Oracle? Is it true? Where will we all go? How will we get there? How? HOW?

SILVER: [*sighing*] You'll go down to the otherworld, the rest of us will go where the light guides us. It will be as it is supposed to be, Delphina. You must trust the water. [*Silver jumps forward into the water and swims a breaststroke out into the pool*]

DELPHINA: But you said that was for the loose ones. I want us all to stay together.

SILVER: That was never an option. When the time is right—

LAUREL: [*shouting from the changing cubicle*] NO!

DELPHINA: [*turning to where Laurel is hiding*] Laurel, come out.

LAUREL: [*not coming out of the changing cubicle*] No, Delphina, you can't leave me. We can't not be together—

DELPHINA: I don't want to be on my own.

SILVER: [*gripping the edge of the pool and kicking his legs out*] It's nearly time.

LAUREL: [*shouting from the changing cubicle*] NO!

SILVER: Oh, Laurel, you know what has to be—

LAUREL: [*rushing out the changing cubicle and spinning on the spot*] NO!

DELPHINA: How long have I got?

SILVER: A few weeks. We've been delaying them as much as possible. The water goddesses are sending punishing rain. I've been keeping the workmen away . . . Look, Delphina, I'm hoping, we're all doing what we can, but—

DELPHINA: But . . .

[*Silver doesn't speak*]

DELPHINA: But you've always known how this would end.

SILVER: You won't be alone.

DELPHINA: But the people who live down there [*looks over to the grid, the gateway that leads to the underwater reservoir that they call the otherword*], what are they like? Are they all like Maddie? She scares me.

KESTER: [*shouting from the viewing gallery, down to Delphina*] There's water in the underground tombs.

POLLOCK: [*shouting at Kester*] That's a bit cryptic.

[*Kester and Pollock laugh in a manic way. Silver and Delphina look up to Pollock and Kester and then turn their attention back to each other*]

SILVER: We're running out of options. Arthur is the key.

Arthur

EARTH: (*Water. Air. Fire.*)

Reference No: 10-013338
Name: Philip Huntley
Missing Since: 12-Nov-2000

I swear this place's like a huge yellowy magnet and I'm a twatting paperclip. No matter how hard I try, I can't stay away. It's like everything I've ever wanted and everything I'll ever need to be happy are here. So it isn't long before I'm exploring the place. And it isn't long before I'm trying to find clues 'bout Delphina and Laurel. Or maybes I'm looking to see if there's kiddies locked up in any of them rooms upstairs, with them two paedos dancing around them naked. Delphina's said Kester and Pollock are her mates but, if I'm honest, I don't know what to believe. Finding Delphina is all a bit too good to be true.

And that's why I'm shitting my pants and that's why I'm upstairs in the dark, armed with a plastic sword. It's that one from my first time here, Delphina'd lifted it from the pool. She'd kept it for me, said I might need it again and then she'd laughed. And that's why it's in my sweaty hand now. And that's why I'm jumping at shadows, lunging at them with my sword. 'Cause this place's creepy as fuck. It's like the silence has noise, it's like I know I'm in danger but I'm brave when I'm in here. I'm a different me when I'm in The Oracle.

So I'm upstairs, near the entrance to the viewing gallery, walking from room to room, pretending to be a twatting ace explorer. I'm like Dora the Explorer but less Spanish. Above the pools, in this fuck-off-huge building, everything's faded and broken and a reminder of what was once significant and proper. Doors lead to tiled corridors, the tiles are chipped, some missing, but they hint at having been important once. The doors have signs: 'Steam-baths', 'Slipper-Baths', 'Turkish Baths'. The doors are closed, like they're embarrassed, like they're not supposed to be there any more. I keep walking, my arm outstretched in front of me, with the plastic sword guiding the way.

But I can't shake the feeling that I'm being followed or watched or both. It's dark, none of the light switches seem to be working and I'm tripping over my own feet as I shuffle along. And that's when I let out a squeak, as two shadows jump across the open doorway of a room that doesn't have much light. I stay still, just for a moment, catching my breath, before I take tiny steps to the door that says 'Office'.

Inside's a dusty room full of ciggie smoke and noise. There's one light bulb, hanging by a wire from a hole in the middle of the ceiling, then there's two desks, proper old wooden desks and loads of metal filing cabinets. But the things that my eyes can't help but focus on are the two blokes who are running their arses off from one filing cabinet to another, from one side of the room to the other. They've got to be twins, identical twins, I'm staring at their pointy features and trying my best to spot the difference.

'Popcorn, popcorn, popcorn,' one says, the other laughs.

It's them, it's them two old blokes from the viewing gallery, Kester and Pollock.

'Indigestion, popcorn cures my indigestion,' the first old man says to the second old man, then they both laugh, again, like they're off their heads.

I look at them, I probs should say something, but it's like my brain can't make sense of what I'm seeing. It's their faces that proper freak me out. Their faces are the colour of chalk, white chalk, with no lines, no marks, no hair, it's like they're no age at all. They're just old.

And that's when I realise that I'm still standing in the doorway and they're still rushing around like they're the busiest blokes in the world. Then they both stop next to one of the filing cabinets.

'Under B,' one of them says, passing a piece of crumpled paper to the other.

'Under A,' the other says, passing the same piece of paper back.

'You fool,' one says. He laughs.

'You old fool,' the other says. And now they're both laughing, like they're proper comedians. And that's when I see that they're holding hands.

And that's when they both turn and look at me. And both of them are smiling. They've got the same freaky toothless smile. I shiver.

'NAME?' they shout, together.

'Arth—' I start to say. I step into the room.

'STOP,' one of them screams. 'You're NOT missing,' he screams. I reckon I'm standing with my mouth open and my feet stuck to the spot. I'm watching the weird fuckers, they've moved apart. One's on his knees now, head in a filing cabinet, and the other's doing some sort of weird tap dance.

After loads of minutes, the one with his head in the filing cabinet turns to look at the other. He says, 'Kester, you fool.'

The other one continues with his weird tap dance, but makes his way over to me. He hands me the piece of crumpled paper that they were looking to file earlier.

'What did he say?' he asks me. I shrug my shoulders.

'You'll have to speak up, me lad, I had trifle for lunch,' he says.

'Trifle for lunch,' the other one says and then he rolls backwards from the filing cabinet and onto the floor. He laughs like he's a nut.

It's 'bout now that I'm wondering what the fuck I'm doing. And then their laughter stops. Silence. I look from one to the other.

'Braxton, ARTHUR,' one says.

'Booked into . . . Males 1st Class. Swimming lesson,' the other says.

'Three thirty,' one says.

'Best hurry,' the other says.

'Don't be late,' one says.

'Changing cubicle 27, Row A,' the other says.

'Goodbye,' one says.

'Goodbye,' the other says.

They're both waving their arms towards the door, so I turn and walk out of their office. And then I'm making my way back to the pool, along the proper-scary dark corridor, when someone steps out from the shadows and I nearly shit my pants.

'Silver,' I say, but Silver doesn't move. A shaft of light flashes over his fat face. He smells a bit, he smells of ciggies and sweat. He's proper hard faced, is Silver, but today he looks worse, he looks serious, angry, like he wants to kill me. And then he speaks, it's almost a growl.

'Run, lad,' he says. 'Run for your life!'

Then he steps back into the shadows and I swear he disappears like he's some evil wizard. I shake my head, I don't run, instead I make my way down to the Males 1st Class pool.

I'm back beside the pool, standing next to the changing cubicles, not really sure what I should be doing next. The plastic sword is at my feet. If I'm proper honest, the last thing I feel like is a swimming lesson. Mainly 'cause I hate the twatting water and that alone means it makes no sense why I'm standing here.

Maddie's in the water, singing that same song of hers. It's like I can feel her song inside my chest and inside my head and beating along with my heart. I daren't turn to look at her, something in my head tells me to try and ignore her, so I've my back to the pool. I wish Laurel or Delphina'd appear, they must be near, they must know I'm here.

That's when I count my way down to cubicle 27. I push open the half-stable door and I pull back the pink stripy curtain; don't know what I was expecting to find, but there's nowt inside. I reckon I let out a sigh of relief. But that's when a voice shouts from the viewing gallery. It sounds like one of the freaky old blokes.

'Change . . . NOW,' it says.

But I don't want to change now, I mean who the fuck do these weirdoes think they are? I mean, for one, I've no swims, and for two, I can't swim, so why the fuck would I 'change . . . NOW'? So instead of stepping into the cubicle and doing what some twatting weirdo's ordering me to do, I stay standing still, with my back to the pool. And that's when the singing gets louder.

It gets louder and then louder again. It's bouncing around inside of me, making me need to move, to sway, to spin, to walk to the water. And as I'm turning towards Maddie, the curtain of another cubicle, number 21 I think, slides back and Laurel rushes towards me. And before I understand what's going on, she's pushing me and I'm moving with her and I'm heading towards the water.

Splash! Yes, splash, and I'm in the water and I'm under the water and I'm probs drowning, but I don't seem to give a fuck. 'Cause Maddie's singing, that sweet sweet singing, something 'bout it having been two years, something 'bout the water goddesses needing food, but it don't matter. It's like nowt else seems important. And that's when Maddie grabs me. I think I can feel her tits through my hoodie, but I don't think that for long. We're travelling down, down to the bottom of the pool, down to a grid, and I'm smiling even though her song's not full of happy. But we're going down and down and I can see a light.

But that's when the singing stops and only one voice can be heard. I hear it through the water.

'No – MINE!' Delphina says. 'Arthur is mine.'

And the next thing I remember is waking up, lying on the side of the pool. I turn to look into the pool and into the smiling face of Delphina.

'Did I drown?' I ask, mainly 'cause I'm a bell-end.

'No, Arthur. You're mine, for always,' Delphina says.

Delphina

WATER: (*Earth. Air. Fire.*)

DAY TWELVE

'Reports are coming through of a holidaymaker from Northampton, named locally as Nicholas James, being trapped on the roof of his static caravan at the Four Oaks Caravan Park in Rhyl. Although the site was evacuated several days ago, the reasons for Mr James's predicament remain unconfirmed. Fire fighters are attending the scene.'

Setting: *Late at night. The moon is shining in through the stained-glass windows and onto the pool. Arthur is sitting on the edge of the pool. His black trousers are rolled up. His calves are in the water. He is smiling. Delphina is close to him, but still in the water. She is smiling. She is floating on her back in the water.*

ARTHUR: What you been doing today?

DELPHINA: Swimming. Same, same. You're later tonight.

ARTHUR: Do you swim all the time?

DELPHINA: No, sometimes I float.

[*Arthur laughs*]

ARTHUR: No, I mean you've never been out of the water when I've been here. Is it 'cause you don't want to be near me?

DELPHINA: [*smiling*] No, it's because I don't want you to see me naked.

ARTHUR: [*laughing*] But I already can! I'd like to touch you.

DELPHINA: Well come into the water.

[*Arthur smiles. He does not move*]

[*Delphina winks and then twirls three times*]

DELPHINA: So what you been up to today?

ARTHUR: Been drinking cider.

DELPHINA: Is that good?

ARTHUR: Means I'm drunk, I might say something I shouldn't.

DELPHINA: What does it feel like?

ARTHUR: What?

DELPHINA: Being drunk.

ARTHUR: Like the world's less scary.

DELPHINA: That sounds nice.

ARTHUR: You know I think the world of you. You know I love you.

DELPHINA: Thanks.

[*Arthur laughs*]

ARTHUR: You can't say, 'thanks'. That's a rubbish response.

[*Delphina laughs, she is too scared to tell Arthur how she feels. She thinks that she more than loves Arthur*]

DELPHINA: What's it like?

ARTHUR: What?

DELPHINA: Sex.

ARTHUR: Honestly?

DELPHINA: Of course.

ARTHUR: I don't know.

DELPHINA: But I thought you'd done it with loads of girls.

ARTHUR: [*embarrassed*] I haven't.

DELPHINA: [*smiling*] You lied.

ARTHUR: [*red cheeked*] I didn't, I just sort of implied that I'd shagged.

DELPHINA: [*smiling*] That's lying!

ARTHUR: [*not making eye contact with Delphina*] No. Yes. I just didn't want you to think I was a . . .

DELPHINA: I think it's cute.

ARTHUR: [*making eye contact with Delphina*] Cute?

DELPHINA: [*laughing*] Sexy cute.

ARTHUR: Do you think we will one day?

DELPHINA: [*smiling*] One day.

ARTHUR: I can't wait. God, I've a semi just thinking 'bout it.

DELPHINA: A semi?

ARTHUR: My cock's getting hard.

DELPHINA: [*laughing*] You're funny.

ARTHUR: I like it when you laugh.

DAY THIRTEEN

Dear Sirs,
Outbreaks of heavy rain are expected to continue across North
Wales, the Met Office has said. Yet it has been noted that,
during last night's meeting, a member of the local council
requested the lifting of the hose-pipe ban that has been
restricting use since the summer. I'm not quite sure who'd be
using their hose pipes in this current weather and can only
assume that the local councillor was being ironic. Yet, still,
surely the council should be taking time to put in place meas-
ures to ensure our safety rather than wasting precious meeting
time being utterly pedantic.
Yours,
Angry in Flint

Setting: *Silver is standing in the doorway to the Males 1st Class pool. He has his arms crossed over his chest and is clearly angry. He is whistling. Laurel is hiding in one of the changing cubicles. Arthur and Delphina are at the far end of the swimming pool. Arthur is sitting on the edge of the pool with his feet in the water. Delphina is holding onto the edge of the pool near to Arthur.*

SILVER: [*stops whistling. Shouting*] You again.

DELPHINA: [*shouting to Silver*] Silver, this is Arthur.

SILVER: I know who HE is.

[*Arthur moves his legs out of the water and stands up. He is looking across the length of the pool at Silver*]

DELPHINA. [*quietly*] Arthur, this is Silver.

SILVER: [*shouting from doorway*] 'Bout time you were off lad. [*he uncrosses his arms and taps at an invisible watch on his wrist*]

DELPHINA: [*shouting to Silver*] Don't be silly, Silver. Arthur's only just got here.

SILVER: His type's not welcome around here. He's a bad egg.

[*Silver turns and storms back through the doors. The doors flip back and forth from the strength of his push*]

DELPHINA: Ignore him. I mean, just the other day he was saying you were 'the key'. It'll just be because you're new around here. We don't get many visitors who come here twice. [*Delphina's eyes flick into the water, to the remains layering the bottom of the pool, then to the pile of shoes*]

ARTHUR: What's down there?

DELPHINA: Things that are missing.

ARTHUR: And them shoes? [*Arthur moves his eyes to the pile of shoes*]

DELPHINA: Things that no one missed.

ARTHUR: Like me and you, missing and not missed.

[*Delphina nods*]

ARTHUR: [*whispering, looking towards the door, changing the subject*] Must be nice having someone look out for you.

DELPHINA: [*looking at Arthur*] He's all I've got.

LAUREL: [*shouting from the changing cubicle*] You've got ME!

DELPHINA: Yes, but you're younger than me now Laurel, and I—

LAUREL: But—

DELPHINA: You're my best friend.

LAUREL: I'm NOT. I'm your—

ARTHUR: Why don't you come out?

[*Laurel doesn't answer. Instead she pulls the striped curtain back. Arthur and Delphina can now see her face. Her mouth is moving as she's eating Smarties*]

ARTHUR: Why did you push me into the pool?

LAUREL: [*whispers*] Maddie made me. Said I had to for Delphina to stay alive. I'm sorry. [*starts to cry*]

DELPHINA: [*smiling at Laurel*] It's okay Laurel. [*turning to Arthur*] Come swimming with me, Arthur.

ARTHUR: [*his fingers ruffle the front of his floppy hair*] I don't do water, you know that. And last time . . . [*he looks at Laurel. It is clear that he still isn't happy with her*]

DELPHINA: [*smiling*] I'll help.

[*Arthur smiles*]

ARTHUR: Don't have any swims.

DELPHINA: Swims?

ARTHUR: Something to wear in the water.

DELPHINA: Why would you wear clothes in the water? [*she smiles and then flips away from the side of the pool, backstroking her way over to the wooden stairs*]

[*Arthur watches. Arthur smiles*]

DELPHINA: [*shouting*] Come over here. [*Arthur smiles. He walks around the side of the pool until he is close to Delphina*] If you come in here you can hold onto the side. It's safe, you'll be able to touch the bottom, but it's best you ignore what's down there. Bones.

ARTHUR: [*Arthur nods, not really understanding about the bones*] Delphina, I've no swims.

DELPHINA: [*smiling*] Neither have I.

[*Arthur laughs*]

DELPHINA: I want you to hold me.

[*This is what Arthur needed to hear, he will do anything for Delphina. Arthur starts to take off his clothes. He is clumsy. The sleeves of his shirt stick to his arms. He shakes them loose. His shirt is still on, flapping open, as he slips out of his shoes. He unfastens his black trousers. They fall to the floor, he steps out of them. Delphina laughs as he finally shakes off his white shirt. They look at each other and their eyes connect. Delphina unlocks her eyes from Arthur's and looks down to his boxer shorts. There is an erection. Delphina smiles. She looks back at Arthur's face. Arthur is smiling. Arthur looks scared*]

ARTHUR: [*pulling at the side of his grey boxer shorts*] I'm keeping these on.

DELPHINA: Just lower yourself in. Grip the side. The water won't hurt you. I promise.

ARTHUR: I trust you.

[*Arthur moves to the side and lowers himself to sit with his legs in the water. He twists, he places both palms on the edge of the pool, pushing his weight onto his arms, and begins lowering himself into the water. Arthur enters the water and Delphina takes him in her arms and ecstasy follows. Arthur tastes true love*]

DAY FOURTEEN

'The north-west was the only part of Britain affected by flooding yesterday.

'Large areas of the region were showered, as more than half of October's average rainfall thrashed down in twenty-four hours.

'And forecasters say there will be little respite for at least a week, with downpours set to continue through to the weekend.

'Last night, the Met Office issued severe-weather warnings for the north-west, and said the rain will continue to batter the north of the country today, with winds of up to 47 mph expected . . .'

Setting: *Arthur and Delphina are in the water. Arthur is wearing the same grey boxer shorts. Delphina and Arthur are holding onto the edge of the pool, their legs are kicking out behind them. Kester and Pollock are watching from the viewing gallery.*

ARTHUR: I feel like a right bell-end.

DELPHINA: Why?

ARTHUR: What could be more gay than being scared of water?

KESTER: [*shouting down from the viewing gallery*] Now that's talent.

POLLOCK: [*shouting down from the viewing gallery*] Is there nothing she can't do?

KESTER: [*shouting down from the viewing gallery*] A great girl.

POLLOCK: [*shouting down from the viewing gallery*] An extinct girl.

KESTER: [*shouting down from the viewing gallery*] She's getting extincter all the time.

DELPHINA: [*ignoring Kester and Pollock*] You're getting used to it now, aren't you? Keep holding on to the side and stretch your legs out. I'm here. [*Arthur looks at Delphina and smiles*] I won't let anything happen to you. The water can't harm you. Move your feet and legs together, like a frog would. [*Arthur follows Delphina's instructions*] That's it. Bend your knees and lift your

171

feet up as high as your bum. [*Delphina laughs*] [*Arthur doesn't turn his head to look at Delphina*] That's it. Turn your feet out, move them out . . . great, now in again, to meet each other. You're doing so well, Arthur. Now, straighten your legs with your knees touching.

ARTHUR: I reckon I'm fucking up my chance with you.

[*Arthur lowers his legs down into the water but keeps a hold of the side. His toes touch on the bones that layer the bottom of the pool and he quickly lifts his feet up. Arthur looks at Delphina. He is not smiling*]

DELPHINA: Will you hold me?

[*Arthur nods his head slowly. Delphina lets go of the side of the pool and glides across the water to him*]

DELPHINA: You'll have to let go of the side. Trust me.

[*Arthur lets go of the side. Delphina holds him. Their bodies lock. Delphina's knees grip around Arthur's leg. Delphina's thigh rests against Arthur's boxer shorts. Arthur's arms wrap around Delphina's waist and pull her to him. They spin through the water. Delphina rests her arms on Arthur's shoulders, crossing them around the back of his neck*]

ARTHUR: Oh God. I've got a stiffy.

KESTER: [*shouting down from the viewing gallery*] It's hard to feel sorry for him.

[*Kester and Pollock laugh hysterically*]

DAY FIFTEEN

'Commuters faced rush-hour despair as heavy rain caused signal failures on rail lines. Passengers on cramped trains out of Chester criticised the extreme humidity and there were delays on all lines. Mainline commuters experienced fifty-minute delays caused by electrical supply problems. More on the delays later . . .'

Setting: *Arthur and Delphina are in the water. Laurel is hiding in one of the changing cubicles. Arthur is holding onto the edge of the pool with one hand and attempting to grab Delphina with the other. Kester and Pollock are watching from the viewing gallery.*

DELPHINA: Stop messing around!

ARTHUR: [*grabbing into the water, Arthur misses Delphina as she spins*] Come here.

DELPHINA: Later. [*smiling*] First you need to let me hold your body. [*Arthur laughs*]

DELPHINA: [*smiling*] This is serious. Place your arms out in front, just under the surface of the water. Like this. [*Delphina shows Arthur*] Keep your palms facing outwards, then push both hands out and around . . . like this, like you're drawing a full circle in the water. You try. [*Delphina puts her hands under Arthur's stomach, his body floats rigid through the water. Arthur smiles*] That's ace. Your hands finish by stretching forwards again. Your arms and legs should stay in the water all of the time and you shouldn't splash when doing the stroke correctly.

ARTHUR: So, what do I get for being awesome? [*he reaches for and grabs the edge of the pool*]

DELPHINA: Close your eyes. [*Arthur closes his eyes*]

[*Delphina glides to him. She kisses him gently on the lips. Arthur's eyes stay closed as Delphina moves her lips away from him and floats backwards*]

ARTHUR: [*opening his eyes, smiling*] Best keep practising. I reckon what I'll get when I can swim will be well worth working my bell-end off.

LAUREL: [*shouting from changing cubicle*] You're getting good already.

ARTHUR: [*shouting to the changing cubicle*] When I'm really good, will you come out? Will you come out and talk to me, maybes give me one of them Smarties? [*it is clear that Arthur has forgiven Laurel*]

LAUREL: [*shouting from the changing cubicle*] Maybe.

KESTER: [*shouting down from the viewing gallery*] Here. [*he stands and throws a white lifesaving ring down to the pool*]

POLLOCK: [*shouting down from the viewing gallery*] Waste of time.

KESTER: [*shouting down from the viewing gallery*] Nothing can save Arthur Braxton now.

POLLOCK: [*to Kester*] You old fool.

KESTER: [*to Pollock*] No, you old fool.

DELPHINA: [*looking at the viewing gallery*] Ignore them. [*eyes connecting with Arthur*] The water likes you.

ARTHUR: Talentless twat that I am, but yes, I think it does.

DELPHINA: [*floating over to Arthur*] But there's something bothering you, I can feel it.

ARTHUR: [*whispers*] It's nowt.

DELPHINA: Tell me.

ARTHUR: It's school, they're suspicious, writing letters to Dad asking for a sick note for me, 'cause my attendance is something like 78 per cent. So I went to the doctor's before and he said I wasn't ill, refused to write the note.

DELPHINA: [*confused*] I don't understand, what does it mean?

ARTHUR: It means that it won't be long before social services are knocking on my door and then they'll see the shit hole I live in and how fucking useless my dad is. I reckon they'll send me some place else to live.

DELPHINA: [*smiling*] Is that all?

[*Arthur nods*]

DELPHINA: Let the water help your dad, bring him here.

ARTHUR: If only it were that simple.

DELPHINA: It is. [*Delphina kisses Arthur*]

DAY SIXTEEN

'Earlier indicators of a storm over North Wales are no longer present. The dark-greenish sky, the large hail, the loud roar and the lightning have ceased, thus making the probability of a tornado *unlikely*. There are no tornado watches or warnings in the Greater Manchester area either. I repeat, there are no tornado watches or warnings in the Greater Manchester area . . .'

Setting: *Delphina and Maddie are in the water in the Males 1st Class pool. They have been swimming together for at least an hour. Maddie is not singing. Delphina is aware that something is wrong. Laurel is sitting beside the edge of the pool. She is clutching her rope with one hand and playing with the lids from her Smarties with the other. Pollock and Kester are watching from the viewing gallery.*

MADDIE: You've fucked my head.

DELPHINA: I've what?

MADDIE: I listened to your story, the stuff you've been telling that boy Arthur, and I've got to tell you how you've fucked my head.

[*Delphina stops swimming and looks over at Maddie. Maddie is spinning. She is naked, but she is wearing white gloves that have pink flowers on them. She is carrying a walking stick in one hand and a plastic bag in the other. The walking stick is being held at arm's length as she spins. Delphina is watching to avoid the stick. The white plastic bag is bellowing full of water. Maddie stops spinning and she waves her walking stick over the water*]

MADDIE: When I was a girl I used to live opposite these baths. When that little boy who liked to swim in some public baths

181

or other went missing and it was reckoned that Myra Hindley
had done it, well I used to think that it was me that had
murdered him.

DELPHINA: [*raises voice*] What? What are you saying?

MADDIE: When I got myself a man just like me and when I got
my own baby in my arms, I wanted her to have everything I
hadn't. And that's when it all went wrong.

DELPHINA: [*scared*] I don't understand what—

MADDIE: Dysfunctional families. You have no idea.

[*Maddie is not spinning, she is not singing. Maddie bobs on the spot.
Her voice is dull, monotone*]

DELPHINA: I have no idea? Maddie, you've heard my story, I
wouldn't say I'd had the most conventional of upbringings.

[*Delphina looks to Laurel*]

[*Laurel nods her head but does not make eye contact with Delphina*]

MADDIE: I thought I'd murdered that laddie.

DELPHINA: Did you?

MADDIE: I still don't know. I swim here, I swim down through the
gateway into the otherworld every day, hoping someone might
tell me. Each time I do as the water tells me, every two years
I've obeyed the goddesses and my singing's fed them a life and
I've hoped someone'd tell me. The bastards, they know the
truth, but they ain't for telling me.

DELPHINA: Maybe they don't know the answer.

MADDIE: They do. I know they do, the bastards. How many more
people do I have to drown before they'll tell me? Seven people
I've killed for them. Arthur would've been number eight.

DELPHINA: I quite liked that David, I was only seven when he
drowned. He used to sing when he was working here at night.
And Deborah, four years ago, she was pretty. And Louise, I was
nine, her shoes are over there.

[*Delphina points to scattered shoes beside the side of the pool*]

182

KESTER: [*shouting down from the viewing gallery*] One of them was a vicar.

POLLOCK: [*shouting down from the viewing gallery*] Now he's a missing parson.

KESTER: [*laughing*] You fool.

POLLOCK: [*laughing*] You old fool.

DELPHINA: [*shouting up to the viewing gallery*] QUIET!

[*Pollock and Kester pretend to be pulling a zip across their mouths, but their shoulders are still vibrating from laughter*]

DELPHINA: [*whispers*] Nigel, his name was Nigel Harbottle.

MADDIE: I do what the water tells me to do. My singing brings them here. They keep YOU alive.

DELPHINA: [*tears falling*] I remember all of their names.

[*Maddie spins. Delphina swerves to miss Maddie's walking stick*]

MADDIE: You've no idea what I did to that baby of mine.

DELPHINA: You had a baby?

MADDIE: A beautiful baby girl. Melody was her name.

DELPHINA: [*whispers*] What did you do to her?

MADDIE: I did the worst thing you could possibly do. Can you, poor little innocent Delphina, imagine the worst thing in the world?

[*Delphina nods*]

MADDIE: Good.

[*Maddie swims to the edge of the pool. She lifts her arm up high and throws the walking stick towards the changing cubicles, then she turns to Delphina and smiles. Maddie dives into the water and down towards the grid, to the gateway. She is going to the underground reservoir, to the place they call the otherworld. Air bubbles pop along the surface of the water*]

SILVER: Just ignore Maddie.

[*Silver has appeared. He's sitting with his feet in the water at the far end of the pool, near the main doors. Delphina swims over to him*]

SILVER: She's a broken soul, pet. She was mistreated on too many levels.

DELPHINA: Did she know Myra Hindley? You've told me about her.

SILVER: No she didn't, but I know Maddie. Her husband broke her and she murdered their only daughter.

[*Silver looks over to where Maddie had dived into the water. He shakes his head and then turns back to look at Delphina*]

DELPHINA: She needs to let the water goddesses heal her. She's still fighting them, even after all these years.

LAUREL: She needs a wash.

[*Silver laughs*]

DELPHINA: How can she smell so vile when she's in water all the time?

SILVER: That's the smell of decay, Delphina. She's rotting from the inside out.

[*Silver lifts one leg from the water, then the other. He is wearing briefs. He walks around the pool, to where Maddie dived. Delphina is watching him. Silver sits down on the edge of the pool. He puts his feet into the remains of the swirls and bubbles from Maddie's dive. An arm emerges from the water and a white plastic bag whips at Silver's naked legs*]

SILVER: [*shouting*] Ow, you bitch.

[*Silver swings his legs through the water and up into the air. A wave of water jumps up and covers his body. Silver stands up and makes his way along the side of the pool and out through the swinging doors*]

Arthur

EARTH: (*Water. Air. Fire.*)

Reference No: 10-145537
Name: David Richardson
Missing since: 14-Feb-2002

I've been remembering tales Dad and Mum used to tell me of the sacred spring that fed into the baths at The Oracle. When I was little they'd talk 'bout water goddesses who inhabited the spring and took kiddies as a sacrifice. That's what all the townsfolk used to say. I reckoned that it was a way of keeping us good, like 'behave or them water goddesses will take you away and eat you all up'. The water goddesses were our town's bogeymen. It worked, I mean I never went near the sacred spring as a kid.

So now, what with everything with Delphina and The Oracle, well I've been researching a bit. Turns out The Oracle was built over a spring that the old townsfolk used to think was full of magic water. It's the same water that does that holy well up the hill. There's loads of stuff online 'bout religious folk from all over the world travelling here with plastic bottles just so as to be able to take some of the water from that well. Some people even come once a month, just so they can dip themselves in the magic water and make their diseases go away. I've spent hours on my phone, clicking on links and seeing all these cases of folk with depression, cancer, baby-making problems and other mental shit, 'bout them all being cured by a trip to the holy well.

That's why I reckoned that I should take my dad there, that

maybes Delphina was right. I mean, I couldn't be taking him to The Oracle. I didn't want him pissing his pants in front of Delphina and Laurel. So I reckoned that if I got him to the holy well and threw some magic water over him, then all our problems might start fucking off.

And that's why I'm now pushing a shopping trolley, with my dad in it, up the hill away from the sea front in the twatting rain. Dad's huffing and puffing, like he's a fucked-up steam train, and I don't know why 'cause it's me breaking my back trying to get the fucker up this hill. The wind's not helping, the rain's not helping and mainly I'm wondering what the fuck I was thinking. I mean, like owt can cure my dad. I've told him I'm taking him to his doctor's appointment, he has to have a review every couple of months to see if he's still ill. Usually the doctor takes one look at him and then, no shit, Sherlock, says that Dad's unfit for work. Dad never even has to speak, which mainly pisses me off, 'cause I can't remember the last time I heard him talk. I miss his voice.

But we get by. Dad's not a dad, he's not even a man now. Instead it's me that does all the official stuff. I use a calendar on the wall, I'm proper organised, mark on it when Dad's got appointments and when bills need paying. We don't really have to worry that much 'bout money. Dad was on the sick from work, but eventually he was dismissed. I reckon we could have had a case for 'unfair dismissal' but really I don't blame them. Dad was being a twat and taking the piss. He still is, if I'm honest. And I tried claiming for disability benefits, but it was all 'bout hoops and paperwork and social services wanting to do home visits and I felt like my head was going to pop. That's why I threw all their forms in the bin. I mean we're not flush, but Mum's monthly guilt money covers virtually everything. Our mortgage is paid by the council, our council tax is too. I'm in charge of Dad's bank account, that's easy 'cause me and him have the same name and so I do all the adult stuff while Dad pisses himself on the sofa eating crisps and grunting like the twat that he is.

Sometimes I wish I could just be a kid and not have to worry 'bout budgets for food and bills and making sure my dad never runs out of fucking crisps. But maybes that'll change after today.

That's why I've tipped Dad on the pavement and parked the trolley around the corner. And that's why I've just paid our entrance money, fifty pence each, to go and look at the holy well and the spring attached to it. Dad's walking around, with no shoes on, like a fucking zombie. His eyes are on the floor, he's bent like an old man and he stinks of piss. I tried to get him to change his trousers before we left but he was having none of it.

I want to hate this place, mainly 'cause the bloke taking the money looked at me like I was a piece of shit on his shoe, but straight away I can feel that there's something 'bout here that's calming. I can feel the beats of music under the soles of my feet and I'm sure I can hear laughter, proper belly-wobbling laughter, but I can't figure out where it's coming from. I want to explore, but I can't trust Dad on his own. So instead I'm guiding him, and I get him to the well.

So now, we're both standing next to the well, in this cave thing, not really sure what the fuck we should be doing next. The plaque on the wall says it's a crypt, 'into which the well rises'. I'm saying it's a cave, in a hill. I reckon Dad would say the same, if he wasn't a mental. I look down at the well. I mean, there's no barriers, no safety fence, just a big round hole that's the size and depth of a kiddie's paddling pool and claiming to be a holy well. There's rocks forming a tiny wall and there's water over the other side too, but I can't be getting a good look without taking my eyes off Dad and I daren't do that. So instead we're both standing, looking at the water and I'm stopping myself from pushing Dad in, 'cause I reckon that only a full-body dunking will cure the twat.

But that's when Dad turns to me. And that's when Dad lifts his head up. He looks straight at me. His long greasy hair's falling over his eyes and he's swiping it away with the back of his hand. But it's his eyes that look different. His eyes are proper glaring at me. I think he's going to speak. I swear I'm willing him to say owt, just a word, even a shit one. And that's when he lifts his finger to his lips and kisses it, then he breaks eye contact. And that's when his eyes seem to fix on something else. I watch as Dad shuffles over to the far side of the well. He stands still for a bit, staring at one of the rocks. Then he falls down to his knees like a twat, still staring at the same rock, then he bends forward and kisses it.

'What the fuck you doing?' I ask.

But Dad keeps kissing the rock, I swear he's trying to tongue it.

'Get the fuck up,' I say. But he doesn't. It's 'bout then that he starts mumbling something, to the rock, as he lifts his head from it and starts running his finger over a cross that's been cut into the stone. I reckon it was done by some fucker with a penknife, but Dad seems to think it's important. I watch him, I swear I daren't take my eyes of the twat. And that's when he stands up. He's laughing, but it's a fake laugh and all hee hee hee. And that's when he shuffles his feet round to near me and that's when he stops both his shuffling and his fake laughing. His back's to the well. He looks me right in the eyes, and that's when he winks. My dad winks at me. And then he hoys himself backwards into the water.

Shit! The fucker. The twat!

'Get the fuck out,' I shout. But Dad's not listening. He's screaming. I mean it's more than a scream, it's the longest-ever high-pitched wail. It's like all the pain in him's got sound. And he's splashing around like he's in his very own paddling pool, not like he's drowning, but like he's fighting with the water. And that's when the bloke who we paid our fifty pences to comes over with some proper scary-looking black bloke. And that's when they start dragging Dad, and then me, out into the road.

'Get your twatting hands off,' I yell. But I don't fight and I don't struggle, 'cause, if I'm proper honest, I'm glad they've stopped my dad's wailing.

And that's when I look at my dad and that's when I see he's looking back at me. And that's when my dad speaks.

'Bloody hell, son, you look a right sight,' he says. 'Them trousers don't fit you proper. Fancy a fish-and-chips supper?'

And so I abandon the shopping trolley, and me and my dad, who's dripping wet and still not wearing any shoes, walk down the hill to the seafront. Dad's asking loads of questions 'bout school, he's spinning around saying how proper the rain feels, he's asking whether or not I've got a lass and I'm not really saying owt, even though there's a million things I want to say. I mean, my dad's talking, I mean he's not nodding or grunting, he's proper talking. I mean all that shit I've been reading 'bout The Oracle must be true. And right now I don't care if it never stops raining, I mean I'll worship the twatting gods of water if that'll help; I mean I'll sell my soul to the rain clouds, just as long as they keep my dad talking.

I've still not said owt by the time we reach the chippie on the seafront. We're standing outside, both of us, Dad looking in through the window. Dad's dripping wet, with no shoes on, looking like a right tramp, and all I seem to be able to do is stare at him. There's a couple of tables inside and Dad asks if I'd like to have my tea there. I put my hand in my pocket, feeling 'bout to see how much change I've got.

'I've not got enough money, Dad,' I say.

His face falls and I reckon I hold my breath, not knowing if he's going to speak again.

'I'm sorry, Arthur,' he says.

I nod and I smile. I know he's not just meaning 'bout us not having enough money for fish and chips.

'How much you got?' Dad asks.

'Enough for a couple of cuppas,' I say. And that's when Dad throws one arm round me and moves me towards the front door.

We step inside, Dad all dripping and tramp-like and that's when a woman practically dives out from behind the hot counter and holds an arm across Dad to stop him moving forward.

'And where do you think you're going?' she asks Dad. Her badge says 'I'm Stella'.

I watch Dad, mainly 'cause I'm willing him to speak. Dad's watching Stella. His eyes are going up her and down her and then his eyes meet her eyes and he smiles. And I look at Stella and she's smiling back at Dad.

'Sorry about the state I'm in . . . Stella,' Dad says. His words are smiling. 'I've just taken a dip in the holy well up the hill.' He turns towards the door, lifts his hand up as if pointing and then he turns back to me. 'Well I never,' Dad says. 'Looks like the sun's shining, Arthur.' Then Dad drops his arm and turns back to Stella.

I turn and look out the window and across the seafront. Dad's right, the rain's stopped, the sun's out. I smile a proper smile.

'We had hoped for a fish-and-chip supper, but I've come out without my wallet, so it's two teas please. And a towel, if you've got one?' Dad says.

I think I'm holding my breath. It all goes silent a bit, a bit too long, if I'm honest. Stella's smiling and staring at Dad and Dad's smiling and staring at Stella and I'm standing staring at them both

194

and feeling like a twat. I swear, somehow, I don't know how, but I reckon my dad's pulled.

A million seconds later and Stella speaks. 'Course, pet,' she says to Dad. 'You two go and sit your arses down and I'll bring you a towel and something hot.' Then she giggles and Dad laughs.

'I'm Arthur,' Dad says. 'And this here's my son, Arthur.'

'Stella,' Stella says, pointing at her badge, but I reckon Dad's looking at her tits. They're huge.

'Nice,' Dad says, then he laughs and Stella giggles and that's when I tell Dad that I'm going to nip home and get him his shoes and his wallet. But also, I'm giving him some space, 'cause for the first time in years I reckon my dad's alive.

'Course, the leaflet for the meeting was on the doormat when I nipped back for Dad's shoes and some money. It was a meeting for local residents to put forward their case for the protection of The Oracle. And it was starting in less than ten minutes.

That's why I ran my arse off with the sun shining down on me. And that's why I'm now panting like an idiot, on one of the back-row chairs in the main hall at school. And that's why I'm trying not to worry if Dad'll be okay in the chippie without his shoes and wallet.

'Ladies, gentleman, please. If you continue to shout together, we'll be here all evening,' the bloke standing on the stage shouts. He's got a posh accent, like he's from London, and he's wearing a suit that you'd not find in Primark. I reckon his clothes alone must be worth more than most of the losers in here earn in a year.

That's when the room goes all quiet. I mean he's that type of man. He speaks and folk listen. The bloke's up there on the stage, all by himself and it's like he don't give a fuck that there's at least fifty of us lot looking at him. He stands like he's famous. Like he's just been walking along a red carpet at a poncey film premier and some tosser of a journo has asked him for a few words. I reckon he's pretty cool, in an old-man kind of way. There's photographers clicking and a couple of journos are standing up at the side of the hall, pretending to take notes.

'To say that The Oracle is cursed is, quite frankly, nonsense,' he says.

A woman sitting on the front row of chairs puts her hand up. It's like she's at school. I laugh at my own joke. He nods at her to speak.

'My lass killed herself in them baths and the body of her kiddie was never found. No good will come of knocking The Oracle down,' she says. Her voice is all loud and shouty. There's other people in the audience, nodding and saying stuff like 'hear, hear' and 'you tell them'. I nod too.

'And what about them rumours of folk being seen going in The Oracle, and then going missing,' someone else shouts. 'I put together a report. Seven people in the last seventeen years. One of them's my son Philip.'

'My American clients,' the bloke on the stage says, 'know the tragic circumstances behind The Oracle's closure and have looked into the missing-persons reports that you gave to us. There is no clear link that connects the persons missing to the building that is The Oracle.'

'For fuck's sake, they were all last seen near The Oracle or going into The Oracle or working in The fucking Oracle,' shouts a man from somewhere near the front. 'People don't just vanish.' He hasn't put his hand up and they're all facing the stage, so I can't be seeing who said it. All I can tell is that he's pissed off.

'The police have investigated and there is no physical evidence that connects the missing people to The Oracle,' the bloke on the stage continues.

'Bloke's right,' someone else shouts. 'Folk bugger off all the time. I'd heard your Philip fucked off to London.' There's a bit of laughter in the audience, like there's some private joke happening.

'I don't blame any bugger for wanting out of this crappy town,' someone else shouts. I can't keep track of all the voices and yelling.

'Yeah. I reckon knocking down The Oracle'll be a new start for us all. New jobs as well,' a woman shouts out. I can see from the backs of heads that some folk are nodding and, again, there's stuff being said like 'hear, hear' and 'too fucking right'.

'Surely all of this is even more reason to knock down The Oracle and support my American clients in the building of new facilities for this area.'

'My son, David, was last seen working as a night watchman in The Oracle, back in 2002. I know there's a clue to what happened to him somewhere in there. I know the police searched, but if I could just go back in, just one more time,' a lady says. She hadn't put her hand up but I can see where she's sitting 'cause some woman stands up and bends over to her, passing her a white tissue, and some bloke puts his arm around her. 'He went to work and never came back, he was only nineteen,' she says. Then she's sobbing really loud. The bloke on the stage stares at her for a bit. I don't know if it's 'cause he wants her to shut the fuck up or if he's actually got a heart someplace under his fancy shirt.

'I think when you hear what my American clients are proposing, you'll all reconsider your objections . . .'

And then he's off on one.

He's spouting 'bout all the money and jobs the wanky 'Spa Pleasure Dome' will provide. It's all 'bout money. It's like that's the only thing that matters. Then he hits them with something that wins every fucker in the room's vote. He hits them with an 'incentive' of three months' free trial to all within a five-mile radius of the wanky 'Spa Pleasure Dome'.

I swear, he's got them all drooling and wetting their pants by the end of his speech. I just don't get how all their principles, how all their cares and concerns 'bout them missing folk can be bought with the offer of free stuff. I mean them baths, The Oracle, it's part of the history of this shitty seaside town. I mean I've grown up hearing all 'bout the stories, the water-healers, the water goddesses, I mean I've seen a miracle take place in the water that fills them baths, I mean it's part of the landscape, it's part of who we once were. And now, these people, these twats are sitting here with pound signs in their eyes, not giving a fuck 'bout what made us not just any crappy seaside town.

I'm leaving the hall, I'm in the corridor and heading for the door out. I mean the meeting's still going on, but I've had enough. They're all licking the bloke on the stage's arse and now they're signing up for their free membership. Bunch of tossers. That's when I hear my name.

'Arthur Braxton,' he says. 'Stop right there, young man.'

I stop but I don't turn, mainly 'cause I know I'm in shit and I've got to play it cool.

'Arthur Braxton.'

I turn slowly. Mr Dodds, the headmaster, is standing in the corridor.

'Yes, Sir,' I say.

'Nice of you to join us,' he says, 'cause he's a funny twat.

'Yes, Sir,' I say.

'We have been trying to contact your father for a number of days now. Nice to see you're looking well, Mr Braxton. I had feared that you were dead,' Mr Dodds says, 'cause he's a funny twat.

'I've had the splats, Sir,' I say. 'Food poisoning.'

'Again?' Mr Dodds says. 'Yes, we requested a doctor's note. I'll expect you, and the note, waiting outside my office nice and early tomorrow morning. Shall we say eight thirty?'

'Yes, Sir,' I say and then I turn and walk towards the door, squeezing my arse cheeks together 'cause I swear I'm going to shit my pants any minute.

And that's when I almost bump into them. They're standing outside the main doors, both of them under one of them huge umbrellas, huddled close 'cause they're clearly gay. It's raining again, I don't understand why it's raining again already. They're smoking a ciggie and talking like no one else can hear. It's them same two blokes that I saw at The Oracle, them American tossers who are all set for knocking it down and building something poncey instead.

'Well that was easier than expected,' one of them says.

'Yeah, fickle. Ever seen so many wastes of skin in one place?' the other says.

'Just Building Regs to worry about now,' the first one says.

'Fucking shambles,' the other one says. 'I think it's time to take matters into our own hands, don't you?'

'What you got in mind?' the first one asks.

'Something hot.'

And then they laugh. And then they hoy their ciggie stumps into the air and they turn to me.

'All right, twats,' I say, 'cause I'm that hard.

'Arsehole,' the first one says. Then the other one closes his umbrella, shakes it so that it pisses all over me, then they both laugh and they walk past me and back into the school.

Delphina

WATER: (*Earth. Air. Fire.*)

DAY SEVENTEEN

'And over to Lucy Carter for local travel advice.'

'We can *urge* the public to listen to our broadcasts and act accordingly. We cannot *prevent* all flooding, but what we can do is *urge* the public to prepare themselves and their property. This will lead to *reducing* the damage. We are now *advising* the public to take additional care on the roads. The AA's water-rescue crews *will* be working in our area due to the increased risk of flooding. Drivers are *advised* to consider the wet conditions. We *urge* you to take your time, to keep your speed down, and this is *crucial* if you see surface water ahead. Do remember that any water entering your car's engine can *ruin* it and it is incredibly difficult to gauge just how deep surface water could be. Our standard advice to you is to *avoid* driving through floodwater if at all possible . . .'

Setting: *Arthur and Delphina are swimming in the Males 1st Class pool. Arthur's confidence in swimming has grown significantly.*

ARTHUR: Someone on Facebook said that you can't get pregnant if you have sex in the water.

DELPHINA: I don't think I can anyway.

ARTHUR: [*smiling*] So we've nowt to worry 'bout.

DELPHINA: [*smiling*] You've nothing to worry about.

ARTHUR: [*Arthur's eyes connect with Delphina's eyes. Delphina and Arthur smile*] I don't think I'd mind if you were, if you did, you know.

DELPHINA: You're too young.

ARTHUR: [*smiling*] But it wouldn't be the end of the world.

DELPHINA: [*serious face*] It won't happen, Arthur, really, It won't.

ARTHUR: I know, but if it did . . .

DELPHINA: [*breaking eye contact with Arthur*] It won't, Arthur. You can't get me pregnant.

ARTHUR: Not ever? Have you had tests?

DELPHINA: Not ever. I just know. We're not the same. I'm not like you.

[*Arthur turns to swim away*]

DELPHINA: Come here.

[*Arthur turns back to Delphina. Arthur smiles. His eyes flicker, a slight shift, a slight sparkle of mischief*]

DELPHINA: And you'll have to take your boxer shorts off . . .

DAY EIGHTEEN

'And here's your latest travel news. M60 Greater Manchester is reporting slow-moving traffic on the M60 clockwise between junction 12 (M62, Eccles Interchange) and junction 13 (A572, Worsley), as surface water continues to cause congestion . . .'

Setting: *Arthur and Delphina are in the Males 1st Class pool. They are swimming in the centre of the water.*

DELPHINA: It's all in the breathing. You can do the leg-and-arm movements no problem now . . . and look how your head starts to lift naturally at the end of the cycle. [*Arthur swims breast-stroke*] Yes, like that . . . so now all you have to do is lift your face out of the water and take a breath in through your mouth . . . [*Arthur does as directed by Delphina*] Yes, that's it. You learn so quickly. Now, put your face back into the water. Breathe out through your nose and mouth, as you stretch your arms forward . . . [*Arthur does as directed by Delphina*] Perfect. Now do it all again.

[*Delphina floats alongside Arthur as he swims up and down the length of the pool. Arthur's movements are now effortless and he is a natural swimmer. Delphina is smiling. She is proud of Arthur*]

[*After five lengths Arthur grips the edge of the pool. Delphina moves near to him*]

ARTHUR: What a total bell-end I was, being scared.

DELPHINA: You're doing so well, Arthur, we're all so proud of you.

[*Delphina looks around for Maddie, Laurel, Kester and Pollock. They are not there*]

ARTHUR: I don't think anyone's ever been proud of me before.

[*Arthur and Delphina's eyes connect*]

ARTHUR: What are you scared of, Delphina?

DELPHINA: Being replaced, being forgotten, being insignificant.

ARTHUR: You'll never be any of them. Come here.

[*Arthur and Delphina move together. Their arms thread and twine together. Their thighs loop and their knees grip*]

ARTHUR: My cock likes you.

DELPHINA: I like it too.

ARTHUR: One day I'll get to taste you properly. Without the water.

DELPHINA: I'd like that. Very much.

[*Arthur smiles*]

[*Kester and Pollock appear at the opposite end of the pool. They are naked. Kester is climbing down the steps and into the pool, Pollock is waiting to climb down the steps and into the pool. Arthur sees them*]

ARTHUR: Oh God, no.

DELPHINA: [*turning to see what Arthur is staring at*] What, Arthur, what is it?

ARTHUR: [*pointing at Kester and Pollock*] They're fucking paedos, they're getting in here with their cocks out.

DELPHINA: Oh, Arthur, of course they are. It's what folk do. That one's Kester [*points at Kester*] and that one's Pollock [*points at Pollock*]. They're just having a swim. The water heals them.

ARTHUR: It's not right.

DELPHINA: When will you understand, my Arthur? The water's magic.

DAY NINETEEN

'The local council is asking for able-bodied volunteers to fill sand bags. Would any community-minded people interested in helping the authorities to prepare local flood defences, please muster on the steps of Mold Town Hall, this Thursday at 1700 hours. And don't forget your spade!'

Setting: *Arthur is sitting on the edge of the pool. His black trousers are rolled up and his legs swinging back and forth in the water. Delphina is holding onto the edge and kicking her legs through the water.*

DELPHINA: Tell me about the rain?

ARTHUR: It's utter shit.

DELPHINA: But to stand and feel the water falling on you. I mean the water goddesses are blessing you—

ARTHUR: Goddesses?

DELPHINA: The water goddesses offer blessing. They want to be noticed, for someone to question why.

ARTHUR: Why. what?

DELPHINA: Why so much rain

ARTHUR: It's North Wales, Delphina, it's what it does here.

DELPHINA: No Arthur. Silver says that they know of the impending demolition, they're full of fear. That's why they're communicating so much.

ARTHUR: [*laughing*] Seriously Delphina, you don't half talk bollocks sometimes. I mean, I'm not surprised, you're surrounded by weirdoes.

DELPHINA: But, the rain—

ARTHUR: Delphina, the rain's utter shit. It's not like this.

DELPHINA: This?

ARTHUR: [*holding his arms out to indicate the building*] You're sheltered living here in The Oracle. For you, being here in this water, this feels natural, you proper love it.

DELPHINA: Yes, but I'd love to be out there, feeling the rain falling on me from the heavens.

ARTHUR: So do it.

DELPHINA: It's not as simple as that.

ARTHUR: It is. I conquered my fear of water. I mean being that 'scared of outdoors' thing, it's nowt to be ashamed of. I'll help you. You just have to trust me.

DELPHINA: I do, but—

ARTHUR: The skies are grey, everything out there is grey. You're not really missing owt. But—

DELPHINA: I'm missing everything, Arthur. Sometimes I wonder if there's a point.

ARTHUR: A point?

DELPHINA: Of this, of me, of this nothingness that I'm supposedly living.

ARTHUR: [*smiling*] You have me now.

DELPHINA: But for how long?

ARTHUR: [*smiling, not understanding what Delphina is saying*] As long as you want.

DELPHINA: We're living on borrowed time and one day, one day soon you'll—

ARTHUR: [*smiling*] One day soon, you'll meet me outside and we'll dance like twats in the rain.

DAY TWENTY

'A breakdown recovery worker from Chester was killed in a motorway accident yesterday, as the freak weather continues to wreak havoc across the region.

'The forty-year-old man, who has not yet been named, swerved out of control due to surface water on the M53, whilst attending a breakdown call-out. The accident happened in the early hours of yesterday morning.'

Setting: *Silver and Delphina are in the Males 1st Class pool. They are swimming lengths and talking. Kester and Pollock are watching from the viewing gallery.*

DELPHINA: There's no future. I know that, Silver. I'm not stupid. I know that I should go away.

SILVER: [*a weak smile*] But you like it here, don't you, pet? Me and you, we're a team.

DELPHINA: Yes, and I know I could go down to the otherworld. I know there's a whole world there, I know he'd never find me there . . .

SILVER: It's not your world, though, is it, Delphina? Not yet.

DELPHINA: It'll never be my world, not without you and Laurel.

[*Silver nods*]

SILVER: You'll have to go someday, but then there'll be no option and—

DELPHINA: This isn't about me, though, is it? This is about him, this is about making it easier for Arthur. If I'm not here—

SILVER: You've fallen for him, I knew this would happen. He's just a kid, pet.

DELPHINA: He's mine.

217

SILVER: [*raising voice*] No Delphina, he's not. We've discussed this. There's not this fairy tale future that you've dreamed up. We can't, all of us, be living here together happily ever after. What you're doing has to end. It's the way it has to be, pet.

DELPHINA: I know, I know. I should say goodbye, let him find a girl, a normal girl, with a super-straight fringe, a fancy mobile phone and a Facebook account.

[*Delphina is crying. Delphina dives down into the water. Delphina emerges through the water. Silver is laughing. Silver stops. He swims to the edge of the pool. Delphina continues swimming her lengths*]

SILVER: Is this about Facebook?

DELPHINA: Oh Silver! I should let him have a normal relationship, one where he can walk down the street holding hands and tongue-kiss at a bus stop. That's what he needs, that's what you said normal teenagers do.

SILVER: It's more that it's going to end at some point, pet, more that there can't be a future for you and him in this pool. The Oracle will be demolished at some point soon. We can delay, but there's no preventing it. You can't leave this water and he's not realised why yet. Maybe he won't. He's not the brightest of the bunch. [*Silver laughs*]. It's best you end it now to avoid extra heartache later, pet. It's the way it's got to be.

KESTER: [*shouting down from the viewing gallery*] Let the girl be.

POLLOCK [*shouting down from the viewing gallery*] She's found love.

KESTER: [*shouting down from the viewing gallery*] Precious love.

POLLOCK: [*shouting down from the viewing gallery*] Slept with one eye open.

KESTER: [*shouting down from the viewing gallery*] Didn't sleep a wink.

POLLOCK: [*to Kester*] You fool.

KESTER: [*to Pollock*] You old fool.

[*Silver looks up at Kester and Pollock from the side of the pool. He is cross*]

SILVER: [*shouting up to Kester and Pollock*] Shut the fuck up. [*turning to Delphina*] Carry on.

DELPHINA: All those people who have drowned for nothing. [*looking to the pile of shoes*]

SILVER: They drowned so that you could stay alive. That's not for nothing, it was the only way. The water goddesses demanded it and Maddie obliged.

DELPHINA: But it's so wrong, Silver. Seven people sacrificed for me to have this half-life. You shouldn't have let it happen . . .

[*Silver doesn't swim to Delphina. He doesn't look at her. He clings to the side of the pool and kicks his legs up and down through the water*]

DELPHINA: So what about now? Why can't I just live for now? Try and make this mean something.

SILVER: That's how normal people live, pet. We're all about the future, about what's coming. It's my curse.

[*Delphina nods*]

DELPHINA: And his future's going to be better without me in it?

SILVER: His future will be the way it has to be. But that doesn't mean it'll be good. I mean, that doesn't mean that the life Arthur's going to be having will be better than the life you'll be having.

DELPHINA: I wish I could be a girl from a fairy tale, one with a happily ever after already mapped out. Girls in fairy tales hardly ever eat either.

SILVER: You know you can't ever be normal. Thank fuck, pet. [*Silver laughs*]

DELPHINA: I know, but can't I just wish for a bit?

SILVER: [*looking straight ahead and never at Delphina*] Wishing's not good for you, pet, you are what you are. And the future's coming whether we like it or not.

DELPHINA: But I don't want to be me. [*Delphina starts spinning through the water. Her voice increases in volume*] I want to exist, I want to feel significant. I want to go on a date, I want him to feed food to me on a fork, in public, in a restaurant with everyone looking and saying things like, 'aren't they sweet'.

SILVER: [*laughing*] But you don't eat.

[*Delphina tries to glare at Silver, but she is spinning too much*]

DELPHINA: I want him to fall in love with me, to get down on one knee and ask me to be his wife. I want to squeal and spin on the spot, on the ground. I want my feet to be on the ground. I want to be out of this water. [*Delphina stops spinning. She looks at Silver. Silver looks at Delphina*] I want for him to laugh. I want to feel forever. I want him to take me home.

SILVER: It's only been a couple of weeks, pet, these things take years.

DELPHINA: The way we are, the way me and Arthur are, there aren't rules like that. It's bigger than normal. It's like we've always been. It's like we're the same person. He makes me want to breathe. You don't understand. How could you? You haven't ever loved . . .

[*Silence*]

DELPHINA: [*looking sheepish*] And our wedding day would be perfect, I'd wear white and he'd beam a smile as I walked down the aisle. Then we'd buy a cottage, with a swing in the garden and I'd give birth to a baby girl.

SILVER: [*after a loud sigh*] What would you call her?

DELPHINA: Emily.

SILVER: [*laughing*] That's a bit normal, isn't it?

[*Delphina is floating on her back. The water beats with her heart. They are the only two sounds heard*]

DELPHINA: [*whispers*] But none of it can happen, can it, Silver? And somehow I've got to make him go away and meet his princess and live his life and love someone for real. And while he's out there, loving and living and forgetting about me, I'll be dying forever. I'll be all alone, I'll be living in the otherworld. I'll be failing to recall what it feels like to be alive.

SILVER: You'll always have me, pet.

DELPHINA: But I won't, will I? Because this place is going away too.

SILVER: Not—

DELPHINA: It's NOT enough, Silver. I want him. I want him so much that sometimes I forget to swim. I want what I can't have. I'm a freak. A fucking half-person. I can touch happiness with the tips of my fingers, I can smell it in the air, I can see it skipping away.

SILVER: You knew you couldn't—

DELPHINA: [*shouting*] Fuck the 'told you so'. Because me and him, we fit together like we've always known each other, like we're cut from the same stepping-stone, like us not being together is the worst thing conceivable. So what do I do? How do I say goodbye to the person I'm supposed to be with?

SILVER: [*after a loud sigh*] But you can't be with him in this world.

DELPHINA: But I need to—

SILVER: [*raises voice*] But you can't be.

DELPHINA: So how do I tell the one person who makes me feel alive to go away? How do I say goodbye to the person who gets me, who lets me be me?

SILVER: You'll find a way. Things happen as they should, pet.

[*Silver swims away from the edge of the pool. He swims over to the wooden steps*]

DELPHINA: [*shouting*] I know I'm being selfish. [*Silver carries on swimming*] I know that I should let him go, that I should push him away and into a world where he can find a nice normal girl. But I can't.

[*Silver stops. He turns around in the water, his movements are slow. His voice is gentle*]

SILVER: Delphina, you and Arthur, pet, it's not real. It can't be what you're wanting it to be.

DELPHINA: To say goodbye to him would leave me with nothing.

SILVER: You have me, you have Laurel.

KESTER: [*shouting from the viewing gallery*] You have Pollock.

POLLOCK: [*shouting from the viewing gallery*] And Kester.

DELPHINA: [*ignoring Kester and Pollock*] It's not enough, Silver. Can I just pretend, for a bit longer?

[*Silver sighs*]

SILVER: You'll never be alive, pet. You know that. You and that boy, it is what it is. [*Silver sighs*] It will be what it needs to be.

DELPHINA: I know there's no future for me and Arthur, that our worlds don't cross, but when I say those words out loud it's like my core's breaking and I want to throw up. We should say goodbye.

SILVER: Yes.

DELPHINA: I can't, not yet, not now, not today.

SILVER: You will, soon. It's how it has to be for events to unfold.

DELPHINA: What am I, Silver? What am I supposed to be?

SILVER: You're a water nymph, Delphina, the most beautiful water nymph to ever be.

DAY TWENTY-ONE

'Severe thunderstorms have attacked the Northern counties of Wales, disrupting transport and instigating power outages and flash flooding. Forecasters said the area was close to suffering its wettest month since records began. Blackouts still persist in some parts . . .'

Setting: *Delphina is looping the surface of the water and down to the bottom of the pool. She is talking to Laurel. Laurel is lying down, on her back, next to the edge of the pool. There are three empty tubes of Smarties next to her. Her eyes are closed, she is not moving and her rope is next to her. She is pretending to be asleep.*

DELPHINA: And then he'll not come back, he'll meet someone else. It's like I can see them, inside my head. They're sitting on the edge of a bed, like the one Silver had delivered here once. Arthur and her, they're sitting on the bed together. I can see the little touches. I can see the folding of their two hands into each other. I can see the first kiss, the cheeky biting of his bottom lip, the gentle pushing of his tongue into her mouth. I can see them falling back onto the bed. There is no water, there is no stupid water. They are a million miles away from my world.

[*Laurel sneezes. Delphina looks to her, but Laurel does not move*]

[*Delphina swims quickly around the pool. She is pirouetting through the water. She stops and swims over to the edge closest to Laurel*]

DELPHINA: And all the time I'm thinking about Arthur. I'm thinking about the hugs hello that he gives me. He'll kneel on

225

the side of the pool, his arms around my shoulders, not quite touching my breasts, his head resting on the very top of mine. It's his energy, how it mixes with my energy. There are sparks, real sparks, Laurel. Sometimes he kisses my wet hair and I smile. Or other times I'll watch him stripping off his clothes and I'll watch him climb down the wooden steps into the pool. Now he can swim, I love to watch him crawl through the water to me. That's when he hugs me close, when I breathe in his smell. He's clumsy, it's agitated but I'm calm. I don't tell him how much I like to feel all of his naked body close to mine. He's warm, I'm always cold. I like to feel him growing against my thigh.

[*Delphina lets go of the side of the pool and drops into the water. Minutes pass and then she re-emerges. The skin around her eyes is red. She is visibly upset*]

DELPHINA: [*to Laurel*] Sometimes, swimming around here in the dark, on my own, it makes me crazy. Tonight I feel that I'm tipping over the edge. I have so much energy, too much energy. I need to scream, to leap, to spin, to stop this pain. But tonight I'm trying to be sensible, to think about other things, to concentrate on the water and the twirling and the swirling that folds around me. But, still, he keeps entering me, Arthur persists on creeping into my head.

[*Laurel sits up. She crosses her legs and nods to Delphina to continue*]

DELPHINA: And tonight I'm thinking about the hours we spend talking about absolutely nothing, talking about everything, skimming over talking about things that we probably should. I know his favourite colour, I know what foods he likes and how they taste, the delicate flavours that he tries to describe in words. The words have no edge, no aroma. I will never know taste. I know what he feels when he walks in the wind, I know of snow, I know of books, I know of Facebook and I know what it feels like to not understand how adults can hurt each other like they do. I know of guns, of matches, of squash, of big houses and posh accents. I know where he buys cheap alcohol, of the first time he tried a cigarette, I know that his parents have left him not knowing what it is to be loved. [*Delphina is crying*] I know of the school he goes to, of the music he really likes to listen to but couldn't possibly tell others at school, I know that those songs are on his iPod. I know of the bullying, I know of the humiliation, I know how injustice makes his insides bubble. [*Delphina and Laurel lock eyes for a moment*] I know that he doesn't like chocolate, that cheese makes his head hurt, that once he fell off a wall and hurt his foot, that one day he'd quite like to learn how to play the guitar. I know him. I know the sound of happy, of laughter that has no restraint.

LAUREL: [*crying*] I've never loved anyone, apart from you. I'm sorry, Delphina, for everything.

DELPHINA: [*wiping away tears with her wet hands*] I know that the minute he leaves I think of a million things I forgot to ask, that I forgot to say, that I wish he was there, here, always. Because the minute he leaves I wish he'd come back. I wish I could phone him, I wish I even knew how the phone worked, I wish I could shout my million questions into his head and he'd shout his million answers back and we'd keep talking to each other through space and through time until we ran out of things to say. I honestly don't think we ever would. There is never enough time. He always leaves me wanting more.

LAUREL: [*sobbing*] Tell him to stay. He can live here with us . . .

DELPHINA: [*swimming around the pool*] But tonight I'm thinking about the conversation I had with Silver. It's like because I've said those words out loud, I can't be squashing them back inside my head. I'm a water nymph. I will always live in water, in this

water. And when The Oracle stops being, then the water will
go back down through the gateway, to the underground reservoir, to the otherworld—

LAUREL: [*shouting*] Don't! Don't say it.

DELPHINA: We both know that I will too, Laurel. Tonight I've been
realising that one day, that one day soon, I'll have to tell him
to leave The Oracle, and that he'll just go. And that he'll walk
onto a new path where he'll meet the person who can give him
everything that I can't. I'm not being stupid, I know how young
he is and that there are bound to be at least a thousand girls
and ladies before he finds the one he'd quite like to live in a
house with. A house, not a pool full of freezing-cold water.
A house with a bed, where they can lie down and make babies
together.

[*Delphina stops talking. She swims to the edge of the pool and grips
it. Laurel's sobs echo around the pool*]

DELPHINA: [*to Laurel, crying*] I can't bear it. I want to crack my
head open and scoop out all the images that are dancing around
inside. But how, really how? How can something so utterly
perfect be wrong?

LAUREL: [*sobbing*] It isn't wrong, Silver told me—

DELPHINA: And lately, every day, I've seen him changing. He's
growing in strength, he's shifting. I love that he is. I love how
confident he is around here, how he smiles, how he laughs,
how silly he can be. But I also know that every day he grows
in strength he's taking a tiny step away from me. And that
because he's strong, because the water's made him different,
that when that day comes, when I tell him to go, he will. And
one day, one day soon, him loving me won't even exist.

LAUREL: [*sobbing*] You'll never be forgotten. How can you say that?

DELPHINA: But for me it'll never be over, I'll never find someone
else. There can be no one else, there'll never be another Arthur

Braxton. Bitter-sweet, that's what they say this taste is. I don't understand. One day, one day soon, he'll walk away from The Oracle and he'll not look back. Silver's told me. Silver's said that I have to stop being attached, that no good can come of it, that Arthur and me can't be.

LAUREL: You don't underst—

DELPHINA: [*ignoring Laurel*] But all the time he said it, I was thinking that he was wrong. That he was talking rubbish. That Arthur and me are meant to be. So tonight I'm left thinking that one day, one day soon, I'll be left with snippets of conversation, with flashes of memories, of looks, of touches, of moments when I knew what it felt like to be alive. There were moments when I wondered if Arthur and me being together could be magic, if somehow, if him and me being together would mean that I'd be able to leave this pool and walk out through the front door and into the rain. And if I'd be able to splash through puddles in my bare feet. One day, I'll be left with echoes. Echoes of hope.

LAUREL: [*sobbing*] I'm so sorry. I should never have—

DELPHINA: I will never blame you. I'm saying that I get it. I understand how heartache works. And that, one day, I'll wonder if my memories were true. One day I'll start thinking that maybe I'm a bit insane and maybe my mind's been playing cruel tricks and conjuring Arthur up from the gutter. Then maybe one day I'll realise that I invented a boy, that perhaps the water tricked my head into inventing a somebody to keep me company, just so that I'd be complete, just because the reality of what I have is just too lonely to bear.

LAUREL: But I'll be here to tell you that he was real. I knew him too.

DELPHINA: [*tears falling from her eyes*] And one day he'll wake up in the arms of another, she'll be petite, with tiny features and skinny legs and a squeaky voice and hair that never curls. And one day he'll look at her and he'll realise that what he was feeling for me wasn't love, that it couldn't have been love because proper love doesn't just disappear without a linger of loss remaining. And that day he'll look at her and realise that she's whole and that she's uncomplicated and that she's enough. And that's when he'll smile the best smile he's ever smiled. But me, well, I'll always be left with a gap. I'll always remember that once upon a time I was nearly alive.

[*Delphina lets go of the edge of the pool. She flips forward and loops through the water*]

[*Minutes pass. Delphina swims underwater*]

[*Delphina re-emerges*]

DELPHINA: Like Silver said, Arthur's young, Arthur's needy, Arthur's bored. Arthur needs somewhere safe, for now, somewhere to grow, somewhere to find his feet. Silver said that all of this has happened too quickly, so it can't even matter, not really. People would laugh if they knew. And I've been thinking about that a lot. I mean, it's not like I've anything else to do. Silver said once that he'd buy me a TV, but it's not like I could ever change the channel. Electricity and water don't really go together too well. Nature likes to be wild and free and not stuck in front of a box of lights. I guess the reality is that Arthur coming here was a distraction from his rubbish life. That's how he started. He'd come here and for that time he'd be accepted and he'd be able to be him, to escape from all the shit that'd been thrown at him by others. I gave him that distraction from real life, but that isn't love.

LAUREL: [*shouting*] No, NO, Delphina, you're wrong. I know love, he loves you. You're connected.

DELPHINA: Sometimes I wish that I'd had the courage to say all of this to him. I see how his face falls when he declares his love

230

and I whisper a thank you. He thinks I feel nothing for him. And that's so far from how I feel. How I feel about him, about Arthur Braxton, that's more than love. It's deeper, truer, for always. It's beyond the words that people throw about. Arthur says he loves lots of things – squash, Abba, Meatloaf, a T-shirt with words from a book I've never read. It's like the word 'love' is everyday, all used up and spat into a gutter. How I feel for Arthur doesn't even slightly fit around that word. There's nothing easy and normal about it. And when this thing that Silver says has to happen, when it does, when Arthur leaves, when he breaks me, well I don't think I'll ever mend. And I'll never understand why the water guided him here, to me, to The Oracle.

DAY TWENTY-TWO

'Flintshire, Wrexham, Denbighshire, the Wirral and Greater Manchester have issued a "boil water advisory" for water customers in the area. It is advised that all drinking water be boiled prior to consumption, as a safety precaution . . .'

Setting: *Arthur and Delphina are in the Males 1st Class pool. They have been swimming around for hours. Arthur is swimming towards Delphina. Delphina has stopped swimming. She has flipped onto her back and is floating. Her eyes are open, they are looking up to the ceiling.*

ARTHUR: [*reaching Delphina*] I've got something I want to say.
[*Delphina turns her head to make eye contact with Arthur*]
ARTHUR: Are you my girlfriend? [*Arthur laughs*] God, that sounded gay.
[*Delphina does not speak*]
ARTHUR: Delphina?
[*Delphina turns her head back to look to the ceiling*]
DELPHINA: [*whispering*] I don't think I can give you what you need. I think I'll keep hurting you and making you feel rejected and hurt and—
ARTHUR: [*looking at Delphina*] I know you love me.
DELPHINA: [*still looking at the ceiling*] You're young, too young. It's all happened too quickly. One day you might want children.
ARTHUR: [*smiling*] Not for ages.
DELPHINA: But I can't ever give them to you.

ARTHUR: One day you might be able to, we can have tests, there are ways. Nowt's impossible these days.

[*Arthur is watching Delphina. Delphina is swirling in the middle of the water. She does not turn to look at Arthur. She is crying*]

ARTHUR: We'll deal with it when we have to. For now let's just enjoy this.

DELPHINA: This? [*Delphina stops spinning. She swims to Arthur, but stops before they touch, and makes eye contact with him*] But what have we got? There's no future, Arthur. I can never give you what you need, what you deserve.

ARTHUR: [*smiling*] But you already do. [*Arthur pulls Delphina to him*]

DELPHINA: [*pulling away*] Don't, Arthur. Not tonight. Tonight, let's talk.

ARTHUR: You don't realise, do you?

DELPHINA: Realise what?

ARTHUR: How I feel. How much I love you.

DELPHINA: [*cringing*] Thank you.

[*Arthur's face changes. His expression is sadness and hurt. Delphina is crying, she loves Arthur but is trying to protect him*]

ARTHUR: [*swimming towards the steps*] I'm fucked off with this. You need to get out the twatting water. It's messing with your head. I'll wait for you outside.

[*Delphina laughs. Her laugh is full of nerves*]

[*Arthur climbs out of the pool, grabs his clothes, kicks the pile of shoes and walks out through the main door. Delphina watches him go*]

Arthur

EARTH: (*Water. Air. Fire.*)

Reference No: 10-158551
Name: Louise Gurr
Missing Since: 05-Nov-2004

I'm straddling the front wall outside The Oracle. The blue fences are behind the wall at the front of the building, so there's space for me to sit and wait. There's no shelter from the rain, but at least I can see most of the options for where Delphina'll come out. I reckon she'll use one of the three front doors, what with her living in The Oracle.

I said to her something like, 'Meet me outside, I've had enough of this twatting water'. And she just laughed, so I guessed she was okay with me waiting for her.

But of course Delphina still hasn't come out. I mean, she knows we need to talk, away from everyone else, out of the water, but still she doesn't come out. I mean, what the fuck does that say 'bout how she feels 'bout me?

And what's made it even worse is that this proper weird woman's come and sat down next to me on the wall. I mean I saw her shuffling along the road, pulling one of them tartan shopping trolleys on wheels and I thought, what the fuck?, 'cause it's raining and her trolley was getting all wet and crapped. But then she didn't carry on walking by. No, God no, instead she decided to sit next to me on this little front wall and she's not said a word yet. So I'm looking at her, I mean proper staring. She's little, not like-a-dwarf little but not far off and she smells like piss. She's wearing one of them plastic rain bonnets that tie under your chin and she's got a yellow plastic mac on that squeaks when she moves. She moves a lot. It's annoying as fuck. It's freezing cold but still she's sitting next to me, staring out into the darkness, out to the sea.

That's when she shuffles and squeaks down from the wall and bends to reach into her little tartan shopping trolley on wheels. She pulls out two cans of Diamond White. She hands one to me. Then she shuffles back onto the wall. She opens her can of cider, so I open mine. I'm not sure what to say, so I keep my eyes on The Oracle and look for Delphina.

She drinks the rest of her can of cider in silence and hoys the empty over her head, over the fence and into The Oracle. I hear it clang onto the concrete and although I'm expecting it, I still jump.

'Drink up, lad,' she says, as she shuffles and squeaks off the wall again, as she leans into her trolley and grabs another two cans. She hands me one.

'Thank you,' I say, mainly 'cause I can't think of owt else to say.

And then she stands up and she shuffles away, pulling her tartan shopping trolley on wheels behind her. 'Been nice chatting to you, Arthur Braxton,' she says.

And I'm mainly left thinking, what the fuck?, while holding two cans of cider, and not having a clue who she was or how she knew my name. But still I reckon the right thing to do is drink them. And I do, I down the cans, it's something to do while I wait. But Delphina still doesn't come out.

And all the time I'm downing, I'm replaying our last conversation over and over, and over again, in my head. I mean I don't give a shit 'bout the other stuff she's saying, mainly 'cause none of it makes sense. I mean we're both young, I mean who gives a fuck 'bout what happens when we're older? I'm not arsed if I never have kids, I'm only just sixteen, for fucking out loud. I swear she's making up excuses to dump me. I just know that when The Oracle's knocked down she's going to piss off without telling me where she's going. She's just like everyone else, a fucking let-down. It didn't take her long to realise that I'm a twatting waste of space and not worth bothering with.

I climb down from the wall and I throw the empty cans of cider over into the grounds of The Oracle. They clang, a proper loud clang, 'cause the only other noise is the bastard rain. And that's when I realise. She's not coming out, she thinks that little of me.

I've no place else to go, so I start walking home. The rain's pissing down on my head and I reckon that it's laughing at me for being such a dick and thinking anyone'd give a fuck 'bout me. I'm thinking all 'bout the crap Delphina's been spouting. I mean if she didn't want me in her life, then why couldn't she just say it, instead of all the bollocks 'bout futures and babies and fuck knows what else she was spouting? And when I get to thinking 'bout that, I get to thinking 'bout how it's hardly ever Delphina who touches me. It's like it never crosses her mind to touch me in any way. It's like she's got no interest at all in going down that route, like when she does it's just to wind me in and make me think she likes me a little bit. Then I get to thinking that it's me always touching her. I mean she responds and all that, I mean I think she does, but sometimes I feel like I'm having to beg her to do stuff. Is that right? Is that how it is?

Fucking hell, is this one big game? Am I going to check Facebook and see links to YouTube videos of me getting a boner in the water?

Yes, I'm the one asking her to kiss me and I'm the one trying to pull her in for a hug and I'm the one looking at her tits and wishing she'd let me suck them. And all the time Delphina's looking around, looking over her shoulder, swimming away, and now I'm wondering if it's like she's almost forcing herself to kiss me. I'm wondering if like inside she's thinking, 'for fuck's sake'. I'm starting to think that maybes she just wants to be mates. Maybes I've come on too strong, I mean maybes I'm just too fucking desperate.

I mean maybes I'm just a waste-of-space loser.

I know she likes me, I mean I think she likes me. I mean I know fucking nowt. I might be pissed off, I might be pissed, I might not be thinking straight. I know she looks forward to seeing me, well that's what she says. But I've got this niggle that we're not on the same page. I mean 'on the same page', how fucking gay a phrase is that? It seems to me that I'm wanting to be so much more than mates and she's wanting to be just mates at best. And now it's all proper fucked up and she's pissed off and she didn't even have the balls to come out and see me and now I've no fucking idea where I stand. I mean all she keeps saying is that I'm better off without her and that I should be with someone normal and all the time I'm thinking that she's everything I'll ever want. I mean, Delphina, she's proper wonky like me.

But now, 'cause she's saying it like a million times, I reckon part of me's thinking that I should stop going to see her. I mean, it's like she's determined to keep pushing and pushing. And if I'm honest I'm sick of this confusion and I'm dreading that day when I go and she's just disappeared forever. I mean at least this way I'll be in control of jibbing her off. I've no idea what's going through Delphina's head. I don't know where I stand, I mean she never even says 'I love you' even though I've said it to her like a million times. And all her talk 'bout not being normal and not being like others, I mean what's that all 'bout? She likes swimming, she wags off school like I do, so what's not normal 'bout that?

But then when I'm with her, it's like none of these thoughts even matter. 'Cause, when I'm with her, proper with her, when it's just me and her twirling in that water, it's all so easy. It's like she can see into me and sometimes I don't even need to talk. It's like she's the only person in the world who gets to see me, the proper me and I know that I can tell her owt. It's like I see other stuff going on, what with Dad and Tommy Clarke and wagging off school and all that cock stuff with Estelle Jarvis and I'm feeling like I want to be sick in my mouth and I've no idea what any of them'll do next. I mean I'm wagging school that much and I missed that meeting with Mr Dodds, it's only a matter of time before he calls in social services. But then I go to the baths and I get into the water with Delphina and we swim and talk and kiss and it's like all of that shit disappears. For them hours I'm proper me.

I guess she just doesn't fancy me. I mean, I don't blame her. She's fit, God, yes, she could have anyone she wanted and me, well I'm the lad with a famous cock, and not for good reasons either. I know there's nowt I can do to make Delphina want me. I mean sometimes with all the asking to be kissed and all the touching I'm doing, well I'm sure she's thinking that I'm a right horny twat. But I can't help it. I mean being with her, like proper being with her, it's all I can think 'bout. But maybes I'm just useful, for now. I mean she's lonely, I mean she's always training right hard with her swimming and Silver's always on her back. And she's not got no one like me to talk to and I'm there and I'm not going no place and I'm willing and maybes it's just 'cause there's no one better yet.

But sometimes, when we're swimming together and when we're laughing 'bout something that bit daft, that's when she makes me feel normal. But that makes me want her even more. I know we're at different places up the tree and all that crap, but just for them hours when we're proper together it's like none of that other shit in the world exists. But I mean it's not like she's ever said she wants to go on a date or be seen outside with me. It's like she's proper embarrassed of us and doesn't want no other person seeing us together. I get it. I'm a twat, I'm a loser. If I was her, I'd be the same. It's stupidly simple. She keeps asking me where I see the relationship ending. She asks me over and over again, 'cause really she knows the answer and she wants me to say them words out loud. It's like she doesn't want to be cruel, like she wants me to do all the thinking and breaking up.

But how do I say goodbye to her? I mean does she expect me just to not go back there? I guess when the pool gets knocked down, then it'll be simple. I don't even know where she'll live, so it's not like I can go around her new house and bang on the door.

It's utter shite, that's what it is.

I pull my phone out from my pocket. I flick it on. My hands are shaking. I'm either cold or fucked off. I'm staring at my screen, wanting it to hurry up. I know what I need to do. The rain's falling on the screen but still I press the icon for Facebook. It takes a second to load. I go to my profile and I press 'status'. It asks me what's on my mind. I type: 'arthur braxtons in a relationship'. I mean I know I should just be changing my relationship status but my brain's all mashed and I can't be arsed with complicated.

All I need to do now is convince Delphina that she's in a relationship too.

But there's no chance of that being sorted tonight, 'cause she couldn't even be arsed to come out The Oracle and talk to me. So instead I start flicking through my news feed while I'm walking, even though my hands are so cold I think they're dead, and even though I don't even know why I'm bothering going home. I mean, it's not like I'll be able to get any sleep, I mean I'm all pumped. But still I'm walking, and still I'm seeing that all my so-called bastard 'friends' on Facebook are still talking 'bout my cock. And every time I see one of their comments or click on who's 'liked' one of them comments it makes me want to be a little bit sick in my mouth and my hands are proper shaking like I've got that old-man disease.

It's not even five minutes later when I hear him.

'Alrite gay?' he says. 'What you been up to, then?'

I turn, I'm still clutching my phone with Facebook still open. That's when I realise that he's sneaked right up on me without me even noticing. It's Tommy fucking Clarke and his merry bunch of utter twats. And Tommy Clarke's got a knife.

'So what you been up to in The Oracle then?' Tommy Clarke asks. He's hitting the knife at the palm of his hand. I reckon it must be with the blunt side, as I can't see any cuts or any blood.

'Nowt,' I say.

'The queer says "nowt",' Tommy Clarke says to his bunch of twats. He says the word 'nowt' in a gay voice and makes his hand all floppy. He's a twat. 'We've been watching you, boyo,' Tommy Clarke says. 'And we're not so sure we likes what we sees.'

God, he's a bell-end. I know he's after doing some more 'gay-bashing'. I keep walking. I mean the rain's pissing down on my head, I'm soaking wet, I'm still pissed with Delphina and the last thing I want is some twatting bunch of cocks giving me grief.

'You got nowt better to do with your time?' I say.

'Well now we've all seen your cock, it's like we're connected,' Tommy Clarke says. 'I'm almost a bender like you.' I don't look at him, but I know that he'll be all skin-head and twattish. He's shorter than me, a bit of a fatty, but he has that scally swagger bad-boy thing going on. Then I reckon he must high-five one of the twats, 'cause I hear something like a hand clap, but I keep walking and not looking back. I mean, I don't even know where I am. I'm walking down a street, there's terraced houses, nowt else. 'So you been doing gay stuff in the Oracle?' Tommy continues.

'I mean, that's the big question, the answer we're all waiting for. Are you bumming your dad, boyo?'

I stop walking, I turn to face Tommy Clarke and his bunch of twats. I'm so not in the fucking mood for him. I don't give a shit any more. I mean what can they do to me? I mean he put a photo of my cock on Facebook, he kicks the shit out of me whenever he can, I reckon there's not that much more he could do that's worse than that. Maybes, just maybes, I'm hoping he'll stick his knife in me, but when I look to his hand he's no longer holding it.

'You know what,' I say. 'I think you should FUCK OFF!' Then I turn back around and start walking that little bit faster than I was walking before.

But, of course, that's not the end.

'Fuck off? Is that the best you can do, boyo?' He's back. Tommy twat-head Clarke has legged after me and now he's right next to me.

I stop. He stops. I don't think the rain stops, but for that moment it's like it's not important.

'What do you want me to say?' I ask.

'Were you doing bum in The Oracle? I've heard that place's where benders hang out,' Tommy Clarke says.

'Did your dad take you there?' Big Cliff, one of the twats, says.

'You're sick in the head,' I say. I still don't move.

'So, you gonna introduce us to your bum chums?' Tommy Clarke asks. He's doing a 'gay' voice again. He laughs. His bunch of twats laugh too.

'No, but I'll introduce you to my girlfriend,' I say. Oh God, no, I'm such a dick. The words are out and I didn't even want them to be out. I'm hoping Tommy Clarke hasn't heard, but of course he has.

'YOU'VE got a lass?' he says.

'Is she a spaz?' Big Cliff says.

'No,' I say. 'She's fucking gorgeous. She fingers herself in front of me and everything.' What the fuck? I swear it's like some extra-super dick has taken over my mouth.

'Nice one, lad,' Tommy Clarke says.

'She got any mates?' Big Cliff says.

'Yes,' I say. 'A lass called Laurel, but she doesn't swim naked like Delphina.'

'That why you've not been in school?' Tommy Clarke asks. And already he's treating me different. It's like his voice has gone all mellow, like maybes, just maybes, he's got something like respect for me.

'Too right it is,' I say. 'Been getting my end away every day,' I say. 'Cause I'm an utter dick. 'Right big nipples and she shaves her pubes,' I add, in case I haven't been enough of a twat.

'Stinky fingers too, I bet,' Tommy says and laughs. Then he comes over to me and hoys his arm round my shoulders. 'You just been with her?' he asks.

'Yeah,' I say. I get a flash of all that shit Delphina was saying 'bout us finishing and I reckon I've a right to say stuff to my mates now. I've broken my promise to her but, I mean, it's not like she gives a shit 'bout me.

'Right then, boyo, let's be going back there and you can intro duce us lads to your lass and her mate.'

Oh God, no, I think. Oh God, what the fuck've I done?

But of course I've no time for regrets. Oh no, 'cause me and the lads, we're splashing through puddles and making our way back to The Oracle. It's still pissing it down and I'm either shaking 'cause I'm freezing my tits off or 'cause I'm shitting my pants scared, but either way it don't matter 'cause me and the lads, well, we're walking in a huddle. I swear, it's like I'm part of their pack, me and my lads, we're like the same. They've all got their heads down, Tommy twatting Clarke is up front with me and the other lads are keeping up with our pace. It's like I belong and I fucking love it.

I'm thinking Delphina's going to be proper pissed off with me, but at least it'll get Tommy Clarke and his bunch of twats off my back, and I reckon Delphina'll understand that. I mean, eventually.

We get to the fences and walk round them.

'Quite fancy one of them "Keep Out" signs for my bedroom door,' Tommy Clarke says, and Big Cliff starts ripping one down for him. I keep walking. 'My mam's right excited 'bout the "Spa Pleasure Dome",' Tommy Clarke says. 'She's signed us all up for three months' membership.'

I don't speak. I can hear music from inside. I wonder if Maddie's told Delphina that I'm outside. I swear Maddie's a witch, she can sense me a mile off. That's when I reach that part of the fence that isn't quite connected to the part next to it. The chain and padlock are lying on the floor, like always. I stop and I look down at the chain. I reckon there's something in my gut telling me that what I'm doing is pretty stupid, but I don't listen to my gut. The other part of me's looking forward to seeing Delphina again, and, if I'm proper honest, to showing her off to my mates.

I step over the chain and padlock and push open the gap, just enough for me to squeeze through, but then Tommy Clarke and the twats do the same. That's when I notice that the rain's proper lashing it down and I start running. I run past the skips, through the surface water that's covering the yard and over all the broken pieces of furniture lying on the floor. I know the way without really thinking 'bout it. Tommy Clarke and his twats follow me. They're laughing and one of them's singing as he runs.

'Fucking ugly building,' one twat says, even though he's running.

'I heard some lass killed herself in there,' another twat says, even though he's running.

'I don't give a shit, I'm going to get me some fanny,' Tommy Clarke says. We all laugh.

Next I'm up some more steps and running along the narrow alley leading to a backdoor. I've done this run a million times before now, reckon I could do it with my eyes shut, but this time feels different. I don't know if it's 'cause Maddie's singing at full belt inside or 'cause Tommy and the twats are running with me, but this time it feels like it's going to be major.

I guess, if I'm honest, I'm just hoping that Tommy'll lay off the beatings and let me get on with school and life. And I know that makes me a selfish fucker. And I know I promised Delphina. And I know I'm a twat.

We reach the wooden back door.

'What do you think of the singing?' I ask Tommy Clarke. He's bending, gasping for breath like an old man.

'Oh that lad Cliff's got the voice of an angel,' he says. I look and he's slapping his arm round Big Cliff. Big Cliff's got some sort of growing disease. He's not even five foot but he's hard as.

I wonder if Tommy Clarke can't even hear Maddie. But I've no time to dwell, 'cause all of us are proper soaking. I'm just 'bout to open the door when I stop. I realise I've shown them how I get in and that means that Silver, that Kester, that Pollock, that Laurel, that Maddie, that Delphina, that none of them will ever be safe again. I'm a twat. I'm a twatty twat. But I can't stop now.

I open the door. Maddie's singing gets louder.

'What, they don't even lock this place?' Tommy says.

'Nope, the twats,' I reply. I'm a dick.

No time to stop, though, as we're off again. There's Tommy Clarke, his five twats and me. This time we're running along the passage, leading into dark, but it's okay as we're heading towards the music. I'm the one running in time, listening to the beats, Tommy Clarke and his twats are all clumsy and out of rhythm and not giving a fuck. I reckon a couple of the twats must've bumped into something, 'cause I hear them saying 'fuck' and 'bollocks' and 'ow' but I don't stop, not for them. I want to get there first, I want Delphina to see me before she sees owt else. I get to the end of the passage. I turn left and go down a few steps. That's when I reckon we're under the pools. The corridor's narrow. There's pipes every now, every then. They're stretching down from the ceiling to the floor. Lights are flickering on across the ceiling as I take my steps, as they take their steps. I know how to avoid the pipes, but Tommy Clarke and the twats don't. I run through the water, I jump, I avoid, I leave them trailing behind. I'm running my way towards the stairs at the end.

And that's when I realise the music's stopped.

I reach the pool first.

I swing open the doors and I practically jump inside.

'Honey, I'm home,' I say.

But there's no one there.

But worse than that it looks like there's been no one there for years. The whole place looks different. It looks all battered and rubbish and like no one's been in there for years and years and maybe even more years. I mean there was always shit scattered round the pool, but this is different. I swear, it's all dusty and there's loads of broken bits of furniture tossed around. I mean there's sinks and toilets and beds. I mean, what the twatting fuck's going on?

But worse than any of that, the water's all green and filthy. I mean the pool's rotten. It stinks. I swear it wasn't, what, a couple of hours earlier? I swear Delphina was there, there was water, there was me, in that water. There was life, there was warmth, it was clean. Not this, not this freezing cold dirty shit. I look at the pool, I look at the water. I mean, what the fuck? I don't get it. I swear I was, I really was in that water a few hours ago, I was with Delphina, we were swimming. I'd conquered the whole water thing, I knew how to swim, I fucking well knew how to swim. But it wasn't that water, it wasn't full of shit. I'm losing it, I've turned into my dad.

What the fuck? I mean, what the cunting twatting fuck is going on?

Why's it so quiet? Where's Maddie? Where's Kester, where's Pollock? I look to the floor, I search for trails of Smarties, for fragments of their tubes. Where are the shoes? There's nowt. All of the changing cubicles' doors are open, all of the curtains are pulled back neatly. Everything is in its place, untouched, dead.

I don't move. I can't move. Tommy Clarke and the bunch of twats are right there next to me.

'Alrite gay?' he says. 'So, where's this naked swimming lass of yours?'

And that's when he starts laughing. Laughing like I'm the funniest thing in the world.

Him and his five mates start walking round the pool. They're one behind the other, all jumpy, like they're on Haribo, like they've downed a few cans of cider. They're loving it. They're shouting and laughing and the noise is echoing and making like I'm some-place I've never been before. Then they've got their phones out and they're taking photos. That's when one of the twats turns to me.

'Smile,' Tommy Clarke says. Then the twat snaps a photo of me standing looking like the cock I am.

A couple of the twats start kicking the stable doors of the changing cubicles, trying to make them come off their hinges. Big Cliff rips down a couple of the stripy curtains and wraps them around his head. Twat. For a moment I'm scared for Laurel, but she's not anywhere to be seen. Of course she isn't.

While they're walking around, kicking and pulling and jumping, I stand there watching.

'You say you've been swimming with this lass of yours tonight?' Tommy Clarke asks. He's on his knees at the side of the pool. I nod. 'Not being funny, gay, but this pool's filthy. There ain't been anyone daft enough to swim in here for years.'

'But—'

'You've been getting it up the arse, haven't you?' Tommy Clarke says.

'Like father, like son,' Big Cliff shouts from the other side of the pool.

I don't know what to say. I can't move. I look up to the viewing gallery and there's no one there, I look back into the pool and Tommy Clarke's right, there's no way there could've been swimming in there for weeks, months, forever.

What the fuck's wrong with me?

I turn and I walk. I want to leave Tommy and his twats to do whatever damage they want to The Oracle. And that's when I realise that I've lost her, that she's gone forever, that I'm not even sure if she ever existed in the first place. I get to the swinging double doors.

But there ain't no way Tommy and his bunch of twats are leaving it at that.

'Where do you think you're going, boyo?'

I hear his voice before I see him. Then Tommy Clarke's next to me. He's not touching me. He's just that little bit too close and I reckon I'm holding my breath. That's when Big Cliff jumps in front of me, blocking the door and my way out. I reckon he must have run, he's out of breath.

'So you think you can spout shit and get away with it?' Tommy Clarke continues.

'No, Tommy, I don't,' I say. I sigh a little bit too much. 'I don't know what the fuck's happened. My lass—'

He pushes me, I stumble backwards. 'Save it, gay,' he says.

I turn around, scanning the room for another way out. But Tommy Clarke's bunch of merry twats are closing in on me. They're circling me, I know what'll happen next, I've been here before. The circling starts bigger, then they move in tighter, there'll be nowhere for me to run. Ring-a-ring-o'-fucking-roses. I'm spinning on the spot. I'm feeling dizzy. I'm a twat.

'Your bum hole must be right loose, what with all the cock that's been in it.' Tommy Clarke laughs, his bunch of twats laugh too. I'm still spinning on the spot, they're moving in.

'I'm not gay,' I say. I'm keeping my eyes on the floor, I daren't look at any of them, I'm trying not to throw up.

And that's why I don't see it coming. Tommy Clarke punches me in the face. Fuck, it stings. My hands go up to my nose, it's bleeding, my hands are covered in blood.

'Not got the balls to say you're gay?' Tommy Clarke says.

'I'm not fucking gay,' I say. It's a whisper, I'm not really helping myself.

'*I'm not fucking gay,*' Big Cliff says, but in a high voice, like he's fucking hilarious. They all laugh, mainly 'cause they're twats.

And that's when Tommy grabs hold of me by the shoulder. I'm all hunched and not looking up. And that's when he pushes me back. I stumble over one of his twat's feet and then I'm on the floor.

And that's when they start with their beating and their kicking and that's when I curl up and that's when I hear Maddie. I mean the beating and kicking doesn't stop, but I open an eye and I see Big Cliff's not joining in my beating. Instead he's walking away, he's walking towards the pool. I'm trying to see, but I reckon my eyes are fucked. I think I see Maddie, I'm wondering if the water's still full of shit, I'm wondering what the fuck is happening. But those thoughts are all in a second, in between a kick into my balls and a punch in my belly. My eyes close, fucking pain, but I force them open. I watch Big Cliff, his eyes are locked with Maddie's, he can see her too, he's walking quickly, he's walking towards the water, he's not going to stop.

I hear the splash. Maddie stops her singing.

'Big Cliff,' I whisper. It hurts to speak.

And that's when Tommy twatting Clarke says, 'That'll do for now, lads.' And that's when they all laugh and run out through the swinging doors. I don't think Big Cliff is with them. I don't think they realise he's gone.

Delphina

WATER: (*Earth. Air. Fire.*)

DAY TWENTY-TWO

'Officials are investigating seventeen reported fatal cases of Legionnaires' disease in the north-west area, to determine whether there is a common source. It is believed that ten of the fatal cases occurred in patients of a north-west hospital, but official spokespersons are currently denying this claim . . .'

Setting: *It is only an hour since Arthur and his friends left The Oracle. The damage they have left is very visible. They have ripped the stripy curtains off and thrown them into the pool. They are floating on the water. They have kicked off some of the doors to the changing cubicles. They are scattered around the pool. They have broken several stained-glass windows. They have urinated up the walls of the building. The water is fresh again. Delphina is in the water. She is holding onto the edge, next to Silver. Silver is sitting on the edge of the pool with his feet in the water. Pollock and Kester are in the viewing gallery. Laurel is just a little bit behind Silver. The pile of shoes is back next to the side of the pool.*

SILVER: [*angrily*] The lad's too young Delphina, he can't be trusted.

DELPHINA: We hid, we did what the water goddesses advised us to do. The water hid too, in its own way. And Arthur, well he went away and I doubt very much he'll ever be back. I guess now he's not even sure if I existed. I'll be forgotten when the rain stops. That's nothing to do with age or trust.

SILVER: [*angrily*] He's put us all in danger. Another young lad's lost his life, sacrificed for them water goddesses to keep you alive. And all because your Arthur brought him here.

DELPHINA: Cliff. His name was Cliff Harris.

SILVER: [*whispering*] Another life.

DELPHINA: When you fall in love with someone, I reckon it's like they become your unicorn. [*Delphina is looking up to the viewing gallery and not at Silver*]

LAUREL: [*touching and counting the leaves that are drawn on her left arm*] One, two, three, four, five, six, seven. I'm scared. Eight, nine, ten. The water changing scared me. Eleven, twelve, thirteen.

DELPHINA: [*ignoring everyone else*] And when they're your unicorn, you believe in them, in their beauty. You believe in them being the most precious, the most fragile person ever created.

SILVER: [*speaks with a gentle voice*] But we don't all love like you, pet. I don't think he felt the same way that you do about him or we do about you. If he did, pet, well he'd not have . . .

DELPHINA: I know that now. Because I think loving someone means you should want to protect them, to keep them safe, to nurture and guard their honour, their dignity, their very being.

LAUREL: [*touching and counting the leaves that are drawn on her arms*] I'm scared. One. Two. Three. The water changing scared me. Four. Five—

SILVER: [*ignoring Laurel*] You're talking to the wrong person, pet. I've never—

DELPHINA: Arthur brought his friends here into our place, into my place, to expose me, to let them laugh and point and ridicule.

SILVER: [*angrily*] The bastard, I should go after him and—

[*Delphina looks up to Silver and then back down to the water*]

DELPHINA: He was prepared to take away my safety for a few moments of belonging . . .

[*Silver nods*]

DELPHINA: I feel so utterly foolish. I know I've let everyone down.

I can tell. I know how disappointed you are in me.

SILVER: We're not, pet.

DELPHINA: I trusted him with who I was, I gave myself to him completely. But now this, this rejection. He's chosen the world he wants to live in. My being me wasn't enough for him.

SILVER: It's what human lads do, Delphina. You're different, you're guided by the water, by them water goddesses. That Arthur don't know the meaning of the word 'respect'. He's a coward, he's a little lad and—

DELPHINA: [*crying*] I know you're right.

LAUREL: [*crying*] Arthur brought his friends here to laugh and to point—

DELPHINA: And to show all of his mates the freak that I am.

SILVER: [*raising voice*] You're not a freak, pet.

DELPHINA: I know what I am, Silver. But what was I supposed to do? Swim up to them and introduce myself? Or, swim around naked, doing flips and flops?

SILVER: We were guided by the water goddesses. You did the right thing. We all did the right thing.

DELPHINA: This world, The Oracle's world, is all that Arthur and I had. The trust that connected us was threaded with water. We're fragile, this world is fragile, it needed tender movements and all the words in the world to protect it. How could Arthur fail to see that?

SILVER: [*whispering*] He's just a little lad and all human lads are driven by one thing . . .

DELPHINA: I guess that the reality, the situation I'm staring at, is that me, this, us, it was never enough for Arthur. He needed others to be part of us too.

SILVER: You're thinking too much, Delphina. Human lads aren't that deep.

DELPHINA: [*crying*] My mind's full of blanks, Silver. I'm trying to imagine the conversations that he must have had about me. I'm left wondering about the laughter, the discussions that are so far removed from those that we shared. How has he described me to others? How has he explained what I am, who I am, what we had?

SILVER: He'd have said you were fit.

[*Silver laughs. Delphina looks angry*]

DELPHINA: But that's not him. I swear, when he's with me I see him. I see a boy, a nearly-man. I hear tender words, we laugh with each other. I trusted him with my soul. I wanted to spend my forever with him.

SILVER: But you knew it'd never be straightforward, pet.

DELPHINA: I knew that it'd be hard, but I believed in us. I believed that we'd find a way to be together because of our connection, because it was us. What I failed to recognise was that all that I felt and all that I thought we had wasn't enough for Arthur.

SILVER: You're from two different worlds.

DELPHINA: He needed others, he needed friends who would look at me and pat him on the back for sharing a freak with them. He would be congratulated on a job well done, for bagging himself something different, something unlike anything they'd ever imagined. Arthur needed to be accepted, to belong, to fit into a normal world with normal people. A world without water, a world where he'd never find me.

SILVER: And you can't leave this water, my little water nymph. This is the way it has to be.

DELPHINA: I guess that him bringing his friends here speaks volumes. He must have known how I'd react. He must have known how I'd HAVE to react. He knows the reasons why I have to hide, he knows I'm not supposed to exist. I told him that I'm a secret, that I'm supposed to be dead. But more than that, he promised me he wouldn't tell a soul . . . [*Delphina sobs*]

264

[*Laurel sobs*]

SILVER: He's thick, pet.

DELPHINA: But he knows that no one can know about me being here. He promised me, he crossed his heart, Silver.

[*Delphina pauses. Tears stream from her eyes*]

DELPHINA: My hiding from Arthur and from his friends has broken that fragile connection that joined us. It's snapped, it's ruined, it can never be as it was.

SILVER: It should never have been.

DELPHINA: [*raising voice*] But it was, Silver. And it was beautiful. But now it's not.

SILVER: It'll get better. This is how it has to be.

DELPHINA: [*calmly*] No, it won't. But I don't want to be something that's laughed at, that's prodded or poked or displayed and used to make him feel part of a group.

SILVER: You deserve more than that, pet.

DELPHINA: I wanted Arthur to love me for me. I thought he did. I can't believe how very wrong I've been about this. It's no longer safe here for me, but I don't want to go.

[*Delphina lets go of the edge of the pool and flips backwards into the water. She needs to swim. She spins underwater. She swirls a corkscrew until the tip of her head is a fraction from the bones that layer the bottom of the pool. She stops and she closes her eyes. She lets the water take her*]

[*Silver is still sitting with his feet in the water. He is watching Delphina. Laurel moves slightly to be lying flat on the floor, either she is pretending to be dead or sleeping. Pollock and Kester have moved down to the front row of the viewing gallery. They are watching and they are unusually silent*]

DELPHINA: [*swimming closer to Silver*] I feel like my stomach's ripping apart. I feel like I can't breathe. The thought of never seeing him again is tearing me apart, Silver.

SILVER: It'll get easier, pet. It's time.

[*Silver moves his legs up and down through the water*]

DELPHINA: [*raises voice*] NO! It can't be time. I'm not ready. [*crying*] This is how it feels to be broken, this is how Laurel must have felt just before she threw me into the pool.

[*Delphina looks over to Laurel and at that moment Laurel sits up. Laurel looks at Delphina and she smiles. It is the first time that Delphina has ever seen Laurel smile*]

LAUREL: I'll miss you.

[*Laurel closes her eyes. She is blocking out what will happen next*]

SILVER: You have to go, there isn't another option, pet. It's not safe here no more. It's time.

DELPHINA: [*shaking her head and holding onto the edge of the pool again*] I don't want to, I can't, please, don't make me. I know there's no solution, Silver. There's no happily ever after, there's no future for me and Arthur.

SILVER: But you've still got a future, pet. Just not here.

DELPHINA: I feel like the entire world's shattering around me, like all this [*Delphina lifts a hand out of the water and points to the viewing gallery*], like The Oracle's an ice palace and now it's fractured and pieces are falling to the ground.

SILVER: It's not safe here, pet, you knew we'd have to leave sooner or later.

DELPHINA: [*sobbing*] I don't know what to do to make this better.

SILVER: You can't. You and him weren't meant to be in the way you think. [*raises voice*] It's time.

DELPHINA: [*sobbing*] But I can't cope with me, with this breaking, minute by minute. I can't cope with that thought, Silver. With that thought of never ever seeing him again. Of never touching, of never laughing, of never—

SILVER: [*booming voice*] You have to stop this now.

[*Laurel opens her eyes*]

[*Kester and Pollock stand to attention. They seem to be saluting*]

DELPHINA: [*whispers*] I don't know how.

SILVER: You do, Delphina, you've always known what to do.

DELPHINA: [*whispers*] Something changed tonight, with him bringing his friends here. It's like what was pulling us into one world, well it snapped and it fell to the bottom of the pool.

SILVER: He doesn't deserve you.

DELPHINA: [*crying*] I looked at him when he shouted, 'Honey, I'm home', just before I hid, and he looked different, like he'd not be able to swim any more. And when I looked at his eyes, they no longer sparkled, they no longer saw me. Do you see me, Silver?

SILVER: I always will, pet.

DELPHINA: When I looked in Arthur's eyes I could see that we were broken, broken beyond repair.

SILVER: Delphina, pet, it's his loss. He's a little lad, you can't make him what he isn't.

DELPHINA: [*voice altered, sad but resigned*] I know. Someone'd broken Arthur way before we met. I knew that from the first moment I lifted that plastic sword of his out of the water. Then later when he hid up there. [*Delphina looks up to the entrance chamber in the viewing gallery. She is looking for Arthur*] He thought he was being so clever, so discreet, but Laurel and I knew he was there.

SILVER: [*staring at Delphina*] You've got to let it go, pet.

DELPHINA: But I could see into him. I could see the broken fragments mixed with flashes of who he could be. And I wanted him to become that someone. I wanted to see him mend, I wanted to help him. The water could have helped him . . .

SILVER: It doesn't always—

DELPHINA: [*raises voice*] It could have. The water's all I have. It's my world, it's part of me. I talked to it, I asked it to help connect him, to help make Arthur whole again. I guess I didn't ask in the right way, I guess the request wasn't understood, that the water needed someone stronger than me.

SILVER: You need to stop blaming yourself, pet. He's not your responsibility.

DELPHINA: When Arthur said he'd quite like a baby with me— [*Silver tuts*] Oh, don't be cross, Silver, I'm not stupid. I know it's physically impossible. I know it could never actually happen.

SILVER: [*angrily*] I didn't say anything.

DELPHINA: [*with a weak smile*] It's just that it feels like that baby's died now, like I'm grieving something that never existed. Does that make any sense at all?

SILVER: Yes, but—

DELPHINA: [*raising her voice*] But nothing. It's like I should apologise to Emily for us not letting her be born. And you know what's worse than all of that?

SILVER: [*whispering*] Go on . . .

DELPHINA: [*angrily*] Well when I think about never again feeling Arthur's arms around me, or his lips on mine or his tongue or his eyes burrowing into my very being . . . well that's when I realise that it's actually you I hate.

SILVER: [*whispering*] You what, pet?

DELPHINA: I hate you, Silver. I hate you for rescuing me and for giving me this crappy life.

SILVER: Don't—

DELPHINA: No. I mean it. Because without Arthur, this life is no life.

SILVER: [*whispering*] You have me, you have Laurel.

DELPHINA: [*shouting*] I have nothing. You're right. I have to leave here, I have to go down there.

[*Delphina pauses. Her eyes look over to the grid where the gateway to the underground reservoir, to the otherworld, lies on the bottom of the pool*]

DELPHINA: [*whispering*] I wish you'd let me die.

SILVER: [*whispering*] Don't say that—

DELPHINA: [*raising voice*] Why? Because it means that all these years you've played martyr, all these years you've wasted on me have been for nothing, Silver?

SILVER: I can't answer that, pet. I can't help who I am, this gift of mine's been a curse for as long as I can remember. But this ain't about me, pet. You'll go down there. [*Silver looks to the grid, to the gateway to the underground reservoir that is the otherworld*] It's time, pet.

DELPHINA: I'll go down to the otherworld. I've no alternative. I'll live there for a bit. I'll do as you want.

SILVER: There's much that is wonderful down there.

DELPHINA: [*shocked*] You told me—

SILVER: [*nodding*] You'll come back. When the time's right.

DELPHINA: [*angry*] Stop with the 'when the time's right' bollocks. I get it. It's written in my palm.

SILVER: [*laughing*] Come back, just once.

DELPHINA: Maybe. To see Laurel, if it's safe, before The Oracle gets knocked down.

[*Laurel stifles a sob. Delphina looks to Laurel. Tears escape from Laurel's closed eyes*]

SILVER: And what should I tell him?

DELPHINA: [*looking at Silver*] Tell him? Do you think he'll come back?

SILVER: No. [*shaking his head*] But if he does?

DELPHINA: [*whispering*] Tell him, tell him I'm sorry that I wasn't enough for him.

SILVER: Enough?

DELPHINA: [*whispering*] Enough.

[*Delphina lets go of the edge of the pool. She floats backwards slightly. She looks to Silver, to Laurel and then up to Kester*

*and Pollock. Then Delphina dives down into the water, down
to the bottom of the pool and out through the grid and into
the otherworld]*

Arthur

EARTH: *(Water. Air. Fire.)*

Reference No: 10-164790
Name: Ellen 'Nelly' Sims
Missing Since: 10-Feb-2006

'WHERE the fuck is she?' I shout.

I've been up all night thinking that possibly I'm off my head. And now I'm here, I'm back, I mean I had no fucking choice, I had to come back here, I had to come back to The Oracle. I needed to see if there were any signs of all the stuff I thought was real. I needed to give my head one last chance to stop being a dick.

So, I've walked back here in the rain. So, I've come in the normal way, the way I always come in, the way I've come every time. And now I'm standing in the open doorway and I'm fucking furious. I mean I don't give a shit what any of them think no more, I'm that fucking mad.

I mean everything's like it was yesterday, before Tommy Clarke, before Big Cliff, before any of that crap. I mean what the fuck's going on? They're all messing with my head. They're all twats.

I look around, I breathe out. I was wrong, it's not exactly the same, I mean the cubicles are broken, the stripy curtains are ripped to fuck and the windows are proper smashed. But there's water, fresh-looking water, there's singing, there's every one of them freaky freaks, there's every one of them fucking mentals, except for the one I want to see, except for Delphina.

'And you can shut the fuck up,' I shout at Maddie. She's singing at the top of her voice and proper staring at me, like she's trying to lure me into the water, like that's going to happen. I turn and look at the pile of the shoes, then I turn back and stare her out. 'I'm not going to drown, you freak!' I scream.

She stops singing. She dives under the water. I didn't think she'd scare so easily.

I take a step onto the mosaic floor but still I'm standing just in the doorway, the doors are still flipping and flapping back and forth behind me. I think I might have pushed them open too strongly. I don't think I've ever felt this fucking cross. Silver's at the far end of the pool. He's sitting on the edge of the pool with his feet in the water. The water, fresh water, I mean where the fuck was it last night when I needed it to be there?

Silver's staring right at me. He's whistling that same twatting song. Laurel's sitting next to him. She's got her feet in the water too. It's the first time I've ever seen her with her feet in the water. Her rope's over her lap and she's sharing a tube of Smarties with Silver. She's staring at me too and I reckon they both know that I'm proper pissed off.

'She's gone,' Laurel shouts.

'What do you mean, she's gone?' I shout back.

'Down to the underground reservoir, down to the otherworld,' Silver shouts. 'She had no choice. Things happen as they should.'

'What you saying? What the fuck's going on?' I'm running towards them, jumping over the crap that's in my way. I want to proper hurt them. I want to shake them until they stop talking in riddles and tell me where the fuck I can find my Delphina. I need her back, I need her here, I need her to know that I'm sorry I was such a twat.

'There's magical stuff down in that otherworld,' Silver says. It's like he's talking to himself. 'Course I could never tell Delphina that, I had to keep her up here, with us lot. She'll be happy down there.'

'Have you really not figured it out yet?' Laurel asks.

I shake my head. I don't understand what they're saying, I don't understand what's going on, but I reckon I'm calming down 'cause they're calm.

'Best come and sit down over here then,' she says. She's patting the mosaic floor beside her.

And I do. It's like her voice is all soothing. It's like I just know that hearing her story will make everything better. I walk over to Laurel and I sit down, I cross my legs on the mosaic tiles that cover the floor.

'I've fucked up,' I say. 'I've proper fucked up,' I say again.

Laurel passes me her tube of Smarties.

Laurel

AIR: (*Earth. Water. Fire.*)

The Victorious Hero's Wreath:

I'd given into Martin Savage. I know you can't possibly understand why I did, but I had my reasons and he was one of those people who didn't pass my life by. Silver's talked about that to me so many times.

'What's meant for us doesn't pass us by,' he said. The sex, the me lying naked on the cold changing room floor while Martin Savage entered me and filled me, well it happened every day. I had hoped that the once would be enough, that it was all about the chase with him and that he'd move on to someone else, but he didn't. Every day, usually between the end of his six o'clock and the beginning of his half six, he'd call me into his changing room.

I knew the routine. He was always naked when I got there. His willy was all big and hard and pointing. I'd strip off my clothes, I'd lie naked on the cold tiled floor. Then he'd tell me to open my legs. That's when I'd imagine I was a tree. I'd imagine that my hard bark would scrape against his shins, that when he touched me he'd find splinters in his fingertips. I'd imagine that my body was sinking into the tiles of the changing room floor, taking root, growing away from him.

You see, Arthur, I let him go into me. I let him huff and puff and shoot his dirt into me. I didn't move. I didn't respond to his touch, his teeth on my neck, his tongue pushing into my mouth. I hated him. I still hate him

'I want you to love me,' he would say.

I wouldn't speak. Not a word.

'If you won't love me, then I'll make sure that no one gets you,' he would say.

'You are mine, you are sacred to me Laurel,' he would say

Then he'd pull out of me, leaving me lying on the floor with him dripping out from my insides. I would watch him dress. I would watch him sniff his palms, I would watch him lick his fingers with his eyes locked on mine. And all the time I wouldn't say a word. I was a tree. A silent tree.

'There are plenty other women who'd quite like a bit of me,' he would say. And then he'd lift his bare foot and place it over my belly. 'It's only a matter of time,' he would say and he would wink.

But I knew already, I knew after only four times. He'd done something to my insides.

Silver knew too. He started bringing me Smarties again. I'd find a tube lying on my desk every afternoon. I would sit eating Smarties and counting the leaves that I had drawn going up my left arm. One, two, three, four, five, six, seven, eight, nine, ten, eleven, twelve, thirteen. One for every time, in permanent marker, snaking round my left arm. I stopped at thirteen, my lucky number.

Of course, I realised I was pregnant but I didn't do anything about it. I guess I hoped that if I ignored it enough then it'd realise that it wasn't welcome, that it really shouldn't be wanting to be born into this crappy world.

But she didn't go away. Delphina didn't go away.

Instead my baby grew and grew. I tried to hide my bump but my mum figured it out right quickly. She was chuffed, said that

it'd mean we could get a bigger house and we'd have more benefits coming in every month. I felt sick all the time. Don't forget
I'd been told that there were only a few months left before I'd die.
And the thought that Martin Savage would one day get his hands
on my baby was making it all worse. I hated the thought of her
thinking I was some little tart who wanted to mess around with
a married man. I wasn't, I hadn't.

And that feeling, the continuous feeling that I was going to
throw up, that continuous waiting for something really bad to
happen, well it stayed with me. It became part of me.

And that's why I did what I did. That's why I did what I did
to her, to Delphina.

I pushed her out of me in the changing rooms of the Males
1st Class pool. It was during the night and I bit down hard on
my jumper, trying my hardest not to make any noise. 'Course I
made noise, pushing a baby out is like someone setting fire to
your bits. It hurt, but that was okay. I swear, giving birth to her,
to Delphina, was the most alive I ever felt. And when I saw her,
all wrinkled and covered in blood and all squashed, well I reckon
I realised that I'd felt love. I understood love. I knew I'd die to
protect her.

And I did.

We stayed on the floor of the Males 1st Class pool for three
hours. Me, Delphina, the cut cord and a load of blood. She tried
to feed off me and we managed it a little bit. I'd seen Mum feeding
Sammy so I knew what I had to do. None of that frightened me.
And I had a blanket, Sammy's old blanket. I had a babygrow, a
metal shopping basket and I had a rope. I'd been prepared for
weeks, I'd known what I was going to do for weeks.

I dressed her in the babygrow, I wrapped her in the blanket
and I scribbled a note to attach to her with sellotape. 'Property
of Martin Savage'. I was being ironic. Then me and Delphina went

out the changing rooms and up the stairs to the viewing gallery. I tied one end of my rope with a tight knot to the fancy railings and the other I'd already looped. I put my head into the noose and pulled it tight.

That's when Delphina started to cry. There was a moment when I didn't know if I'd be able to go through with it. She was crying and her tiny hands were in fists and she needed me more than anyone's ever needed me. But I knew, I knew that her life would be rubbish. I knew that I'd resent her, that she'd be a constant reminder of my weakness, of all that was wrong with Martin Savage. I had to protect her from him, from me, from this fucked up world. I did it for Delphina. I did it for love.

That's when I put her in the rusted metal shopping basket that someone'd left in the yard. Then I threw her from the viewing gallery and into the pool. Then I climbed onto the railings and I jumped.

My neck broke instantly.

Arthur

EARTH: (*Air. Water. Fire.*)

Reference No: 10-173758
Name: Deborah Cartland
Missing Since: 01-Nov-2008

'Fuck off! You're Delphina's mum?' I ask Laurel. She nods. I'm still sitting cross-legged on the mosaic tiles next to her. I'm still clutching her tube of Smarties. I swear, I've absolutely no idea what's going on.

'Killed by her own mother,' Kester shouts from the viewing gallery.

'I blame her parent,' Pollock shouts from the viewing gallery.

I ignore the weird old blokes. I have a good look at Laurel, like I'm seeing her for the first time. She's proper tiny, she's proper skinny, she's got a little-lass body but her eyes are old. Her eyebrows are black, her hair's black too, but her lips are the brightest red I've ever seen. It's not lipstick, it's the colour of fresh blood. I'm staring at her face and I can feel who she is. I know that she's full of unhappy, I know that she carries all the bad in the world with her. I know that she feels loss, that she carries guilt. Her eyes are proper intense, it's like they scream out pain, it's like they scream out sorrow and it's like they scream out for me to listen. It's like she's waiting to be found.

I look at her arms. Her jumper sleeves are pushed up to her elbows and I can see the leaves that she drew on her left arm all them years ago. I count them. Thirteen.

'But she's older than you,' I say. 'Cause, clearly, I can think of nowt else to say.

'She wasn't then,' Laurel says. I nod. Of course she wasn't. I'm a twat.

'And you're dead?' I ask.

'No shit, Sherlock,' she says. I think she smiles. She's been listening, she knows I like that phrase.

'But if you're dead, then how come I can see you?' I ask.

'It's something to do with this place, with being close to the water. It's all to do with Delphina.'

'Shouldn't you be in heaven?' I ask. I'm staring at her. I mean 'heaven', what the fuck's that all 'bout? I don't even believe there's a God. And Laurel's not see-through and she's not got any loose skin flapping from her. I'm thinking that all them zombie and ghost films were proper bollocks.

'I've got to look out for Delphina. I keep her company,' she says. 'That's why I'm still here.' I look at her arms and I count the leaves again. I count to thirteen, again.

'Delphina talked about Martin Savage . . . She said you loved him,' I say.

'I didn't. Lots of women did,' Laurel says. Her eyes are sad. 'They all wanted him, but I didn't.' I nod.

'I get that,' I say. 'I mean it's starting to make sense. I mean . . . Oh, twatting, shitting, fuck,' I say. 'Could I have been any more of a dick?'

Laurel laughs, it sounds awesome. I'm still thinking it all through. I swear it's like my head's fit to burst.

'But if Delphina was hoyed into the water and you were hanging, then how isn't she dead now?' I ask.

'That's where I come in, lad,' Silver says. He's still sitting with his feet in the water, but he turns to look at me. 'Come sit next to me, lad,' he says. And I do. I uncross my legs, I stand up and I move over to the edge of the pool. I take off my shoes and socks and I roll up my trouser legs. I sit next to Silver and lower my feet into the pool.

He smells a bit. He smells of ciggies and sweat. He's fat, he's old and he hangs out with dead people. I'm looking at his face and I'm seeing that it gives nowt away. He's proper hard-faced is Silver. But really it's his hair that bothers me the most. It's silver, I mean it sparkles, it glistens and I reckon it's threaded out from his scalp. My mind's wandering, thinking what came first, his hair or his name.

'Who are you? I mean, who are you really?' I ask.

'I'm no one,' Silver says. 'I'm just here to look after Delphina,' he says.

I nod.

'I reckon it's about time you joined all the dots together, don't you, lad?' he says. I snap out of my thinking 'bout his hair.

I nod. I mean, there's nowt else I can do but nod and listen.

It's like I'm now seeing him for the first time too.

Silver

EARTH: (*Air. Water. Fire.*)

I told her to run for her life. That's what I always did. But with Laurel I knew it'd make no difference. It was all there. Her death was a-coming. And all I could do was sit on me arse and watch.

It was me. I found them. I woke in the night knowing. I was outside in my caravan but I still heard Laurel screaming when Delphina was coming out of her. But I left her to her private stuff. I knew what I was coming in here to find. I wasn't brave or anything like that, but I knew it had to be me who found them.

I walked in here right slow. I walked through them doors and Laurel was hanging from that viewing gallery. She was dripping her blood into that pool. And the baby, Delphina, well the baby was lying face-down in that water. There was a few seconds where I didn't know who to help first. I guess I stood still in that doorway. My eyes watching from one to the other. Then I turned round, ran into that hallway and up them stairs. I screamed to the heavens for Madame Pythia to come. By the time I got to her flat's front door, she was there with her dressing gown wrapped around her. I didn't say no words. She knew. Like me, she knew. I turned and I ran back down them stairs. Madame Pythia hoisted up her dressing gown and she ran after me.

Something broke in me that day. I don't reckon I've ever said them words out loud, but something did. Because Laurel should have been able to do so much with her life. She had what them teachers call potential. Inside her head was full of plans and smashing ideas. But that day her mum took that job notice down off that corkboard in that butcher's. And that day that Laurel decided to apply for a job here at The Oracle. Well that's when all them new lines appeared on them palms of hers. And once them palms had been engraved, well there's nowt I could do to erase them. Consequences for decisions. That's what life's all about. Even if the decisions are made with the sweetest of intentions.

I was back in Males 1st Class. I screamed. I dived into that water fully clothed, even though clothes weren't allowed. I swam to the baby. I grabbed her. She'd fallen out of that metal shopping basket. That was on the bottom of that pool. I started swimming to the edge, clutching her, and I was going to lift her out of that water. I was going to lift her onto the side. I wanted her to rest in peace. My swimming, with only the use of one arm, was all clumsy. Water was going in my mouth and up my nose. I was spluttering. That's when I heard Madame Pythia screaming at me.

'Do not remove that baby from the water. Do not!'

I stopped my swimming. I treaded water and I looked up at her. Water was all in my eyes and I was struggling to stay afloat. Madame Pythia was stripping off. She sat naked on that edge of this pool and lowered herself into that water. She swam to me and the baby. She took the baby from my arms. I saw her pulling in her breath before sinking under that water with the baby in her arms.

At first I didn't know what she was doing. At first I was thinking that maybe she was trying to drown the baby a little bit more. Then I realised that she was giving the baby mouth to mouth under the water. If I'm honest, nowt made sense. None of it made sense to me, not even a little bit.

Then Madame Pythia came back up out of that water. She was gasping for breath. She rocked the baby over the water. And that's when I saw the baby open her eyes.

Arthur

EARTH: (*Air. Water. Fire.*)

Reference No: 10-230397
Name: Nigel Harbottle
Missing Since: 19-Feb-2010

'What? She opened her eyes?' I say.

I swear, I think they're pissing with my head. I mean, Laurel's dead, Silver knew she was going to kill herself and let her, Delphina was drowning and then alive. I'm off my head. This is it, I've turned into my twatting dad.

'She lived,' Silver says.

'We all live, sort of,' Laurel adds.

I look at Silver and he's smiling at me. His whole face looks different, he looks gentle, like I'd reckon Santa Claus would look if he'd gone off the rails and was recovering from an alcohol addiction.

'But that makes no sense, how can a baby survive being face-down in water?'

'They can't,' Maddie says. 'And I should know.'

'I always knew it would end that way, lad,' Silver says. 'There was nowt I could do to stop it. Things happen as they should.'

'That's bollocks,' I say. 'No one can know the future.'

'That's where you're wrong, young Arthur,' Maddie says. 'Silver always knows what'll happen next.'

Madora Argon (Maddie)

WATER: (*Air. Earth. Fire.*)

The story goes that we were desperate for a child.

Jason and me'd met when we were still at school, so he was all of my firsts. There's been no one else. We grew up together, fumbling through arguments and stupid teenage fights that were the end of the world, but never quite. I guess we probably got married because it was either that or splitting up. We were both twenty-three and I guess we were both a bit bored of us. Jason was drunk when he said, 'You know what, me and you should wed.' He gave me one of his Haribo rings that night and we had the most amazing shag ever. We married within six months and those six months were truly ace, because we had something exciting to focus on.

Back then I was a singer. I did the clubs. I mean my voice had been trained when I was eleven, which was unusual, but my music teacher at school had seen potential. My act was 'The Voice of an Angel' and Mum and Dad, later Jason, would take me around clubs and I'd perform my set for pennies. I loved it. I loved being on a tiny stage and losing myself in the words and the rhythm and the sentiment. I sang words about things I'd never experienced, but when they came out of my mouth it was like they were my words, like I'd sat and written those lyrics just after the event they described. When I sang I felt truly alive. 'Course Jason never really understood that, why would he? He worked in car sales, he was all about commission and figures and how much money he could grab each month.

Then the story changed a bit. We'd been married three years and I guess it was others who put the idea out there. Jason's parents, my mum and dad, they started dropping little mentions of babies into the conversation. At first it was funny, but then I started thinking that I'd quite like something that me and Jason had made together. A mini us to show the world that we were secure and for always. Jason wasn't sure at first. He talked about my being out nights singing and his long hours at work and the strain that there already was on us and our relationship. He talked about us being too young and that a baby just wasn't part of his 'life plan' yet. It was about then that I stopped taking the pill, not that we were having much sex. And it was a couple of months later when Jason figured that I'd stopped taking the pill. I mean, he was cross at first, but then I cried and I told him that I needed a baby. I explained how it was a female thing, how it was all I could think about. I cried and cried for days and eventually Jason gave in and said we could try properly.

And so it was that, cycle after cycle, the bleeding came. And cycle after cycle the bleeding chipped away at our relationship. Every month I'd do a test, every day from day twenty-five of my cycle. I'd buy them cheap from a shop in town. It became a routine. Lavender bubble bath, exfoliating facial wipes, pink razors, tea-tree shampoo, Tunnock's teacakes and four pregnancy tests. I'd do the test on day twenty-five, then day twenty-six, then day twenty-seven, usually it was all over by day twenty-eight. I was like clockwork, I was. But those days before, those days when I held a negative test in my hand, well I'd deny it. I'd try to ignore that hope was buried in the bottom of the black binbag with each of them soiled

308

sticks. I swear I'd convince my head that it was just because it was too early and I'd curse myself for wasting our pennies, but it'd be the same every month. And so every four weeks I'd feel like a failure. And every four weeks, when I told Jason that I'd come on and how I felt, he'd never say that I wasn't a failure. His eyes would simply look sad, disappointed and sad. And that made me feel like a failure even more. I mean I couldn't do anything right, I couldn't even give my husband a baby.

After a year of trying, I was all for going to the doctors, but Jason wanted none of it. He said he didn't want no doctors judging us and writing in our files about how crap our sex was. I mean, there were days when we laughed, because when we were teens and having sex every place we could, we were so scared that I'd get pregnant. I mean sometimes Jason even wore two condoms, just to make sure. And with Jason's opinion of doctors, well it was pretty clear that he wouldn't even entertain the idea of IVF. His argument was that he wanted it to be all natural, that he didn't want anyone prodding and poking around in his bits, and he'd heard from some mechanic at work that sometimes the doctors used their own sperm instead of the patient's and Jason said that if we had an IVF baby, then he'd never know for definite if it was his.

That ruled out adoption too. Jason said that we'd have no idea what kind of mental-health issues we were letting ourselves in for, that we might be letting some nutter's baby into our house. He said that all adopted babies had 'issues'. I knew he was talking utter bollocks, but at that time I didn't want to rock the boat. I mean, I was the failure, it was my fault that I couldn't give my husband a baby, that I couldn't do that one simple thing that all the other women in the world could.

That's when I reckoned that The Oracle might help. It was when Laurel worked here, close to a year before it closed down, actually. I turned up one day and I remember seeing Laurel, nose stuck in a book. I thought the water might help, that maybe it'd heal my insides. I didn't realise then that it was Jason that was faulty, not me. His sperm was crap at swimming and my coming here, well I reckon the water goddesses had a right laugh to themselves. Anyway, that day I got here, Laurel was reading at her desk and I remember standing watching her, not knowing if I should interrupt her or not. It was a good five minutes before she saw me. I told Laurel that I needed an appointment and she looked into the book and said that Silver was the only one of the healers that was free. I remember feeling a bit pissed off because everyone had said that Madame Pythia was the best, that she was the one to see. But she was booked up for weeks and I was desperate.

That day I went through to the Females pool and I sat on the side, all naked and self-conscious. Silver came over and sat down beside me.

'Let me see your palm,' Silver said.

'I'm not here for any of that witchery,' I said.

'I don't heal unless I know there's something worth healing,' Silver said to me, and I turned over my hand and stretched it out to him.

I remember that I started to relax and I wondered if he was gay because not once did he look at my nipples. But then Silver started to cry.

'What?' I asked.

'Run for your life,' Silver said, and he let go of my palm with a deep sigh. I watched him steadying himself, trying to get to his feet. I watched Silver walking away.

'But I've no place to run to,' I shouted after Silver.

'And there's nowt I can do to stop what's got to happen from happening,' Silver shouted back, not turning to look at me.

'What the fuck?' I shouted.

'When you get to the end, come back and see me,' he shouted, as he pushed open the door and left me sitting stark bollock naked with my feet in the cold water.

I didn't know what to do, I mean I had no idea what he was talking about and part of me wondered if he was a nutter, if he got his kicks from upsetting women. That's when I jumped into the Females pool. I plunged in, my feet touching the floor and the water rushing past my body.

I swear that when my ears were submerged I heard a voice, I heard the most beautiful voice I've ever heard. 'Soon you'll be mine,' the voice whispered and even though my head was underwater and even though I had no idea what the hell was happening, I found myself nodding slightly, just before I pushed myself from the bottom of the pool and up to the surface to gasp at the air.

It was about that time that things between Jason and me became cold and stale and negative. I'd find myself snapping at him for the least bit thing and he'd respond with words that were full of negative, full of anger and hatred. He'd go to the pub after work and come home with a bag of chips, throwing the food that I'd made him in the bin.

I stopped my singing. I didn't want to be performing. The words suddenly meant too much and one time I found myself crying, I mean there were tears streaming down my cheeks and I didn't even realise until the third repeat of the chorus. My voice coach adored my coloratura soprano. She spoke of how my voice was flexible, of how it was agile, of how I could execute vocal runs and leaps with brilliance. Sometimes it felt that so much of the operatic music, its ornaments, its trills and turns, sometimes it felt as if those songs were composed just for me. And with that I had a pride, I felt like I'd achieved, like I was good. And that's why I had to stop singing.

That's why I'd spend days lying on the sofa, watching *Vanessa* and sometimes even contemplating phoning up the show and getting Jason on there with me. I never did. Instead, over time, I stopped washing, I stopped caring and Jason didn't give a fuck.

It's fair to say I gave up. It's also fair to say that sometimes Jason came in horny and drunk and I'd pretend to be asleep but he'd still shag me. Everything about our relationship was broken. All the joy was gone, there was nothing positive to cling to, just negativity and resentment. And because our sex life was shattered and because the thing between us was gone, I'd stopped buying tests and I'd stopped paying attention to my cycle. I mean some days, I'd just let the blood soak through my jogging pants and onto the sofa. I reckoned the stain was needed, because I had no words to speak to Jason.

It's said that it's only when you stop trying that what's meant to be is allowed to be. And that's what happened. There was a month where I didn't come on. And if I'm honest, I don't think I noticed for a few days. I had all the symptoms for coming on, the sore boobs, the odd taste in my mouth, the pulling in my tummy, but I didn't realise at the time that all of those symptoms signal a baby forming. I had none of the hope from the early days of trying left in me. I think that my initial reaction was that maybe I was ill, that maybe my period not coming was because there was something seriously wrong with me. I didn't even tell Jason just how worried I was, but when the worry was keeping me awake in the middle of the night, well that's when I figured I'd have to go and see the doctor.

The story goes that seven days after my absolutely clockwork period was due, I made myself an appointment. I reckon I was all set for the doctor to tell me that I was seriously ill, or that I was starting with an early menopause. I mean my mum was late thirties when she started and although I was still in my twenties, I reckoned that all the sadness that I'd been feeling recently could have triggered the start of something ridiculously chemical in my blood. I mean when I was sitting in the waiting room and when I was flicking through the pile of old magazines on the little table, I even started thinking about how I could write to *Take a Break* and maybe they'd run a feature about my early menopause and then pay me a few hundred quid. I even thought about what I'd spend the money on, I was thinking maybe a holiday for me and Jason, maybe a bit of sun was what we'd need to try and get back some joy.

But the doctor didn't even mention the word menopause. Instead he asked if I could be pregnant and I said that I reckoned there was no chance as I'd been trying for years and nothing had happened. And then the doctor asked me straight if I'd had unprotected sex and I nodded and blushed, like I'd been caught doing something naughty. That's when he asked me to go and pee in a little plastic sample bottle.

I scuttled off to the toilet and my hands were shaking as I held the bottle under my fanny and tried to aim my trickle of wee into it. I peed all over my hands and managed a tiny bit into the sample bottle. But that was enough. A little bit was all the doctor needed.

I watched the doctor poking a thin test strip into my pot of pee. I'd seen a million of those tests before, I reckon they were cheap ones like I used to buy from the shop in town. I watched the doctor looking at his watch and then putting the test down on the sink and then he came back to his desk and started writing things about me on the card in my file. That's when I thought about Jason and how pissed off he'd be if he knew that details of our crap sex were floating around the doctor's and that anyone who wanted to could open the doctor's files and find out Jason's secrets. I sat all quiet, listening to the tappity-tap of the doctor's fingers on his desk. It made me think about wearing tap shoes on the pavement. Then the doctor stood up and walked back over to the sink. He picked up the test, let out a big sigh and all the time I was trying to read his eyes and wondering what he was thinking was wrong with me.

'Do you want the good news or the bad news?' the doctor said.

'The bad news,' I said, because that's what I always wanted first.

'You're going to have to see me a lot more often,' the doctor said and smiled. I still had no idea what he was talking about. I mean, call me thick.

'Shit, am I dying?' I asked.

'No,' he said. 'You're pregnant.'

And that's when I threw up onto my skirt.

I don't know if I've ever said this out loud before, but that day, when I was walking out the doctor's surgery, and even though I stunk of vomit, I reckon that I was the happiest I've ever been. I mean, at that very moment I didn't feel like a failure any more.

'Course, when I told Jason he was initially shocked. I think he said something like 'Are you sure?', and then 'It's mine, right?' And I didn't rise to his words, I didn't shout back like I'd normally shout, because I figured he was shocked. I mean he'd had no indication at all that I possibly could be. Then he moved towards me, from the doorway into the centre of the room, and he picked me up and swung me around. When I was back on my own two feet, I looked over at him and his eyes were smiling. I think it was the first time I'd seen him smile for weeks and weeks.

That night we sat around the kitchen table, with special fried rice from the Chinese around the corner. Jason bought four cans of Stella to celebrate, but I didn't take a sip. I'd already decided that I was going to give our baby the best possible chance at survival. That night it felt right between us. I told Jason all about my being late and my thinking I was dying and my going to the doctor's expecting the worst news possible. At first Jason laughed, but then he went silent and then he said words about how sorry he was for not having been there for me and about how horrible it must have been to have had to go through all of that on my own. We talked about how things had been bad between us for weeks and weeks, we talked about how the joy had gone and about the resentment that had been bubbling. I mean we said stuff that hurt each other, but at least we were talking, at least it was all out in the open. That night, while finishing off his last forkful of fried rice and while downing half a can of Stella, well that night Jason promised me that things would be different. And that night Jason made love to me. It was gentle, the kisses were tender, it was very quick.

And things did change, and things did get better, for a little while. Jason started coming home on time, we'd eat together and watch *Coronation Street* together and sometimes we'd talk about the baby. We'd talk about whether we thought it was a girl or a boy, about names, about how big the baby would be inside me at that very moment. We scheduled doctor's appointments, midwife meetings, NCT classes and scans, all around dates and times that meant Jason could be there, could be part of it all. And when we talked about the baby, well Jason's eyes still sparkled.

But even then, even when he was making all that effort to be with me, to make us better, there was no love, there was no real intimacy, there was never a moment when I felt that he looked at me and I took his breath away. And, I mean, if I'm totally honest, well I knew that Jason was with me for all the wrong reasons. I knew that the only reason Jason and me were still together was because of the tiny miracle baby that was growing in my belly.

I can remember when it all started going wrong again. It was just after my twenty-week scan. We'd found out that our miracle baby was a girl and Jason had admitted that he'd really hoped for a little girl. I'd had that flicker of hope again, right there when I was lying on my back on a bed in the ultrasound department. But then Jason had had to rush back to work. After that he was distracted for days, not quite there when I'd been trying to talk to him. His mobile had been ringing late at night and he'd been going upstairs, into the spare room and closing the door to take the call. When I asked him about it, he'd said that work was crazy, that there was talk of a takeover and that he was stressing that he'd not make that quarter's sales figures. He'd said that everyone was feeling it and that's why the phone calls were happening. I believed him. But that night, a few nights after the day of the twenty-week scan, that night Jason didn't come home until past eleven. I was waiting up for him in the front room, fretting that something had happened to him. He'd not been answering his mobile all evening. That night Jason stood in the doorway to the front room, his eyes glaring at me.

'I wish you'd fuck right off,' he said to me, before turning and walking upstairs.

The next morning he apologised, said it was the work pressure and that he'd had too much to drink. But that night had marked a change in him. From then on he'd come home late every night, he'd have meetings at the weekend, he'd be called into work for health-and-safety courses on a Sunday afternoon. And every time he came back he'd smell of beer and cigarettes and sweet perfume. It was about that time that I started checking his pockets for receipts. I didn't find any. But I'd see condoms in his wallet. I'd mark the packet with a tiny dot of biro on it and the next day the biro mark would be gone. I'd start writing little initials on them and they'd be gone too. Sometimes the type of condom would be different, extra-safe one day, super nobbly the next. He never tried to hide them, maybe he thought I'd not notice the detail. I never questioned him about it. That's when I started sniffing his boxer shorts, that's when I'd see white stains, that's when I'd check his pockets and see the occasional notes from her, or ones he'd written in reply, waiting to be delivered. They were never there for long, he thought he was good, he thought he was an efficient cheat. But it was always enough to make my stomach feel like it was trying to push its way out. I'd shake as I read the words that he used when talking to her, she was a 'hottie' and he couldn't wait to 'taste' her again. I never said anything. Instead I clung to the hope that it would all change again when our miracle baby girl was born.

And she was born.

Her name was Melody.

She was beautiful. I know that all mothers should and some do think that of their children, but Melody was. She had the biggest blue eyes, with eyelashes so long that they weaved tears between them, like a web, like a beautiful glistening web. And Jason adored her. It wasn't a simple love, the love you might feel for a cat or a purse or a nephew you see every other weekend. No, Jason adored Melody, their love, their bond was more than I had ever anticipated. Every moment that he spent in our home, he spent it with Melody. This is no exaggeration, Melody even slept between us in bed and it wasn't long before I realised that his love for her was stopping what little love and affection he may have had for me from reaching me.

Some days I'd hide in shadows. I'd watch him through cracks in doors. I'd see him scooping her up to his shoulder, his rocking her, his whispering words that I'd never know, as he walked slowly around the room or padded from foot to foot. Their bond, their love, it tore into me, it ripped my heart out. I swear, it was as if Jason could love anything and anybody except for me. I felt unlovable, I was marked with the scars of his child, yet still he brushed me aside for another, for a baby, for a lover, for anyone and everyone who gave him all that I never could.

It was at that time that I stopped loving Melody.

I looked at her and all I saw was inadequacy, all I felt was hatred of the love she could evoke, and even at that stage, even after a couple of hate-filled months, I was beginning to realise that the best way to get to Jason, the best way to punish him for what he was doing . . . well, it was clear that Melody was the key.

Because my suspicions were 'beyond doubt'. I mean a woman knows, doesn't she? She knows when the person who has been hiding in the shadows of her relationship with her husband suddenly steps forward and starts taking the piss.

It happened that day, a Saturday. Because that day I followed him. I guess he'd been getting away with it for too long, I guess he'd been getting away with it for so long, I guess that's why he'd let down his guard. I guess there was the possibility that he thought I wouldn't care. But I did care. That day he said that he had to nip into work for a meeting regarding the changes to their commission rates. He'd given a long and overly complicated explanation and that was the first clue. That day I followed him with Melody in a sling attached to the front of me. I strapped her in so that she was looking forward, so that she'd see what I could see, so that she'd understand why I would have to do what I already knew that I would do. To her.

That day we followed him by foot, ready to nip behind thick tree trunks, ready to slow in pace, but we never really needed to, as not once did Jason look back. It was clear that he had no idea that we were following him. That day we followed him to a house and we saw her open the door. It was Corinne. She was Jason's boss' youngest daughter. She was single, blonde, thin, twenty-one. Daddy had bought her a house, Daddy had given her a job doing practically nothing for lots of money, Daddy had given her everything she wanted. And one of the things that she wanted was Jason. Daddy had given him to her too.

I stood, we watched. We saw the smiles, the look of absolute joy, as she flung her arms around Jason and kissed him in a way that I never had. We, Melody and I, could see the passion, the need, the all-consuming joy that they had. I stood, we watched, as they broke off their embrace and walked into her house.

That's when I stroked the soft wisps of hair on my beautiful daughter's head. And that's when I walked a slow walk back to our house. And that's when I decided that I had no other choice. That's the day that I killed Melody.

I went back to our house, the rocking of my steady strides lulling Melody to sleep, and by the time we arrived home she was breathing in time with the beating of my heart. Fast, little breaths, the occasional gasp. I already knew how I would kill her. I'd been lying awake for nights, sleep evasive, my thoughts fuelled with suspicion and dread. I guess seeing Jason with that woman, knowing what he would be doing. Knowing that he would be entering her, making her squeal with delight. Those images burned inside me.

That's why I moved around our house quickly. I was focused, determined. I filled a bathtub, checking that the water was the correct temperature, not that it mattered, but still, even then, I guess there was a part of me that went through the motions of being a good mother.

I put Melody's plastic bath seat into the middle of the bath to help me gauge how high the water needed to be. I didn't add fragrance, no need for bubble bath this time. Instead, I stayed still, watching the water rise, wondering if I'd have the courage, wondering when that killer instinct had been born within me. Melody continued to sleep as I bent to turn off the taps.

That's when I turned and searched in the wall cabinet for the Night Nurse. I filled the baby syringe with an adult's dose and that's when I started to remove Melody from the security of the sling. Her nappy was heavy, full, her eyes still sleepy as she opened them and then her mouth in protest. I emptied the syringe into her mouth, watching as she gulped a swallow in between her growing cries.

For years I've wished that at that moment I'd pulled her close to me. I've played this scene over and over again in my head.

I sat on the closed toilet's lid. I held my baby daughter at arm's length, as she wriggled on my knee. She needed changing, she needed feeding, she needed comfort. Her eyes spoke her confusion, her eyes begged me to make her better. I didn't. I swear, I wish that I had. I wish that I'd been able to bring her close to me, to breathe in her scent, to gently rock her back and forth, to make her secure. I didn't. Instead I looked at her and I thought of Jason and that other woman and I thought about Jason and Melody and somehow, I can't begin to explain why, but somehow, in those moments, it was as if Melody belonged to them. To Jason and that bitch of a woman. And that's why I stood, and that's why I bent, holding my miracle baby awkwardly, and that's when I took out Melody's plastic bath seat and that's why I lay Melody on her stomach in the water.

The water was too deep, she strained to push her head up, her body up. I couldn't stay to watch, instead I turned my back on my child and I left her alone in the bath tub.

It was an hour later, exactly sixty minutes later, when I returned to see her. She was face down in the water.

I guess what distinguishes killers is the remorse they feel directly after the event. I showed no emotion, no tears, no falling to the floor in angst. Instead my hand shook, as I wrote a note to Jason. *Melody is in the bath*, it said. I left that note on the welcome doormat.

It was then that I left our home for the last time. I didn't take anything with me, there was nothing I would need. I remember that it was raining. I mean of course I remember that, it was the last time that I felt the cold, the wind, the beating of rain on my skin. I had no place else to go, other than here, to The Oracle, even though it'd closed a few weeks earlier when Laurel had died here. I just walked around the building, found an open door and came inside. I didn't know for sure if Silver would be here, but his words, 'When you get to the end, come back and see me', were all I had left.

The truth is that Silver always knew how it'd end, he knew I'd come back here and he was waiting for me. I'd like to think that was the only reason he was here, but back then both him and Madame Pythia were caring for little Delphina. I mean it was all a bit screwed up. When I got here I couldn't even see the little water nymph Delphina and the spirit of Laurel, my sight was so very clouded over with anger and hatred. I mean I tried, for a whole day, I tried to see and hear but I couldn't. That's when Silver told me that he reckoned I was too screwed up with guilt and grief and sadness.

That next day, after no one had come looking for me, Silver talked me through my options. Live or die. Simple, really. I knew that I had nothing left to give, I knew I had no more options and really there was never a choice. It was Silver who showed me how to die. Nothing dramatic, ropes, stones, tied tight so that no matter how hard I wriggled, there was no way out. The water took my life.

But I guess the water had the last laugh. The water decided that my voice would always be heard. My coloratura soprano, the vocal runs and leaps, the trills and turns they sang with the water. They twisted and turned and brought people to them, to the water goddesses. My voice became their voice, their way to be fed, to feed, to lure, to protect. Those eight missing persons, one every two years, all those bones that line the bottom of this our home, all those innocents who became her nourishment. They had to die to keep Delphina, to keep all of us alive. I did that for them, for the water goddesses. I sang, they came here to drown.

So now I sing, I sing when the water orders me to sing. She is my mistress, she fuels me, she protects me from my own pain, from my own grief. I feel nothing, I am calm, I am one with her. I'm a siren. And when I sing, those that the water desires come to me, to this pool, to their deaths. And each death pleases her, each death fills a need within her, each death reminds me of Melody and all that I cannot replace within me. Make no mistake, I am wicked. I am a killer. The bones rattle and shake. I deserve no pity, I deserve no joy. My mistress demands attention. She seeks others to ask questions, but those questions are not being heard. Our time runs out.

But hear this, sweet Arthur, the water saved you. You should have been my eighth. My voice lured you here, but the water let you live. Delphina claimed you as her own. You may believe that you are in control of all that is happening, but you're wrong, oh so very wrong. The water allowed you to resist my voice.

You are chosen. Just as I was chosen. We each have a role to play in Delphina's story.

The water tells me that you are Delphina's one. And, I urge you, I urge you to listen to the water, I urge you to be true to your destiny.

Arthur

EARTH: (*Air. Water. Fire.*)

Reference No: 10-348710
Name: Cliff 'Big Cliff' Harris
Missing Since: 11-Nov-2012

'Be true to my destiny?' I say. 'What the fuck you going on 'bout now? I swear you're all off your heads. You're all fucking—'

'Arthur, lad, have you ever seen Delphina out of the water?' Silver asks.

'I don't—' I start.

'Think, lad,' Silver says. 'Think about it.' I'm still sitting next to him. But now he's staring at me and his eyes are gentle and he's not scary and he's not angry no more.

'She's always swimming, always practising,' I say.

'But why do you think you've never seen her out of the water?' Silver asks. He's talking right slow, 'cause he thinks I'm a dick.

'I always thought it was to do with her body. Like she was too shy to have me looking—'

'Lad, she was stark bollock naked. Do you really think she was arsed about you seeing her body?' Silver asks.

'I thought she had that scared-of-going-outside disease, agro-something,' I say.

'Have you ever seen me out of the water?' Maddie asks.

'You're not always here, so I just assumed—'

'You assume too much,' Silver says. He's smiling so I know he's not pissed off with me.

'I cannot leave the water. It is me, the water is me. When I'm not here, I'm in the underground reservoir, in the otherworld, with the others,' Maddie says.

'The others?' I ask. It's like suddenly I'm realising what a brainless twat I've been.

'The other water nymphs,' she says. She laughs. Silver laughs. I reckon they must think I'm a right thick twat.

'Of course, water nymphs, yes,' I say. I'm absolutely positive they're all off their heads. I've no idea what they're talking 'bout. 'And how do you get there?' I ask. 'To the otherworld?'

'Through the gateway,' Maddie says and she points to the other side of the pool. I follow her pointing and I nod, not that I can understand what she's going on 'bout, but still I nod. 'Down there we have no worries. Down there is happy, it is whatever your heart desires, it is full, full of music, such pure music, but they keep sending me back up here.'

'All this lad, all this that's been happening, it's how it had to be. We had to get you here so that you could love Delphina,' Silver says. Then he breaks eye contact with me, like he's not telling me something really important.

And that's when I proper get to realising what they're trying to tell me.

'And Delphina,' I start to say.

'She's a water nymph too, lad,' Silver says.

'You what?' I say.

'A water nymph,' Silver says.

'She likes to shag in the water?' I ask.

'No, lad,' Silver says. He smiles.

'What then?' I ask.

'Like a siren.'

'A what?'

'Don't they teach youse anything in school?' Silver asks. 'Like a mermaid.'

'A mermaid,' I say. I reckon Silver's proper mental.

'But without a tail,' Silver says and then adds, 'She lives in the water.'

'What the fuck are you talking 'bout?' I ask.

'She can't ever leave the water.'

'What do you mean, she can't ever leave?' I ask. This is proper doing my head in.

'In simple terms, my lad, the water is keeping her alive. Did you honestly not wonder why she never left the water?' Silver shakes his head. He looks proper disappointed in me.

'I just—' I start to say.

'It's this place!' It's Kester. He's shouting from the viewing gallery. I've been so busy concentrating on Silver and Maddie I haven't even realised the two old blokes are here.

'This place is keeping us all alive.' It's Pollock.

'And when this place is knocked down . . .' says Kester.

'Then we're all knocked down,' says Pollock.

'Like three blind mice.'

'Like London Bridge is falling down, you fool,' says Pollock. He laughs.

'You old fool,' says Kester. He laughs. I turn my attention back to Silver.

'But why are you here then?' I ask Silver. But before he can answer I get to thinking a bit more and I shout up to Kester and Pollock. 'Are you two dead, too?'

'Something like that,' Kester says.

'Are you sitting comfortably?' Pollock asks.

I move slightly. I'm still staring up at them in the viewing gallery, but I move a bit of a wiggle, then I nod my head and I wait.

Kester and Pollock

AIR: (*Water. Earth. Fire.*)

'Something like that,' Kester says.

   'Are you sitting comfortably?' Pollock asks.

   'You've said that,' Kester says.

   'What was that?'

   'What?'

   'That!'

   'I liked Laurel talking best.'

   'She was telling him—'

   'Why she's like that with that thing she carries.'

   'What?'

   'It's called a rope.'

   'Smarties.'

   'She likes them, so she does.'

   'Laurel's a nice lass.'

   'She is that.'

   'Shame that man messed with her.'

   'Was indeed.'

   'Wasn't rare, what was done to her.'

   'Wasn't well done either.'

   'Something's wrong with my ears today.'

   'What's wrong with them?'

'I can't hear with them.'

'Try harder.'

'I will.'

'Do you think Delphina will bring us some popcorn when she comes back?'

'Course she will.'

'You old fool.'

'No, you old fool.'

'Our mam always said that the water here was magic.'

'Yip, 'twas the water that got her up the duff.'

'Not that waste-of-space dad of ours.'

'Not him.'

'She came here.'

'Our mam did.'

'Just like that witch at the well said.'

'Followed instructions.'

'Right clever like that, was our mam.'

'Our dad said we was born from an egg.'

'Old fool.'

'He was, old fool.'

'But when we was born something funny happened.'

'Funny ha-ha.'

'Funny odd.'

'I was sick.'

'Me never sick.'

'Our mam reckoned you had all the good.'

'And you had all the bad.'

'Put us together and you get—'

'One wonky . . .'

'Old fool!'

'Inseparable we was.'

'Inseparable we is.'

'Our dad didn't like it.'

'Said we was queer.'

'Made him be a boxer.'

'Made him be a runner.'

'Put us together.'

'One old fool.'

'That's why our dad buggered off.'

'Met some lass down the pub.'

'Left our mam with just us.'

'We had to look after her.'

'And we did.'

'We got us two of a kind.'

'A set of twin lasses.'

'Identical.'

'Like two potatoes.'

'You old fool!'

'Them lasses were betrothed.'

'To the Corinth twins.'

'Right buggers they was.'

'But us two were right charmers—'

'Back then we was lookers too.'

'Wooed them lasses.'

'We did.'

'We did.'

'Caused holy hell when them Corinth twins got wind of it.'

'Right scrap we had.'

'Got myself a few kisses better that night.'

'And the rest.'

'You dirty bugger.'

'That's when a war started, on our estate.'

'The stealing was the worse.'

'Stole mam's dog.'

'Found it dead.'
'The bastards.'
'But we still married our lasses.'
'Had meself a son.'
'Same for me.'
'Bonny lads the pair of them.'
'Born within a week of each other.'
'It was when we was wetting their heads.'
'Down the pub, we was.'
'That was when it all went wrong.'
'Them Corinth twins was out.'
'They'd been on the ale.'
'They didn't take too kindly to us celebrating our good fortune.'
'They were itching for a scrap.'
'Punched you.'
'Punched me.'
'Knew I was a boxer.'
'You boxed them back.'
'But it made no difference.'
'They'd punched me onto a wall.'
'Did your head in, that wall did.'
'I felt it in here.'
'You felt it in there.'
'Knew you was leaving me.'
'You acted fast.'
'I brought you here.'
'To The Oracle.'
'Madame Pythia was running the shop.'
'Gave us some options.'
'Used the water.'
'Used you'
'Used me.'

'Your blood.'

'Mixed us together.'

'Into one.'

'Sacrificed one.'

'To save t'other.'

'Two half-lives.'

'One whole.'

'We can't leave here though.'

'We've no place to go.'

'We need the water.'

'One naked swimming a day.'

'No more, no less.'

'Just enough to keep us going.'

'Going forever.'

'Or maybe not.'

'We're aging.'

'Too fast.'

'Too soon.'

'Old fool.'

'You, old fool.'

'That wasn't supposed to happen.'

'One was living forever.'

'The other was dying when old.'

'Then it was traded.'

'Forever for a life.'

'And never seeing our lasses.'

'And never seeing our boys.'

'But at least we have each other.'

'You.'

'And you.'

'And popcorn.'

'Is someone bringing us popcorn?'

'It's hard to feel sorry for them without popcorn.'
'Nothing will save us.'
'Nothing will save them.'
'The end is coming.'
'The water has spoken.'
'Something's wrong with my ears today.'
'What's wrong with them?'
'I can't hear with them.'
'Try harder.'
'I will.'

Arthur

EARTH: (*Air. Water. Fire.*)

Reference No: 10-348752
Name: Arthur Braxton
Missing Since: 13-Nov-2012

The old men speak too quickly. They're shouting down from the viewing gallery. They're all laughing and high-fives and all I can do is bend my neck upwards and watch.

We're a right odd bunch. There's Laurel, she's now lying on her back and looking up at the viewing gallery. Silver and me's got our feet in the pool and we're both watching the two old men putting on a weird kind of show. And Maddie, well she was here, but she's gone again. I can't help but wonder if she's gone down through the gateway or if she's climbed out the pool when we've been watching Kester and Pollock. I mean today, this whole fucking unravelling of bollocks, I mean it's all a bit far-fetched for my liking.

'So, let's get this straight,' I say. 'Everyone here's dead?'

Silver laughs. 'Not quite, I'm still here.'

'But the others are all dead?' I ask.

Silver nods.

'So what are you, some kind of caretaker of dead folk?'

'I'm responsible,' Silver says. 'There's stuff I have to do. That gift of mine's been a curse for years, lad, and when Laurel did what she did, well I've been here since. I've got a responsibility to them, to Laurel and Delphina. I didn't have the balls to save Laurel and stop all this from happening, so I'm stuck here until I can make it all good. And I will, lad. I will. It's nearly time. Do you believe in happily-ever-afters?'

I nod. I don't know what else to say to him.

'But why am I here?' I ask.

'There's a reason, lad, it'll all be clear soon.'

'And those eight folk,' I ask.

'All dead, lad,' Silver says. I nod.

'Big Cliff's one of them?' I ask.

Silver nods. 'Sacrificed for the water goddesses,' he says.

I nod.

'Do you know when Delphina'll be back?' I ask.

'She's down in the otherworld.'

'Can I see her?'

'No, lad, no humans can go down there. Not even me,' he says. 'It's a magical place, it's where she'll find happiness and she'll forget all that has ever caused her pain. She'll forget all of us, lad.'

'Did she say owt 'bout me, before she left?' I need to know.

'That she was sorry she wasn't enough,' Silver says. He's looking at me with his sad eyes. He looks like he's going to cry.

'I've fucked it all up,' I say.

And that's when I realise that my tears have been falling without me realising. I feel like I'm choking, like all the emotion, like all them years of nowt, all them years of shit at school and Mum leaving and Dad being off his head, it's like they're all stuck in my throat. I'm coughing and spluttering and sobbing. Snot and tears are flowing and there's nowt I can do to stop the pain. Silver puts his arm around my shoulder and there's nowt I can do but put my head on his shoulder and sob.

*

It's been hours, fuck knows how many episodes of *Waterloo Road*. Just me crying and Silver sitting statue-still and letting me sob onto him. Laurel's stayed beside me too, but she hasn't spoken a word of comfort. I don't think she can.

'I need to see her,' I say. I'm wiping my eyes and my nose onto my shirt sleeve.

'That's impossible,' Laurel says. 'None of us can be with Delphina again, only water nymphs can.'

'Then I'll be one of them,' I say.

'You can't,' Silver says. 'Only the drowned and only then the chosen few. There's no way of knowing if you'll be one of them. Being chosen is the ultimate gift from the water goddesses.'

'I can try,' I say.

'You bringing those mates of yours here, that's what drove Delphina away,' Silver says. 'You put us all in danger, lad. You need to be making that better.'

'I'm sorry, I'm so fucking sorry,' I say. I'm crying again, 'cause I'm a twat.

'She had to hide, we all did, we can't be showing ourselves to just anyone,' Laurel says. She's playing with the lids from her tubes of Smarties again, spelling out words on the mosaic floor.

'Will she come back? Like Maddie,' I ask.

'She's not her, lad, but she might, just the once. I can let her know that you know the truth,' Silver says. 'But she'd need to know you were going to help make it all better, make her story end like it's supposed to end.'

'I'll do whatever you want,' I say. 'And all that talk 'bout us not having a future, it was all 'cause she was a water nymph. Not 'cause she didn't like me?' I ask. I need to know.

'You're her unicorn,' Laurel says.

'Her what?' I ask.

'Her unicorn.'

'So I still have a chance?' I ask.

'Maybe,' Laurel says. 'She more than loves you.' Her eyes seem to be smiling.

'Look, lad,' Silver says. I turn to look at him. 'You can't ever get into the otherworld, but I think this'll help you.' He hands me some pink swimming goggles.

I don't understand,' I say, 'cause I don't.

'I could tell you a load of stuff 'bout water nymphs and water goddesses, and all the sacrifices that have been made here, 'bout how happy Delphina'll be, but I doubt you'd believe me. So best take a look yourself. Go on!'

And so I do as I'm told. I stand and I strip down to my boxers, then I pinch my nose with my right hand, I hold the pink goggles in my left hand and I jump into the pool. As I surface I look to Laurel and Silver, they're smiling.

'Put them goggles on,' Silver says. 'Big breath and then go down the way you've seen Maddie go.' He waves his arm over towards the opposite end of the pool.

And I do as I'm told. I swim across the water. I mean there's nowt graceful 'bout my swimming, but for me it's a reminder of Delphina and just how fucking amazing she is. I know I'm crying.

I get to near where Maddie always dives down to the otherworld. I tread water, badly, trying to get the goggles over my head and over my eyes. And then I take like the biggest breath ever and dive down into the water. 'Course, 'cause I'm a bell-end, my breath's not big enough so within something like a few seconds I'm back above the water and gasping for air.

'Deep breath, lad,' Silver shouts. I wave over at him, take in a huge breath and dive back down.

My dive's fucked. There's a moment when I wonder if I've enough strength to go down, but I have. There's a moment when I wonder if the water'll let me, but it does. And it's then that my body gets sucked into something like a water bubble, 'cause I seem to be able to breathe under the water. It's all so fucked up, but I keep going, I keep swimming, down, and down some more. It seems that the grid is much further away than I imagined. I don't understand how the pool's suddenly this twatting deep, or how I'd never spotted all the fish that swim in here. They swim down with me and one swims into me, it's the brightest blue I've ever seen. I apologise to it, I say sorry, even though I'm underwater. I'm sure it smiles at me, I'm also sure I'm losing the fucking plot. And as I'm thinking that, I'm working with the bubble and we're getting closer to the gateway, to the grid that leads to the other-world. There's light coming from between the metal bars, beautiful sunlight, the most beautiful light I've ever seen. And so I reach out, I grab hold of the metal grid, my body bobbing through the ripples and that's when I realise I'm breathing normally, that I can talk and smell and taste. And, also, that none of that is freaking me out. When did this become my normal?

I hold on with one hand, I take off the pink goggles and I look around, trying to figure out how far down I've travelled and how that's even possible. And that's when I see the bones. I panic, I almost let go of the grid. The bones are lining the bottom of the pool, skulls, big and small, bones, big and small, children's bones, adults' bones, they're dead people's bones. So many sacrificed for the water goddesses. I mean I'd been told, I mean I knew what was going on but, if I'm honest, I don't know if I even thought it was real. I don't think I've even thought 'bout what the fuck I've got myself in to. 'Cause I'm hanging out with killers, serial killers. I'm looking to help them, I'm keeping their secrets. I'm one of them. I feel sick. I think 'bout all them eight who've been sacrificed, I think 'bout how lucky I am to have been saved. But still all of them thoughts and all of them feelings are quickly pushed aside. 'Cause mainly I look. I look through the gaps into the grid and I see the otherworld, Delphina's world. And that's when I realise that nothing else matters, that the only thing that matters is Delphina and that really I'm not even sure I want to live without her.

I stare through the metal bars. The otherworld is the stuff of wet dreams. Proper fit, naked water nymphs swim in and out of the underwater tunnels, they're laughing and singing and dancing and none of them's got any pubes. I mean I'm calling them water nymphs, but really they're just fit lasses who happen to live in water and not wear clothes. I'm trying not to over-think, I'm trying not to be too freaked out. I look at them, their long hair fans out behind them in the water and their nipples are all huge. White skin, smooth skin, perfect bodies, my cock is ready to burst. I mean it doesn't mean I want Delphina any less, or that I love her any less, just that these lasses are proper fit. I watch them dance through the water, but it's not all water through there. The sun's shining on them, not the twatting rain we've had, no, they've sunshine, perfect sunshine. Butterflies are flittering around, some of the lasses sing, some chat, I don't see any lads. But mainly I'm realising that watching them fills me with happy, they're all so happy, like they've nothing to worry 'bout, like there's nothing bad in the world. It's like they're on holiday, no school, no Mr Dodds, no social services, no twatting Facebook, no Tommy Clarke, no beatings, no feeling like the world's full of bad.

And it looks like the water's a deeper blue through there. I think I hear an ice-cream van, I think I see deckchairs on rocks, I wonder if that means they can leave the water, that somehow, through there, they can exist, they can sleep in beds, they can taste. And that's when I realise that the otherworld is a reward. It's where you get to go when you've had a shit childhood or even crap as an adult, it makes up for all the twats and all the crap that's been thrown at you, it makes everything better. I understand why

348

Delphina needs and deserves to be there. I understand why Maddie thinks she doesn't deserve to be there.

And that's when I see someone who looks a bit like Maddie, Maddie the beautiful monster, but it's not Maddie. This one turns and looks me straight in the eye, she's not singing or dancing. She swims over to the other side of the grid. I don't move. I smile at her, I want her to see that I feel happy too. This one's not got teardrops that are pearls. Her flesh is like Maddie's, practically see-through and her eyes sparkle, like she's 'bout to say something cheeky, but not in a good way. But, mainly, she smells of dead things and the smell makes me be a little bit sick in my mouth. I'd quite like her to move out the way so that I can look into the otherworld.

But she's right up close to the other side of the grid, there's probably only a few centimetres between us. And that's when she opens her mouth to sing or to speak or to eat me up, and that's when fish swim out. I scream, 'cause I'm a twat, I panic, 'cause I'm a twat. I let go of the metal grid.

And that's when I manage not to be in the water bubble and that's when I realise that I can't breathe and that's when I realise that I need to breathe. I panic, I panic like a twat. I try to swim up, I need to go faster, I think I won't make it, I think I've miles to go, but I haven't. I'm there, in no time at all, I'm on the surface and I'm gasping for air.

'Did that help?' Silver asks, as I grab the side of the pool and try to breathe like someone who's not shitting his pants.

'Weird as fuck down there,' I say. 'But beautiful too,' I add. Silver nods.

'Yes, lad, but more pressing issues, lad,' Silver says. 'We need to see what we can do to stall them knocking down The Oracle. We've been working hard with the water goddesses to delay stuff, but we're running out of ideas.'

'What can I do?' I ask.

'I need you to listen and see what else you can find out. I need to know what them American suits are planning on doing next.'

'But aren't you a psychic?' I ask.

'Trust me, lad, you need to act. I know how it should end. This story was never about me,' Silver says. Then he closes his eyes and falls forward into the water. The splash is huge and I can't help but laugh.

I'm back in my house. I'm sitting on the stairs, almost at the upstairs landing. Dad's not lying on the sofa. I popped in a bit ago, was thinking I might tell him what was happening and maybes ask for his advice. I thought he'd left me, too, just for a minute, then I remembered the holy well and Stella.

I'm reading the mail, 'cause it was unopened and on the mat when I came in. There's a letter from the school 'bout my attendance. Mr Dodds is threatening all sorts and asking for an 'urgent meeting', since I missed our last one. I wonder what Dad'll do now. I'm thinking he might kick Mr Dodds's arse. But what does it matter? I've no intention of going back to school. I mean why the fuck would I go to school knowing that Tommy Clarke and his bunch of twats are going to kick the shit out of me? Oh God no, there's no chance of that. I've had it with school, I've had it with the bunch of twats who go there too.

And that's when I hear giggling from upstairs, like someone's play-fighting and jumping on a bed. I'm thinking, what the fuck? Then I think, shit, Tommy Clarke. But then I realise I'm hearing the bed's headboard banging against the wall and the bed's springs are going for gold and Stella's squealing for my dad to 'Give it to her right hard'.

I'm smiling. I mean it's as weird as fuck, but I'm glad my dad's getting some.

I'd wanted to tell Dad 'bout Delphina and Silver and Laurel and Maddie and Kester and Pollock. I'd wanted my dad's advice. I'd wanted him to tell me what to do next, I'd wanted him to help me sort out this fucking mess, but I can't. I mean my dad's alive again, he's back in the shagging saddle and by the sound of it he's doing a good job. And the sound of Stella screaming in delight and the fact that the water from that holy spring has made all of this possible, well it's like it's all clicking into place.

I need to see Delphina again. I mean I know she'll be happy in the otherworld, but I need her to see that I'm sorry and that I've changed, that I'm not a complete twat.

I pull my phone out my pocket and switch it on. I flick on Facebook. I've a million new notifications. Two make me feel a bit sick. The first's from Estelle Jarvis:

Well, you are really really lovely, hilarious, always there for me, legend, utter babe and we have THE BEST chats ever;) . . . you always know how to help me and how to cheer me up when I'm down, you're such a special child;) . . . I havent seen you in ages though. sorry I couldn't . . . come today:/ need to meet up soon, k?:) EMINEM. we are just hilarious when we sit there texting each other photos of your cock, hahahahahah. you're my bezzie;) heheheheheh:) don't want to lose you! :/

I reckon she's trying to milk the whole 'get Arthur to show his cock' for all it's worth. There's a hundred and fifteen likes on it. She's a cunt. I don't respond, it's like she's not even important no more. That whole cock thing feels like a lifetime ago now. But there's another notification, another post on my wall that makes me feel a bit sick in my mouth. It's off one of Tommy Clarke's bunch of twats. It says:

tommy clarke says you can tell arthur braxton that ive deleted
him and i hope he burns in hell for being a fuckin gay.

And something in my gut tells me that the worst is still to come.

And so I do what I have to do. I do what my gut tells me to do
and fifteen minutes later I'm back at The Oracle. Mainly 'cause
it's where I feel safest, but also it's like something in me told me
that I had to be there, that I had to be doing something and not
sitting on the stairs in my house looking at Facebook and hearing
my dad shagging Stella.

None of the others are around, so it's just me sitting on the
edge of the pool, dangling my legs and feet into the water. I guess
there was part of me that was hoping Silver or Laurel had managed
to convince Delphina that I'm not a dick and, just maybes, that
she'd be willing to give me a second chance. But they haven't. I'm
hoping that they haven't all pissed off. I don't know what I'd do
if I never got to see them all again.

That's when I hear voices.

Loud, American voices.

I lift my feet out from the water and I leg it into one of the
changing cubicles, one of the few that Tommy Clarke and his band
of twats didn't destroy. I jump up on the wooden seat inside, I
close the door and pull over the stripy curtain. I reckon my breathing's so loud it's echoing around the whole fucking pool.

They come into the pool area. I reckon it's the same two posh-
looking businessmen that I saw when I hid behind the skip that
time. The two that chatted under huge black umbrellas. I don't
know for sure, I mean it's not like I can look, but their voices
sound the same.

'Jesus. The rain in this godforsaken town,' one says.

'Workmen are now saying that the water damage is going to

need to be looked at by local council. That's two, maybe three months on the schedule,' the other says.

'We can't wait that long, this place is eating at our budget,' the first one says.

'So you want me to do something?' That's a different voice, a familiar voice. I can't help it, I need to know who it is. I let myself peep through a tiny gap in the stripy curtain and there he is, the fucker.

Tommy twatting Clarke is here, in The Oracle, talking to the American suits. His bunch of twats aren't with him.

'The building needs to disappear,' the first one says.

'Yes, we'd like to propose you do a little job for us, in return for payment,' the first one says.

'How much?' Tommy Clarke asks.

'Five hundred pounds in cash and we'll supply everything you need,' the second one says.

'Five hundred quid. Piece of piss,' Tommy Clarke says. With that, one of the Americans hoys his arm around Tommy Clarke and lets out a proper loud laugh. They turn around and start walking towards the double doors.

'There has to be enough damage for a total rebuild to be the only option,' the first one says.

'Like I said, piece of piss,' Tommy says. They all laugh, like they're super-villains, then they carry on walking out through the double doors and into the entrance hall.

I don't move. I stare at the rusty hinges on the door. I daren't move. I mean what the fuck am I supposed to do now?

I feel a bit sick. I guess that's why I stay all scrunched up on the little wooden chair in the changing cubicle. I'm thinking I stay like that for at least two episodes of *Waterloo Road*. I'm surprised the chair holds all of my weight, but I can't seem to move. I'm replaying all that I've heard over and over, and over and over again. I'm trying to understand what the fuck it all means.

Tommy Clarke and no doubt his bunch of merry twats are going to destroy The Oracle. That'll mean that everyone will go away, that Laurel and Silver, that Maddie, that Kester and Pollock, that they'll all have to find someplace else to live. But, mainly, I'm thinking that it'll mean that Delphina'll never come back, that I'll never see her again, that there'll be no way of letting her know just how sorry I am for being an utter twat.

I step down from the wooden seat inside the cubicle, I open the stripy curtain, I open the wooden stable door. I walk out, it only takes three steps, and that's when I look down at the pool. It's drained. It wasn't before, when I was there earlier, I'm sure it wasn't. I swear. I was dangling my legs in the water. I mean the pool's totally empty, there's none of them bones that my toes've brushed over, none that I saw through the goggles. I shiver. I'm sure that there was water. I'm fucking sure I'm not a nutter.

But I'm no longer sure of owt. Am I like my dad? Is being off your head a disease I've caught? How long was I in that changing room for? I swear to God, I've no fucking idea what the fucking fuck's going on.

I look down to my legs, my trousers are rolled up still. My feet are bare. I wonder if the American suits or Tommy Clarke saw my shoes over by the entrance, not far from the wooden steps into the pool. I bend down and touch my legs. They're cold, proper cold. They're damp. I haven't pissed myself, they've got to be damp from the water. I swear, there was water. Twatting cold twatty water.

That's when I start running around the pool. That's when I start running and jumping and shouting.

'Silver!' I shout. I know I shouldn't be shouting, I know there are people around. I know I shouldn't be there, that I'd have a million questions to answer if anyone saw me there. But still, again, 'Silver,' I shout.

He doesn't answer. No one does. Not Laurel, not Kester, not Pollock and there's no water for Maddie to appear. That's when I sit down on the mosaic-tiled floor with the palms of my hands gripping my head. And that's when I start to rock backwards and forwards.

It's hours and hours before Silver turns up. It might even be the next day, but it's still dark. 'Course, I'm still sitting on the floor, I'm clutching my knees, trying to make sense of this utter shit situation and in walks Silver. He's whistling some stupid song that I've never heard of before, like he's not got a care in this twatty world.

'They're paying a lad from my year to destroy The Oracle,' I say.

I'm not sure Silver knew I was there. He jumps slightly when I start to speak. He's over by the entrance double doors and he turns and walks round the pool to where I am. He sits down on the floor next to me.

'How do you know, lad?' Silver asks.

'I hid in there,' I say. I point at the changing cubicles.

'What's the plan?' Silver asks.

'Tommy Clarke's being paid five hundred quid to destroy this place, "beyond repair", they said. The American suits are providing all the equipment.' I say it all matter-of-fact, but I'm shaking. I'm proper shaking. 'Where's the water gone?' I ask.

'They've drained the pools,' Silver says.

'But, earlier, I was—' I stop. I realise that I'm sounding like a total gay. 'What'll happen?' I ask.

'Without the water, we don't really have much to protect us,' Silver says. 'Best I can do is let everyone know.'

355

'It'll all be as it's meant to be,' Laurel says. She steps out from the shadow, carrying her rope with her and frightening the fuck out of me. 'I think it's nearly time.'

'Time for what?' I ask.

'Time to say goodbye to The Oracle,' she says.

'These here baths were a playground for the water nymphs, Arthur,' Silver says. 'The underground reservoir, the otherworld's sacred, it's full of magic, and the nymphs have a whole set of other playgrounds they can visit.'

'So if you tell me the other places,' I say, 'then I can visit them and find Delphina and tell her—'

'She's safer without you taking a load of humans for a visit,' Silver says.

'But I need her,' I say.

'This isn't about you, lad. My priority'll always be Delphina's happiness.'

I nod. I get it. None if this was ever 'bout me.

'I've told her that you're sorry,' Laurel says. I see Silver snap his head towards Laurel. I think he might be pissed with her. 'She's still pretty hurt though,' she says.

'Thanks.' It's all I can think to say.

'These things have a habit of turning out as they're supposed to, lad,' Silver says. His eyes are different, they're a bit kind. 'At least this way we can make sure that no one gets hurt.'

'Silver says that what's meant for us don't pass us by,' Laurel says.

I nod. I nod, but really I'm properly hurting inside. It's like I'm proper breaking. It's like my insides are ripping apart. The pain's all splitting and pulling and burning. I daren't speak. I daren't open my mouth in case all of my insides fly out.

I don't go back home.

Instead I stay in the dark, instead I stay in the light, instead I stay with my feet dangling over the edge of the empty pool. I try not to sleep, if I'm proper honest I try not to breathe. I wait, just in case Delphina returns, I wait for her. I want the water to return. Laurel and Silver go away. They said they'd come back 'when the time is right'. I've had it up to the top of my twatty head with their fucking riddles. What is it with this place? Why can't no folk talk straight?

I don't know how long I've been waiting, but they're loud when they arrive.

They bash in through the swinging double doors, they're singing 'London's Burning', even though clearly we're nowhere near London. In fact, I doubt any of them've even been to London. They're standing just in front of the main doors and them doors are swinging backwards and forwards. It takes a while before Tommy Clarke and his merry bunch of twats spot me.

'Alrite gay,' he says. He drops his plastic bags, they all drop their plastic bags, and they start to walk down the side of the pool towards me.

I lift my legs out from the empty pool and I stand up. I move away from the edge of the pool. I'm not in the mood for any of their crap, but seeing them with their bags full of shit to destroy The Oracle, well it's made me pissed. I think 'bout Silver and all the years he's devoted to looking after Delphina and Laurel, I think 'bout Maddie and Kester and Pollock and how this place makes us all feel like we belong somewhere. I reckon something inside of me grows, or maybes it snaps, but I feel proper different. Too fucking different.

'What the fuck you up to?' I ask Tommy Clarke.

He's right close now. His merry bunch of twats stay back slightly, just behind him. I think they might be growling.

'Come to burn this shit down,' Tommy Clarke says. He hoys his arms out wide, like he owns The fucking Oracle.

'I can't let you do that,' I say.

That's when I look at his hand. That's when I realise that Tommy Clarke's holding that knife of his.

'You and whose fucking army?' he says. He laughs. He fucking laughs at me. His bunch of twats all laugh too.

And that's when I proper explode.

'Just me,' I say. It sounds like a growl. I'm so fucking pissed.

I make a swing at him but he blocks me. He pushes me back, double-handed on my chest. I feel the wooden handle of the knife against my chest. I stumble back a bit, but I'm still nowhere near the edge of the pool. That's when I realise that I can't walk away from this scrap, not this time. I know this is it, this is when I get to prove to Delphina that I'm sorry for being such a dick. The merry bunch of twats move forward, but Tommy Clarke shouts at them to stay back.

That's when I move forward and I push him, double hands on his chest. He stumbles back just slightly. He laughs.

'That the best you've got, gay?' he says. The knife glitters as the moonlight shines through one of them broken stained-glass windows. I think I hear Silver whistling.

'Shut the fuck up,' I shout. I sound arrogant, confident. I'm not.

That's when he punches me in the stomach with his free fist. I double over, he takes the moment. One hand, the knife in that hand, pushes up and into my stomach. The other elbow pushes down on my back. It's quick, it doesn't hurt.

Then he steps away.

I don't say a word. I swear, there's not a sound in The Oracle. I look up, I look at him as I start to uncurl. He holds the knife up into the air. Blood drips down the knife and down his arm.

I look down at me, at my shirt, at my stomach. My hand moves onto my shirt then up to my eyes. Red, I see red. My blood. No pain, just blood.

I turn, I'm stumbling, I feel like I'm spinning and all the time I've got my hand up near to my eyes and I can see my blood dripping from my fingers and down to my wrist. I'm numb. I'm tingling. I'm not quite in my body. My body's not quite mine.

Red. My blood on my fingers.

Red. I see red.

But then I look into the pool.

I see the water. The pool's full of water.

And that's when I see her.

She's smiling, she's come back for me.

Delphina. My Delphina.

'What the fuck's that?' Tommy Clarke asks. He must've been watching me. He must've seen me smile. He must've seen my Delphina.

'My lass,' I say. I'm like full of pride. And that's when I walk forward. I walk to the pool. It's like the water's whispering, it's like moving towards that water's the most natural thing in the world. And I don't stop my tiny stumbling steps and I don't even think 'bout what I'm doing.

And then I turn. And then I look at Tommy Clarke. I stare at him in the eyes. I smile.

And then I let myself fall backwards, into the water.

And the last thing I remember is feeling Delphina grab the collar of my shirt and pull me down,

down,

down.

Tommy Clarke

FIRE: (*Air. Water. Earth.*)

I saw him falling into the water.

He was all covered in blood but the gay looked right happy to be dying. And, if I'm proper honest, that's causing me a couple of issues. One, there was no twatting water in that swimming pool a couple of minutes before. And two, who the fuck was that fit naked lass in that water?

I panic. I throw the knife in the pool. I hear it splash.

I turn round to look at the lads.

'What the fuck just happened?' I ask. 'Has one of you fuckers spiked my cider?' I ask. 'Own up, you bastards!' I shout.

The lads don't answer, none of the fuckers own up. But then one of them pipes up. 'Where's the water gone now?' he says.

We all turn and there's no trace of water and there's no trace of Arthur Braxton, there's no trace of the fit lass and there's no trace of the knife I threw in there like a minute ago.

I'm thinking, what the fuck? I mean, I'm thinking, WHAT the fuck?

I lift my hands up right close to my eyes. I mean my fingers are still covered in his blood, it's all over my hands and down my nails. I look down to the floor and there's stuff on the floor, I mean I can see Arthur Braxton's blood on the fucking floor, but there's no sign of a body and there's no sign of my knife and there's no water, I mean not a fucking drop of the shit.

I've killed someone, I think I've fucking killed someone, I mean I stabbed him. I look at my hands again. I lick one of my fingers. Blood, I can taste Arthur Braxton's blood.

Fuck, shit. FUCK. I'll go down for this. FUCK.

This isn't what I wanted, none of this shit is what I wanted; this was about the money, five fucking hundred quid.

I can taste Arthur Braxton's blood in my mouth. And that's when I bend over and I throw up into the empty pool.

'Tommy lad,' one of the lads say.

'Some fucker's spiked my drink,' I say, wiping my hand 'cross my mouth. I can still taste blood, Arthur Braxton's blood. I start heaving, the noise echoes around the empty pool.

I need to hold my shit together, I need to figure out what to do next. I take a few moments, none of the lads say a word.

'Fucking weird shit,' I say.

'What the fuck?' one of the lads says. 'None of this makes no sense, Tommo.'

I nod. I nod my head, 'cause really I can't think of nowt else to do.

'Let's burn this place before owt else weird happens,' I say, mainly 'cause I can't think what to do. I mean, where the fuck is Arthur Braxton? I mean, did I kill him? I mean, where's his body? I mean, what the fuck's going on?

So that's what we do, we use everything the Americans gave us. The liquids, the fuels, the wood, the accelerants, it's all pretty basic shit but there's no doubt it'll do the trick. I try to put Arthur Braxton and the fit naked lass out my head. And all the time I'm trying not to think 'bout him having told the truth and all the times we've given him a beating for being gay.

When we've got everything ready I shout at the lads to get

back out into the reception area. I follow them in there, we use some shoes to wedge the double doors open.

'Right,' I say. 'Not a word of this. We're brothers, so don't be letting us down. I mean there's no body, so it ain't like I did owt wrong,' I say.

They all nod. I mean what I'm saying's right. Without no body I'm innocent.

'But wasn't there a lass in the water too? Do you reckon she got out?' one of them asks.

I turn and look at the empty pool. The lad was right, there was a lass, but now there's no lass, there's no body and there's no fucking water. It's doing my head in.

'I reckon her and Arthur Braxton must have somehow got out,' I say, but I don't think any of them really believe me. 'Right, time I did the honours and flicked the fucking switch,' I say. And I walk back into the pool area. I flick the lid of my Zippo and I let my lighter burn the fifteen trails that we've made.

Fucking fabulous. The smell, the fact that it all goes so smoothly, the fact that it's all going to be over soon. The fire shoots across the floor and around the pool. And within a couple of minutes the smell of burning wood is fucking spectacular.

I turn, I'm smiling like a mental and I walk out to join the lads to watch our handiwork together. But then, just as I'm about to reach the double doors, one of the lads pipes up from the entrance hall.

'What the fuck?' he says. He's pointing into the pool area.

I turn and there, right next to the edge of the pool, is an old bloke. He's lying on a platform of wood, maybe sticks or broken chairs, I swear to fuck it wasn't there before. He's fucking fat and old and I'm not sure if he's already dead, but he's just lying there, like he wants the fire to burn him.

'What the fuck?' I say.

And suddenly I'm running back into the pool area, trying to dodge the heat and the flames and my breathing's already in trouble. I can't be killing some bloke else, that's not in the plan, that's not what I want to be doing. And that's when the old man sits up on his bed of bust-up wood.

'Go, lad,' he shouts. 'This is how it's supposed to end.'

I stop, I mean just for a few seconds because the heat from the flames is fucking ridiculous.

'Come on,' I shout. 'Get the fuck out,' I shout.

'No, lad, I'm staying here,' he says. And I don't know what to do, I mean if I leave him there then I've killed him, I mean it was me that flicked the lighter and torched this fucking place. I mean they'll find a body and they'll investigate. That'll be two killings in one night and that's not what I'm about. I swear, it's not what I'm wanting. I'm no killer. I mean, that'll practically make me a serial killer.

Then I hear one of my lads screaming at me to get the fuck out before it's too late.

I look at the old bloke again. He seems to be waving at someone. I look to where he's waving and see a bunch of others up on the viewing gallery.

'Fuck! What the fuck?' I scream. 'Get the fuck out of here,' I yell. But it's like they can't even hear me.

'I'll miss you, Silver,' a young lass with a rope shouts.

'Take care,' shouts an old man. He's throwing what looks like popcorn.

'You old fool,' shouts another.

'Get out, GET OUT!' I scream.

This wasn't part of the deal.

I didn't plan on murdering loads of people.

I'm jumping up and down on the spot, it's all going wrong, I'm going to be done for this, I'll get caught and I'll go down for life.

What the fuck, what the fucking fuck should I do?
And that's when the old man turns to me, bursts out crying,
and that's when he shouts, 'Run, lad, run for your life!'

Thanking

Mr Richardson – for far too much to mention here, but the 'believing in me' means more than he'll ever realise.

My publisher, Scott Pack – for being patient, thorough and, really, rather magnificent.

Gaspard Royant – for replying to my ridiculous fan-girl messages (never to be public!) and for allowing me the use of his lyric at the beginning of this novel.

Rachel Faulkner, Corinna Harrod and LightBrigade PR – for not shouting at me, even when I was being ridiculous, and for being utterly dazzling.

Dorothy Koomson – for being astute, significant and responsible for my frequent 'What would Dorothy do?' questioning.

Alexandra Brown – for being my writing-buddy and the person I'd least like to see in a Poundland uniform.

Natalie Flynn – for making my days funny and for being wise (never sensible) beyond her years.

Kat Stephen – for posting a stunning photo of herself on Facebook that I (shamelessly) used to help me visualise a water nymph.

Sophia Leadill Taylor – for guiding me through the dance and for being my oldest friend (she'll like that).

Paula Groves, Ryan Groves, Richard Wells and Margaret Coombs – for being my constants and for being my chosen family.

Matt Hill, Jean Ward, Bernie Pardue and Megan Taylor – for the encouragement, friendship and support.

Kate Holmden – for being clever and for enabling me to say this: 'Welcome to the world, Megan Caroline.'

My Twitter friends – for being the BEST company during my tea (and cake) breaks.

Jacob, Ben and Poppy – for holding my hand.

And, finally, Gary – for giving me far more than I'll ever deserve.

Victoria Baths

The inspiration for *The Drowning of Arthur Braxton* started with a place – Victoria Baths on Hathersage Road, Manchester.

When it opened in 1906, Victoria Baths was described as 'a water palace of which every citizen of Manchester can be proud'. The magnificent building provided facilities for swimming, bathing and leisure.

Victoria Baths aided the people of central Manchester for eighty-seven years, until Manchester City Council decided it had to close in 1993. There was, at that time, passionate reaction from the local community, with residents valuing the facilities and the building itself.

The campaign to try and prevent the closure became the 'Friends of Victoria Baths' and a charitable trust was set up with the aim of fully restoring the building, bringing the Turkish Baths and at least one of the swimming pools back into public use.

I have drawn on this building for my inspiration, but the real story of Victoria Baths, including its success on BBC's 'Restoration' series in 2003, can be found at http://www.victoriabaths.org.uk.